The State of Grace

Catherine Donnelly was an award-winning copywriter with a
Dublin advertising agency for some years, before leaving to write
a novel. She became a regular contributor to the *Sunday Independent* newspaper and *Image* magazine, before writing *The State of
Grace*. She is currently working on her second novel.

The state of Grace

CATHERINE DONNELLY

PAN BOOKS

First published 2003 in Ireland by Sitric Books Ltd
And by Tivoli, an imprint of Gill & Macmillan Ltd, Dublin

First published in Great Britain 2004 by Pan Books
an imprint of Pan Macmillan Ltd
20 New Wharf Road, London N1 9RR
Basingstoke and Oxford
Associated companies throughout the world
www.panmacmillan.com

ISBN 0 330 41218 3

1 3 5 7 9 8 6 4 2

A CIP catalogue record for this book is available from
the British Library.

Printed and bound in Great Britain by
Mackays of Chatham plc, Chatham, Kent

All Pan Macmillan titles are available from www.panmacmillan.com
or from Bookpost by telephoning 01624 677237

For Frank

ONE

GRACE TOOK TO SMOKING like a politician to planning applications. It was as though she had always held that small cylinder between her lip, always drawn that column of smoke deep into her lungs, her fingers holding the cigarette lightly, like a flower.

'There's no smoking in the agency building,' said Myles, the managing director, automatically, quickly followed by, 'I didn't know you smoked, Grace.'

'I do now,' said Grace, resting the smouldering cigarette on the edge of her desk while she continued with the task of emptying her drawers of twenty years of working in advertising. Myles Kitchen stood, momentarily discomfited, then strode on, anxious to complete his daily circuit of the agency to assess the condition of his employees. He could spot a hangover at fifty yards, a quickly discarded crossword at seventy. Grace took another lazy pull on her cigarette.

There wasn't much in the end: some letters, an emery board, a stopwatch, and a smooth grey stone. Everything else she threw into the two large bin bags draped over chairs. Normally, she was a person who kept things. Her house was full of unread clippings from newspapers, cracked plates, broken clocks, worn-down lipsticks, and carefully catalogued clothes in long brown boxes. But she found that once she'd consigned the first item to the bin bag, the urge to throw everything away was irresistible. Out went her walking shoes and the stilettos she kept lest an unscheduled meeting with a client occur. Out went the nail varnishes, the CDs she'd bought on impulse, the plant, the framed photograph of her ex-husband, the photograph of her two children – Josh and Emily, another of her ex-husband Lionel and Grace herself, caught unawares, looking away to the left with a frightened expression on her face. What was she looking at that day, she wondered? Probably the dog – what was its name? Ah yes, Gandhi – Gandhi on account of his extreme thinness. He had a habit of darting out onto the road, dicing with death until one day he didn't move fast enough. The owner of the car was more upset than Grace, who had imagined Gandhi's demise so often that she treated the reality with a fair degree of stoicism.

The two bags were nearly full now as Grace dispatched a last jacket into their depths and, finally, the ten awards – heavy, ugly things – which she had won for her work as TV Producer in this advertising agency that she was now leaving.

The cigarette had smouldered down to its filter and there was a greasy, brown burn on the desk. Grace brushed the butt to the floor and ground it into the carpet tile. She picked up her pack of cigarettes and lighter and went out and round to the back of the building where the smokers stood, hunched against the cold.

'Jesus, Grace,' said one of the young art directors, 'when did you start smoking?'

'Oh I think everyone should take up a hobby in retirement,' Grace told him.

TWO

WHEN MYLES KITCHEN had called her into his office three weeks earlier, Grace felt a flutter of excitement. She'd just overseen three commercials on the trot, all of which had gone like clockwork, and the agency was going to make a great deal of money from them. Grace, who was under-paid, felt that this was the moment when the situation would be redressed. She was so busy visualizing the expression on Josh's face when she told him – she was not going to tell Lionel, tempting as it was, lest he use it as an excuse to reduce her alimony – that she had to ask Myles to repeat what he'd said. The only phrase she actually heard from what had been quite a long speech was, ' … and of course we'll miss you.'

'Miss me?' Grace searched his face as though it might reveal the text of all he had said.

'Look Grace,' Myles said, 'we both know this is a young man's industry.'

'And I'm not a young man?'

'A young person's industry,' Myles corrected himself. He smiled at her then, a smile she recognized. It was the one he reserved for a new business pitch. It was a smile that suggested honesty, charm and boyish enthusiasm. It was an expression that used both his mouth and his forehead – which was now furrowed with integrity and kindliness.

'I'm only forty-six – eh forty-two.'

Grace remembered just in time that she'd lopped four years off her age on her forty-first birthday.

'Sometimes I feel too old myself,' Myles said, leaning forward confidingly, 'and I'm only –' Grace could see him doing some rapid arithmetic. He was actually only a year younger than Grace herself. 'Forty,' he said stoutly.

He got up and rested his haunches against the edge of his desk.

'Look, I tell you what, we'll bump up your last month's salary by what – by two thousand, say and you can draw down some of your pension. Start enjoying life, relax, take up a few hobbies.'

'Yes, absolutely. Yes. Yes. Hobbies. Yes.' Grace felt at a loss. She had a huge urge to go to bed in a darkened room, take two sleeping pills and just sleep.

'Now,' said Myles, jovial again, 'you've still got a bit of finishing up to do. You'll be doing the Javelin shoot – oh and you'll need to negotiate terms with whoever's cast in the coffee thing. You're so good at that. So … here's to freedom,' and he raised his coffee mug, which was emblazoned with a picture of Bart Simpson and the instruction EAT MY SHORTS.

That evening, Grace had gone home to her house in Donnybrook with its two granite steps and dark blue door. She'd walked in, her hand automatically finding the light-switch which illuminated the Indian rug that ran the length of the hall and the kitchen on the return with its once-fashionable pale green, rag-rubbed cupboards.

She sat in one of the matching cream couches in the living-room, ignoring the vase of dying tulips, and channel-hopped for a half hour or so. Then, having drunk both bottles of wine she kept for guests, she realised she didn't need the sleeping pills after all. The phone rang twice, but she didn't answer it. Probably Josh. Not Emily anyway. Emily never called.

The next morning she woke with a hangover. This was very bad news indeed as she'd given up drinking fifteen years ago and wanted to keep it that way. She had two Solpadeine, a vitamin C tablet and washed her teeth with more than her usual vigour, although what she really wanted was a treble vodka. Old habits die hard. As she put on her make-up she looked at herself carefully. Was this old? Her face looked back at her, the tiny lines around her eyes, a slight looseness around the mouth and maybe a bit of extra weight. But hadn't someone told her – or maybe she'd read it somewhere – you either keep your face or your body? She applied lipstick in an apologetic shade of peach and climbed into one of the three Louise Kennedy suits she owned which glided over her, concealing her body in a sweep of cream. The tights she was wearing, with their 'tummy-shaper' panels, bit into her waist. Rather unfair, she thought, considering the missed dinner.

The day passed in a blur of simulated disbelief from her colleagues. 'It won't be the same without you,' they said, not meaning it. They imagined they had done it all themselves – *believed* they had done it all themselves: contacted the outside producers, got the reels in, assembled the directors' treatments, beaten down the price, set up the casting, liaised with the director, arranged the terms with the cast and the extras, scheduled the wardrobe and the location scout, caught all the dropped balls during the shoot and sat in on the edit, re-edited after the rough-cut, and thanked the client for being so courageous and helpful when the final cut was approved.

She made the telephone calls covering the last-minute arrangements for the five-day Javelin shoot operating on autopilot. It seemed a long time since her first Javelin shoot fifteen years before. She looked idly at the Polaroids of the three leads. How predictable they were. The handsome one with the floppy hair, the impish one with the shaved head, the brooding one with a dangerous slant to his eyes. Yawn, yawn, yawn, she mumbled to herself. It was a complicated shoot and, with the industry going through a lean time, she suspected the production company had under-quoted.

'How many extras have we got on this bloody thing?'

'Hundred-fifty,' said Mike, her assistant.

'Oh great, bloody excellent!'

'I went through the Polaroids, they're all fine,' Mike said soothingly. 'No one looks over twelve.'

'Shut up, I've no sense of humour today.'

'Sorry.'

Broadcast regulations insisted that everyone featured in a beer commercial had to be over twenty-six and look it too. This posed something of a problem as the target market was considerably younger than this, so they endeavoured to walk the tightrope between station approval and client need to 'push the envelope', as the creative director was fond of saying in those rare moments he was in the agency.

Grace reached over to Mike's desk and lifted up a handful of photographs. She rummaged through them interjecting the exercise with occasional exclamations. 'God, what's that she's holding – a Barbie doll?' 'Ah Mike, this one hasn't started shaving yet.'

'Male or female?'

Grace threw the photos back on his desk.

'Oh who cares?' she said, and then they both shouted in unison, 'Sure no one will see them anyway.' They laughed then because this was the phrase which had comforted them during all the beer shoots of their long association when, confronted with a child actor staunchly maintaining that he was twenty-seven last birthday, the two would nod sagely and mutter, 'Sure no one will see them anyway.'

Next she phoned the account director to ensure there was enough product and branded glasses. 'God I hate beer commercials,' she told Mike, unnecessarily.

She fielded calls from her son Josh during which he talked about solicitors and lump sums always ending with, 'You're so useless Mum. You're so passive.'

'Yes,' she agreed, before holding her hand over the mouthpiece to say evenly to the account handler, 'You complete idiot – does this look like an ace glass to you? The damned branding is all over the place.' The account handler was number three in the shaky chain of command that managed Javelin. His name was Henry and his anxiety about his work had recently manifested itself in an attack of eczema. Grace dusted a drift of white skin off her notebook, trying not to look too disgusted.

'Sorry Grace.'

Everyone was apologizing to her today. It was very wearing. Almost a relief really to return to Josh's hectoring voice, pummelling its way down the phone line. Even as a child he had the certain knowledge that he was always right.

'Look Josh,' she said, returning to the phone, 'I'm incredibly busy just now. I've got a shoot and I'm up to here – all right?'

'Oh for God's sake, it's not brain surgery Mum.'

'No,' Grace murmured. 'It's not.' And she replaced the phone carefully in its cradle.

'Son and heir?' Mike asked sympathetically as he started to staple call-sheets together. 'Grace … ?' Mike had paused in his task.

'Mmmh?'

'You should go for them.'

'How do you mean?'

'They've shafted you. You're just rolling over for them. Maybe Josh is right – y'know?'

Grace ran her fingers through her straight, brown hair, cut in a style she had worn since her twenties.

'I can't be bothered, Mike.' She smiled at him and with an air of purpose took up the phone. 'Best get the kiddies over for a chat.'

The commercial's creators arrived some minutes later. The art director was a sulky twenty-two-year-old called Melvin who had little talent apart from an ability to plagiarize the work of people more gifted than he. The writer, Dion, was even younger and mightn't be half-bad in ten years or so, by which time he would be considered too yesterday and would eke out his days doing press ads for phone companies and cars.

'Well,' Grace asked, 'all set?'

'Pretty much,' said Dion.

'Right,' Grace consulted her call-sheet, 'the call is for seven – be there.' Dion looked excited, Melvin horrified. Eleven was his normal starting time involving a lot of 'the cat was sick on my homework' excuses.

'We're starting with the big club scenes because they're the messiest,' Grace continued, trying to keep the ennui out of her voice, 'and it'll be a long day. Wear something warm, it's like an icebox there for some reason.'

'The Red Ice Box,' sniggered Dion before Grace quelled his good humour with a glare. They were shooting in a club called

The Red Box. It had been chosen because the director said it was 'totally ideal'. The production company then set about dismantling the entire premises, retiling, refurnishing and repainting until it was virtually unrecognizable.

'Is that it?' asked Melvin rattling his Zippo in his hand impatiently.

'No pet, it's not,' Grace said and then, 'oh what the hell. Let's go outside.'

She and Mike followed the others to the door and out to the back of the building where a tangle of bicycles slouched against the wall – a vain attempt to outwit Dublin's traffic congestion.

'Could I have one of those?' Grace took a cigarette, lit it and inhaled deeply. This smoking business was wonderfully relaxing.

There were three messages from Josh when she got home and an irate one from Lionel. What did she mean packing in her job – did she think he was made of money?

'I hope your disgusting twins throw up all over you, you stupid old goat,' Grace told the telephone, feeling instantly better. Lionel had remarried – choosing, predictably, a girl some years younger than his own daughter. Too late, Lionel discovered that behind the taut brown tummy and pert breasts, there was a mother aching to get out and she became pregnant with twins almost immediately. Lionel, as poor a father as Grace was a mother first time round, was an even worse one now. Fortunately for everyone concerned, he spent a great deal of time abroad, writing vivid reports about trouble spots from the comfort of his large hotel, as far away as possible from the smell of death and cordite.

The phone rang again. The answer-phone clicked on and she let it run.

'If you're there, pick up. Mum? Pick up.' It was Josh. He started to say something and then said, 'Oh forget it. Ring me.'

Grace's relationship with Josh was run on diplomatic lines. Their life was one of talks about talks in a series of meetings that had to do with a constantly fluctuating power base. As a child he had chipped and gnawed at her authority – if you could call her lazy parenting 'authority' – until one day the balance had shifted and all of a sudden, she was the child, forever found wanting.

She and Josh had drifted apart just as surely as she and Lionel had. This had to do with the fact that Grace found it difficult to concentrate on more than one thing at a time. So, when Lionel and she had been negotiating the long, slow, last dance of their marriage, the children hardly figured in her consciousness at all.

Then Emily had her problems – actually it was *a problem* but Grace found that the use of the plural somehow diminished its seriousness. And, when Emily's difficulties were Grace's focus, all thoughts of Josh receded so that he became as close to her as, say, someone with whom she shared a plane journey, but less close than her hairdresser.

She'd lost count of the number of times he'd said, 'I told you that Mum!' alluding to some aspect of his life that they'd discussed at length but Grace had forgotten. It would have been easier to admit it – to say, 'I'm sorry, I wasn't listening,' but even Grace knew that you couldn't say that to your child. Not all the time anyway.

There were no more calls that night and she was in bed by eleven. She was awoken by the sound of the phone ringing but this time it was her early morning call. She never trusted alarm clocks on the day of a shoot.

THREE

WHEN SHE ARRIVED, the generators, the catering truck and buses were all in place. She accepted a sausage and egg sandwich, had two bites and threw it away. On the other side of the road, a man in an ancient coat tied with string made his way tentatively to the catering truck.

'Any chance of … ?'

'Fuck off,' said the greasy-haired caterer.

'Ah give him a sandwich and a cup of tea for God's sake,' said Grace, smiling at the old man who didn't smile back.

During the course of the day, she saw him several times, gaining in confidence at every trip to the chuck wagon. He had the chicken curry for his lunch. 'Bad decision,' Mike had said when Grace had pointed out their guest, and louder. 'Never have the curry mate. Never, ever have the curry.'

Grace began to feel quite cheerful in the cold, early morning air. She went to the make-up caravan to check on the actors. The three of them sat with towels bibbed around their necks wearing pristine clothes from Gap and shiny Camper boots. The wardrobe girl, Sam, was ironing the box-creases out of an Armani shirt, its not inconsiderable price tag hanging from the collar.

Grace sighed. 'Sam I thought you were going to distress the clothes. The guys look as though they're doing a mail-order catalogue.'

Sam looked at the actors, her pretty brow slightly furrowed.

'I know Grace, I know – but I was really up against it 'cos they all gave the wrong sizes and I had to race into town last night and re-buy everything.'

'Sam, they always give the wrong sizes. Just the way they always say they can drive, high-dive and ride to Olympic standard, but you don't necessarily believe them.'

Then she turned to the actors.

'Off!'

They looked at her, uncomprehending.

'The clothes. Take the clothes off – and the boots so Sam can make you look as if you have some sort of life outside of applying cream beige foundation and a touch of mascara.'

The three actors looked at each other and then stripped off until they were standing in their boxer-shorts. How thin and white they looked, how young.

'Put sweaters on before you freeze to death,' Grace said over her shoulder as she made a call to the agency and asked to be put through to the creative director, Andrew.

'I've no creatives,' she said. Mike had just come into the trailer. She threw her eyes up to heaven and continued talking into the phone. 'Actually,' she said, 'I'll have no creatives even when they do arrive. No we're fine. Everything's great. Terrific. Are you going to come by? No I'd really prefer if you didn't bring your children. Because they'll be in the way. I see. Excellent. Well, we look forward to seeing all three of you.'

'Bastard's bringing his kids,' she told Mike, pressing the end button savagely.

At the other end of the trailer, Sam was squashing a shirt ineffectually between her smooth, brown hands.

'Look,' Grace told her, 'you're going to have to run them through the machine again – leave them a bit creased – and wash the coloureds with the whites. Please God they'll run. Mine always do. You three can rehearse in your own clothes,' she told the three actors. The shaven-headed one made to speak.

'Yes?' Grace said, ungraciously.

'Will I have to drink in the commercial?'

Grace looked at him searchingly to see if he was making an ill-timed joke, decided he wasn't and said carefully, 'This is a beer commercial. In it you will be required to drink beer. Yes?'

'You see the thing is,' Shaven-head said with a winning smile, 'I don't drink.'

'Neither do I,' said Floppy Hair, coming to life for the first time since he'd been stripped of the comfort of his Gap trousers and sweatshirt.

'I'm sorry?'

Grace looked helplessly at Mike, who gave a great bark of laughter and then said, 'You don't what?'

'Oh this is ridiculous.' Grace sat down and grabbed a cigarette from her pocket.

'I'd prefer if you didn't,' Sam said tentatively and then thought better of it as Grace opened her lighter with a clatter and inhaled copiously. The three actors moved closer together.

'I drink,' the brooding one mentioned.

'Good for you,' Grace said, not looking at him but rather at the other two who were returning her glare with puzzled expressions.

'So you don't drink? I see. Excellent. Wonderful. That's all I need.' Neither actor replied.

'What about non-alcoholic beer?' Mike suggested.

The actors looked mutinous.

'No,' said Grace, 'it looks like shite.'

'Well I'm not drinking,' said Shaven-head.

'Me neither,' said Floppy, a little uncertainly.

'Sweet mother of Jesus is there no end?' Grace ground her cigarette into the linoleum and rounded on the two actors, 'Did it not occur to you to say this at the casting you complete morons? What did you think you'd be doing in a beer commercial – washing baths? I'm calling your agents,' she said and started dialling.

'We could spit it out,' Shaven-head suggested.

'What do you think?' asked Mike.

'Oh I don't know. Yes. I suppose. Yes. But you bloody well better look as if it's the best thing that has ever passed your lips before you spit it out.'

'Jesus,' she said to Mike when they'd stepped outside the trailer, 'when I started in this business the problem was stopping them drinking. At the first Javelin shoot two of them passed out before the end-shot and we had to do an extra day – worst bloody shoot of my life.'

The director, Derek, was an immensely calm man in his mid-thirties who took the news of his two non-drinking leads with equanimity.

'At least they won't get poleaxed before we're done,' he said.

'I'd poleaxe them myself if I had a suitable weapon,' Grace said, lighting another cigarette. At that moment Dion and Melvin appeared from behind the chuck wagon, clutching bacon and egg sandwiches and endeavouring not to drip them on their leather jackets.

'Have you talked to them yet – the creatives I mean?' Grace asked Derek.

'Yeah,' he grinned lazily and looked off into the middle distance. 'Is this their first commercial? 'Cos they don't know fuck.'

'We all have to start somewhere.' Grace felt suddenly tired, the long, long day stretching before her like an illness.

'Ready to rock and roll?' Derek enquired of the cameraman.

'Nearly there,' said the cameraman as men pegged sheets of translucent paper over the huge arc lights called, appropriately enough, Brutes.

'Rehearsal!' screamed the first assistant.

'Oh God, oh God, oh God,' muttered Grace, lighting a cigarette from the end of the one she was about to put out.

'I must say you don't believe in doing things by halves,' Mike said, eyeing her cigarette as the first assistant circled the crowd of extras like a sheep-dog – darting here, chivvying there until the group were all assembled on the dance-floor.

'Thought I'd start with the dance scene,' Derek explained, 'we can see who we'd like to feature.'

'Try to avoid showing the ones who haven't done their Junior Cert yet – OK?' Grace sat down on a pile of beanbags and closed her eyes as a blast of music came out of the speakers. Over the music, she could hear the first assistant yelling, 'I want everyone dancing now. Go go go. Dance!'

'Roll on one a.m.,' muttered Grace.

'One a.m.? God bless your optimism,' said Mike.

At the lunch break, Grace toyed with something called The Vegetarian Option, which was khaki-coloured and tasted in equal parts of raw cumin and burnt garlic. Finally, too nauseated by its colour against the patterned paper plate to eat more than a bite or two, she slung the plate into the plastic bin. She took an apple from a big silver dish and cut it into quarters. It tasted of soap.

At ten that night, they still hadn't gotten the dance shot. Between takes the hundred or so waifs in their cut-off tops and their spindly shoes clambered up the stairs to the mezzanine area of the club and muttered amongst themselves. At midnight, the first assistant called them down for another take. The chatter from overhead ceased.

'Extras on the set – now,' yelled the first assistant.

'We're not coming down,' said a tiny voice.

'Come down this minute,' shouted the first assistant.

'No,' mumbled several small voices.

'Bollix,' Derek said philosophically and wandered over to Geoff, his producer. The two had a whispered conversation for some minutes and then the producer disappeared through the big double doors to the street. Twenty minutes later he returned with several heavy brown boxes that he and the grips carried up to the mezzanine. Grace looked questioningly at Mike.

'Vodka and something nice and sugary,' Mike explained.

Ten minutes later, the extras were back on the floor, dancing their little hearts out.

At five a.m. Grace fell into an uneasy sleep. She awoke not knowing where she was. Mike was looking startled and rubbing his face.

'Jesus Grace, remind me never to sleep with you. You just clocked me one.'

He felt around inside his mouth experimentally with his tongue.

'I think you loosened a tooth. You were completely out of it. "Where am I? Where am I?" ' Mike squeaked using a voice she hoped didn't resemble her real one. 'Anyway, there was one thing I knew I shouldn't reply to that question and that was,' and he dropped his voice to a funereal bass, '"You're in The Red Box, Grace".'

'Ha ha,' Grace said, getting up stiffly.

'Well we're wrapped,' Mike told her.

'I can see that,' she said crossly. 'Oh let's get out of here.' Grace hoisted her bag over her shoulder and they walked out into the dawn to hail a taxi, ignoring Dion and Melvin who seemed to have been sneaking some of the extras' ration of vodka.

'Had a good night then?' leered the taxi driver who picked them up outside the club.

'Oh fuck off,' said Grace.

Four

GRACE HAD GOTTEN INTO advertising by accident. Actually, her entire life was a series of accidents – including Josh and Emily. And Lionel, of course, was the worst accident of all – the relationship equivalent of a five-car pile-up.

She'd met him when she was twenty, in a pub frequented by law students located close to the King's Inns. She was having a quiet drink with her then employer – the editor of the obscure literary magazine where she worked after failing her final Arts exam.

'Little turds like that should be drowned at birth,' Raymond, her employer, remarked as another gust of manic laughter rose from a crowded table in the corner. There were about eight young men, all clad in dark suits, all drunk – all, it seemed, reading from a script more appropriate to Evelyn Waugh than Ireland in the mid-seventies. Raymond sighed and called for another round. They were both drinking whiskey: Raymond maintaining the gentle fog of alcohol that surrounded him all day, Grace, the less practised of the two, a little the worse for wear, although the pint of cold lager that suddenly drenched her sobered her somewhat. There was an abrupt burst of laughter close to her ear and she heard Raymond say, 'What the?' and then Lionel was bending over her, ineffectually mopping at her hair and face with the sleeve of his pinstripe suit.

'It just fell out of my hand,' he laughed, 'wet glass! Jesus!'

Grace eyed her silk shirt, which was absorbing the beer as though it had a raging thirst. Her hair dripped on the table with the steady beat of a metronome. The sour smell of yeast was overpowering.

'It's meant to be good for hair all the same,' Lionel said, his face serious once again.

'Pity you can't hold your drink sir,' said Raymond, rooting through his pockets till he emerged with a grey, somewhat used handkerchief.

'I'm fine, no really, I'm fine,' said Grace as she pressed tissues into the wettest sections of her shirt and squeezed her hair.

'Let me buy you a drink at least,' Lionel said winningly.

'Two large whiskies,' Raymond said with alacrity. He forgave easily when the offer of drink was involved. There wasn't much money in literary magazines.

'Raymond!' protested Grace, but already Raymond and Lionel were shaking hands and Lionel was explaining that he'd just attended a Grand Night at the Inns, which involved the consumption of several beers and a bottle of port. This, he explained disarmingly, was why he was a little more maladroit than would ordinarily be the case. Raymond had moved from his former position and was now of the opinion that such an accident could 'happen to a bishop – happen to a judge even', at which the pair brayed with laughter. Within minutes Lionel had joined them on the faded banquette and he and Raymond were deep in conversation about, amongst other things, the state of the Abbey, the future of Irish poetry, the death of the novel and 'Brits' (the fuckers).

Raymond ordered another round and Grace went to the ladies' to assess the damage. 'Great,' she thought, looking at her reflection in the scarred mirror. Her hair lay slick and tangled against her head; the stained half of her shirt was honeycombed with froth-encrusted crinkles. Her mascara had run and her make-up had formed small tidal bays around the dark streaks. She swiped viciously at her face with toilet paper and rubbed her hair with the cleanest part of the roller towel she could find, then checked in the mirror again. The mascara was gone but she looked as though she had been crying for a very long time.

Prescience, no doubt.

Raymond worked out of a mobile home in the drive of his house. From here, the quarterly review was assembled, proofed and finally printed, generally late – a combination of lack of funds and Grace's ineptitude. Efficiency was a quality that came to her late in life. Aged twenty, her mind was a tangle of crossed wires and half-conceived notions about her future.

'What I can't understand,' Raymond would say, 'is how you can type both slowly and inaccurately. You'd think you might compensate for your lack of speed with precision but ...' and he sighed and took a deep swallow of the cheap red wine he drank during the day – saving the better vintages for the evening when he could concentrate more on 'the nose'.

Four times a year, Grace approached the pasting-up of the magazine for printing. It was a simple enough task. All you had to do was count the lines and then paste them in. Raymond had already decided the order of the magazine. There would be incomprehensible articles about esoteric Russian poets written by American academics; gloomy short stories set in Antrim about old men rowing over smallholdings; big, dense poems about forgotten moments in history; and slender little poems about 'life' that dribbled down the page and ended with a single word. All too frequently when the lines wouldn't fit, Grace allowed that single, final word to drift onto the next page and then, when the magazine hit the bookshops, had to endure the tearful phone call from the poet whose opus had been rendered meaningless. As this latter was a condition that had existed from the outset, she couldn't bring herself to simulate penitence. Grace also proofread the galleys, so there were more angry phone calls about the misspellings and literals that had escaped her less than beady eye. On those days Raymond ranted and raged around the mobile home so that it shook on its foundation of cement blocks.

'What were you thinking?'

He waved the offending pages in front of her face.

'What made you think "gorse" should be changed to "of course"?'

And Grace could never answer satisfactorily because she didn't know. She didn't know what she was thinking. Her thoughts were just a mish-mash of daydreams, regret and fear. Disgusted with her lack of an explanation, Raymond retired to the security of his home leaving her alone in the caravan with its smell of gas and ink and paper.

Grace lived with her parents. That is to say, she lived in a war zone. How her parents had gotten together in the first place was a mystery. Possibly they were the 'opposites attract' syndrome carried too far – the exception to the rule. They were proof that opposites repel. As far back as Grace could remember, they had bickered and sniped at each other. Although they were never physically violent, the threat of it was always present – often articulated in the most gruesome terms. No one could describe evisceration quite so colourfully as Grace's mother, whilst her father's medical background meant he was skilled in the finer points of flailing and eye-gouging and capable of delineating his plans for her mother in minute, stomach-churning detail. Lionel said it was *Who's Afraid of Virginia Woolf?* on Zimmer frames. This was inaccurate. Grace's parents were alarmingly agile – relentlessly shadowing each other around the house, effecting ambushes of verbal grenades and spattering the machine-gun fire of their rage 'indiscriminately' – as Lionel was wont to say in his later war articles.

Oh yes, after that first meeting she and Lionel had started going out. She slept with him on their first date. Couldn't think of a good reason not to. He was attractive, funny, and with all her friends getting engaged, it occurred to her vaguely that he might make a good husband. He'd certainly be better than her last boyfriend, a sleepy, taciturn boy who inhabited a parallel world, thanks to his huge consumption of Colombian Gold which an ex-girlfriend sent him, secreted in carefully hollowed-out paperbacks, from San Francisco. You couldn't do it now, Grace reflected. Grace was in the habit of meeting Lionel after his King's Inns dinners in the pub where they had first met. Bar students were obliged to 'dine' at the Inns four times each term in order to sit their exams. The tradition had come into being so that students could benefit from the wisdom of their more learned colleagues, but now had deteriorated into a boring necessity leavened only by drink. Students were given several beers as an 'aperitif' followed by their choice of a bottle of wine or a half-bottle of port. Future senior counsels and judges ate the execrable food ('What precisely is "fair-end of lamb"?' Lionel would ask rhetorically), drank too much and, occasionally, one or two of them threw up on the polished mahogany tables. The latter habit was rather frowned upon by the benchers – the five or so judges who sat at an elevated table at the top of the room and who had to be 'petitioned' if you wanted to go to the lavatory. But members of the legal profession have short memories and you would be unlikely to be reminded of these peccadilloes as your career blossomed.

When Grace sulked about the endless King's Inns dinners and exclaimed at their anachronistic character, Lionel said he liked it. He thought traditions should be nurtured, held sacred – though not, as it turned out, the tradition of marriage.

In the end they had to get married. When Grace fell pregnant, Lionel seemed to take the news on the chin, but this was only because he assumed Grace would do the decent thing and go to London. And she did go to London. She got the name of a clinic from the web of such information criss-crossing the university, offering far speedier solutions than the present-day Web. She took the plane and waited with all the other women in the waiting room of a tall, redbrick house in Pimlico. She stared at the ceiling while the Indian doctor probed around with one cold, jellied, rubber-clad finger and then, instead of waiting for the minibus that was to take all the women to another location to be terminated, she walked out into the late summer evening and hailed a taxi into the centre of London. She used the money Lionel had given her, £80 if memory served, to pay for a hotel off Oxford Street. Once settled in the dusty pink of a twin-bedded room, she ordered room service. She was surprisingly hungry.

'How did it go, angel?' Lionel asked when she called.

'Fine,' she said, picking a thread of steak from between her teeth.

She didn't tell him for a month. Actually, she didn't need to tell him because by then you could see that her vague tales about how things had gone in the clinic were fabrications. They didn't tell Grace's parents, who simply thought she was getting fat. 'You've turned into quite a big girl, haven't you?' her father mentioned to Grace on their way to the church. Although, in retrospect, this may have been said in a rare moment of kindliness. He was a doctor after all. Grace's mother mumbled indistinct threats, seemingly unaware that this was a strange wedding, taking place at nine o'clock on a Monday with only Grace's school friend, Maeve, and Lionel's brother, Ralph, present. Afterwards they went to a wine bar where Lionel got drunk and Grace got sick – twice.

Josh was born four and a half months later. By then Grace had left Raymond's magazine. He bought her lunch on her last day.

'I'll miss you.'

'No you won't. I was totally rotten.'

'Well yes, you were pretty abysmal, but … we got along,' he finished rather lamely.

Lionel got an allowance from his father to support them till he did his final exams and he went for interviews with various newspapers. 'Can't sit around in the Law Library waiting for work,' he said, a little accusingly.

From the outset it was accepted by Lionel, by Lionel's parents (his father was a very successful senior counsel), and by Grace herself that she had RUINED HIS LIFE. As it was, he got a job quite easily with a daily newspaper and started his journalistic career writing acid little pieces about the day-to-day workings of the District Court. His career burgeoned rapidly thanks to the fact that a foreign correspondent due to cover civil unrest in some African state got appendicitis. In the absence of anyone more experienced, the paper sent Lionel. He did so well – cannily relying on the bar-chats with other reporters rather than his own investigations – that he was sent abroad more and more to those remote places where the paper did not have a journalist on the ground.

And Grace became a mother. A bad mother. It wasn't that she disliked Josh it was just that – well he didn't seem to belong to her. She couldn't cope with the crying, the nappies, and the constant throb of the washing machine. She felt simultaneously bored and exhausted. She was too tired for sex but fortunately Lionel was also too tired. Unfortunately, he was too tired *from* sex.

She started drinking seriously. That is, she tended to head for the off-licence prior to stocking up with baby food. Some people weren't meant to be mothers really. In the hospital she had been the only woman who never asked for her baby to be brought to her and was relieved every time it was wheeled away to screech in some distant glass-walled room. Wine dulled the feeling of intrusion – of being colonized against her will – and, the more wine she drank, the more affectionate she became. She aimed at a level of anaesthesia just short of total drunkenness – a point where she felt a pleasant kinship with the world in general, where she was 'a good mother'.

Lionel either didn't notice or didn't care. 'You sound exhausted,' he would say as he telephoned from the edge of the pool in some hotel in some country that edged some little war, its violence as contained as a struggle fought out in a boxing ring.

Emily was born two years later. Looking back, it seemed as though the baby-years had passed in a dream. She remembered very little of them except the occasional vivid snapshot of a birthday party or a day at the beach when a combination of wind and icy water had sobered her for a minute.

She might have gone on like that forever but for the fact that one afternoon she lost the children. It was a bleak, dank day with yellow-grey clouds hanging low on the horizon. Rain tumbled and slid down the windowpane, the bricks of the house opposite oozed and bled, the living room smelt of soot and wet wool. Grace was not put out by the weather because she was well into her second bottle of cheap Spanish red and was inclined to see the humour in all this dark and melancholy. The high piping sound of Josh and Emily playing some game of pretend of Josh's devising seemed soothing rather than irritating. She dozed for a bit. She awoke to silence and the beginnings of a headache, but another glass of wine soon saw that off.

About half an hour later, she realized the house was quiet. 'Too quiet,' she said in the ominous tones of a TV thriller and then laughed hysterically. She enjoyed her own sense of humour. She got to her feet unsteadily, a little disorientated by a gust of wind in the hallway, and called up the stairs, 'Josh? Emily?' There was no reply. Then she noticed the front door was open.

She ran into the street and looked up and down but there was no sign of them. Some instinct for self-preservation made her go upstairs and run the shower full force over her head and face, the icy water clearing her head. Then, hair lank, sweatshirt sodden, she went out again. At the top end of the road, a window cleaner was tying a ladder onto his bicycle. She ran up to him.

'Did you see two children – four and six – a little girl and boy?'

'Blond?'

'Yes, yes – both blond.'

'They went down towards the pub,' the window cleaner said, pointing to where the main road with its flash of cars strobing past lay at right angles to the street.

'Oh Jesus. Oh God.'

Grace started to turn circles, feeling panic closing its grip. She couldn't think – couldn't move.

'Hold on now.'

The window cleaner had started untying his ladder. He rested it against the railings and climbed on his bike.

'You go down straight ma'am and I'll go down the other road. They can't have gotten far.'

Grace raced down the street he had indicated until she reached the main road. For once the street seemed quiet, although it was jammed with cars that were stopped, drivers looking out their windows asking what was the problem. 'Two kids,' yelled a man some distance away.

Grace ran towards him. She was gibbering a mantra, 'Oh please God, I'll do anything only please, please no.' When she reached the head of the bank of stalled cars, she screamed. Emily was lying in the middle of the road. Josh was sitting beside her. 'I'll tell Mummy,' he shouted.

'Oh no,' tears coursed down Grace's face mingling with the wet of her hair. She heard Emily's stout little voice.

'Won't, won't.'

At that moment, Josh caught sight of her.

'Mummy, she just sat down and wouldn't move.'

' 'Cos you were going too fast for me,' Emily said, jumping to her feet and dusting her pink, sprigged Laura Ashley dress fastidiously. Grace grabbed both their hands conscious of some mutterings from the people who had gathered on the footpath. 'It's a disgrace,' she heard, 'poor little mites.' Grace smiled shakily and, almost dragging the children, made it back to her own street. 'Never, ever, ever do that again,' she said to the bewildered children, after she had caught up with the window cleaner and called off the search. But in her head was that the never, ever applied to her. That she was never going to drink again. And she didn't. Well, until now.

She stopped drinking, got the children into a Montessori school and started applying for jobs. An assistant in the TV production department of Zeus Advertising seemed the best bet – for the moment at least. That was twenty years ago – although, oddly enough, it seemed longer.

FIVE

THE SECOND DAY of the Javelin shoot passed uneventfully.
The non-drinking actors took delighted mouthfuls of beer – and
then spat them into the plastic bucket provided.

'Charming,' said Mike.

'I don't like this at all,' said the client.

'Oh it's just so they can – be at their best all day,' Grace
soothed, 'normally they'd be swilling the stuff.'

She went up to the actors, smiling at them warmly. Still
smiling, she indicated the client.

'If any of you breathes a word about being non-drinkers, I will
personally see to it that you never work again.'

She then spent an hour with the client who didn't like the
colour of the beer.

'It's your shagging beer,' Grace felt like telling him, 'that's the
colour of it.' But instead she told him tranquilly that they'd tweak
it in 'post'.

They wrapped at eight.

'Give you a lift?' Mike asked.

'Thanks pet, I don't think I could cope with a taxi.'

Outside the house, she asked him to come in.

'Only spag bol mind.'

'Perfect.'

There was another message from Lionel who seemed to have forgotten all about his call of the day before and wanted her to send him a newly published novel. He was bored out of his tree and his present assignment was in a country where soothing his soul with alcohol might mean the loss of a hand. Could she send it care of the Hilton?

'Bastard,' she exclaimed to Mike who was opening a bottle of wine he'd found in the fridge.

'Last month he wanted a back issue of *The New Yorker*,' she said, expertly lowering spaghetti into a pot of bubbling water. 'About the only thing I can cook,' she said over her shoulder. They ate in silence for a while.

'God it's good to sit down,' Mike said finally.

'Hah!'

'What do you mean, "Hah!"?'

'You were sat down all day in the make-up van. Flirting with that hairdresser.'

'I was not! Oh all right,' Mike laughed, 'that's hard work too you know.'

'Well you won't be able to do that next time round. You'll be doing my job. Worry, worry, worry twenty-four hours a day and nothing but a new job description to recompense you. Agency Producer! Tah-rah!'

'I must have a plaque made.' Mike twirled his pasta into a nest on his fork and let it fall back onto the plate. 'They'll get someone else in. I won't get it. Don't want it to tell you the truth.'

'They'll have to offer it to you,' Grace took their plates and threw them in the sink, 'just make sure you screw more money out of them.'

She turned round, rested her hips against the sink and smiled at Mike. He was a curiosity amongst all the designer-clad agency people with their studied grunginess, their close-shaved heads, their boots fashioned to scale mountains rather than simply step on their colleagues.

He was wearing a very old corduroy jacket and flannel trousers. His shoes were old too, but looked as though they might have been handmade, which they were. These clothes were set off by a floppy hairstyle that just grazed his collar and a rather diffident English public school accent. He had the appearance of someone who maintained a 'place' in Scotland – the sort of place that provided shooting and fishing but not much in the way of central heating. He looked like 'old money'.

Perhaps that was what had attracted his wife, Annalise. If it was, she had been in for a shock. Mike had indeed attended a well-known English public school – courtesy of a great-aunt who had provided for it in her will. Mike's parents would have preferred the money. His father was a poorly-paid civil servant and his mother worked in a shop.

Still, they comforted themselves with the thought that Mike would make influential friends during his schooldays and this would serve him well later. But Mike didn't make any friends to speak of. He was understandably reluctant to invite any of his school-mates to stay in the pebble-dashed semi-detached in Knocklyon, its window draped with his mother's home-made curtains, the glass-fronted cabinet housing her collection of china animals. He didn't feel like exposing his father, who tended to wear carpet slippers when at home and owned a part-share in a greyhound, to the pitiless gaze of his school-mates – several of whom had titles.

So all he got out of his six years at the school was an accent that embarrassed his parents and the ability to eat absolutely anything, no matter how badly cooked.

Mike did his best to soften the edges of his past. He made a conscious effort to drop the 'g' in 'fucking' and to say 'shite' rather than 'shit' but somehow this only served to highlight the elegance of his vowels and the crisp explosions of his consonants.

Grace reached for a tea towel and ran it under the tap.

'You've got bolognese all over your shirt,' she said, throwing the towel to him.

'Oh shite,' he said, looking down at his pale yellow shirt, speckled with terracotta. He dabbed at it and then took a gulp of his wine. 'Spoken to Josh yet?'

'Not face-to-face thank God.'

'What about Emily?'

Grace started to peel a peach, one long tendril of skin spiralling down from the glistening flesh, and shook her head.

'Emily doesn't talk to any of us. I'm not sure which is worse, Emily the drug addict or Emily post-rehab. Apparently she can't "risk" any contact with her family because, of course, it's all our fault. In any case, she wouldn't have the time, she goes to about twenty of those wretched meetings a day.'

'Never tried it yourself?' Mike said, not looking at her.

Grace, who was having a hard time not reaching across the table and downing Mike's wine in one swallow, told him she didn't need meetings. She'd just stopped. Years and years ago.

'For the children,' she said and noticing how pompous that sounded, burst out laughing. 'Anyway,' she confessed, 'I've started again, just a glass now and then,' she said, going over to the cupboard for another glass which she filled from the bottle on the table.

'Cheers,' she said.

Then, inexplicably, Grace's eyes filled with tears.

'Ah Grace,' Mike shifted uncomfortably.

'Sorry.'

Grace blew her nose thoroughly in her napkin.

'It's just I've always done the right thing – I thought anyway. I was a diligent employee, and while I wasn't a natural mother, I did my best, the best I could. I was a good wife, a good home-maker, I gave up the jar – and in the end I've just made a mess of everything.'

'No you haven't.'

Grace ignored him.

'I was a good little girl – boringly good. I always got good reports, I was captain of the netball team, and I was a prefect. I was a virgin when I got married. Well, no I wasn't.' She held out her glass for a refill. 'But I might as well have been. I was so naïve it's unreal. Then I worked my ass off for those cretins for nearly twenty years – and for what? For bloody what? So they could buy villas in bloody Portugal and change their goddamn car every year?'

'Fuck them,' Mike advised.

'I feel as though I'm going to explode – I'm so tired of being perfect – someone you can rely on no matter what. I want to be unreliable and reckless. I want to be a danger to myself and to other people. I want to shoplift, I want to take drugs, I want to have meaningless affairs with men who are far too young for me – don't look so terrified, you're too old. Do you think I'd even look at someone over thirty?'

'That's a relief.'

'Sorry,' Grace said again, 'I'm just – menopausal probably. Excellent! That's something to look forward to.'

'Grace you need to lighten up. Go on – maybe you should . . . you know, kick over the traces. Though no shoplifting. That's a bit mid-life crisis.'

'Not if it's something really big,' Grace smiled at him wickedly, 'like a car. I quite fancy that. Shoplifting a car.'

'You can't drive.'

'What's that got to do with anything? Anyway, any fool can drive now. You just point it somewhere and press the accelerator. Easy peasy!'

'Whatever you say.' Mike drained the last of his wine and got up to go. 'Better head,' he said, 'another early one tomorrow.'

Finally, it was all in the can. Grace had seen the rushes – the dailies – and it looked OK although Derek would have a horse of a job trying to make it cut. And indeed, when she rang Mike at the edit suite two days later, this turned out to be the case.

'How's she cutting?' she said, followed by a snort of laughter at her own witticism.

'Not too well at all,' Mike said, ignoring her sally, 'you'd better get down here.'

When she arrived at the studio, Grace was directed to edit suite three. She climbed the stairs, nodding at the streams of pretty girls who clattered by her carrying trays of cups and coffee-pots. 'Hello,' they each trilled merrily as though she were the nicest encounter they had had all day.

In the edit suite, Mike was hunched in a couch, smoking. Beside him sat Derek, looking uncharacteristically nervous, while Melvin and Dion had the air of small boys discovered torturing a cat. Mike nodded at the editor who pressed a series of buttons and the commercial appeared.

'Oh my God,' said Grace.

'I'm very happy with it,' said Derek, unhappily.

'Are you?'

Grace smiled pleasantly before asking the editor to go through the commercial again, freezing at the points she would indicate. 'OK,' she said, addressing Derek, 'this is our main drinking shot – am I right? This is that blond idiot taking one drink from one pint. So he's drinking and the pint is half-full. Good Lord! Now it's full. Oh dear, empty. Oh! Now it's full again. How the fuck did you think this was going to cut, you complete idiot? Did you even consult continuity?'

Grace leaned against the wall. Melvin and Dion looked at their hands. Then Grace remembered that Derek's continuity girl had been one of his old flames. Grace had let it pass even though Ciara, the lady in question, used Polaroids as though she were paying for them herself, so there were never adequate records for the last set-up. She also had an unnerving habit of turning to you just before the camera rolled with the query, 'Was his shirt open or closed in the last shot?'

'You're continuity,' Grace had snapped at her more than once, 'you tell me.'

'You could make a feature of it,' Geoff, the producer, suggested timidly from a spot deep in the shadows. Half-moons of sweat gathered in his armpits.

'Look, Grace. I'd a shit of a time trying to get any useable drinking shots. They all turn into a spit before I can get a decent edit in. I can't believe that no one checked that they all drank,' Derek murmured virtuously, 'I mean it seems fairly fundamental.'

Derek was a great man for checking. For example, he always asked every actor if they had the requisite number of fingers. This stemmed from the fact that he had once been careless enough to cast a hand artist who was missing two digits.

'We could do something in post,' the editor suggested.

'OK that's what you'll have to do then.' Grace rooted angrily through her bag looking for a cigarette.

'We haven't budgeted for …' Geoff began before thinking better of it. 'OK,' he said in a beaten voice, 'that's what we'll do then.'

Grace pulled on her coat and wrenched open the door. In the car park, she paused to take some deep breaths.

'Grace?' She looked up to see Mike.

'Well I think you've got the wind up them,' he said, and then in a John Wayne voice, 'I don't mind telling you, you scared the hell out of me.'

Grace smiled at his big, open face. They were so careful of each other, she thought. For example, she never asked after Annalise, who was a serial adulterer. Mike had told her once that he no longer held grudges against any of the men. If he were to avoid contact with all his wife's lovers it would exclude half the population, he explained, so he ignored it. And the more he ignored it, the less important it became. In fact, Grace realized with a start, Mike and Annalise had quite a happy marriage in a way. Once Grace and he had gone to a film, an Argentinian one, she remembered, with subtitles. It was called *We Don't Want to Talk About It*, a reference to the heroine's attitude to her daughter who was a dwarf. The mother simply put it out of her mind – ignored it. When one of her lovers bought the daughter a miniature horse, exactly the right size for a miniature person, the mother was furious. 'What sort of person could ride a horse like that?' she railed.

Occasionally, it occurred to Grace that it might be healthy to talk to Mike about the real reason for Annalise's infidelity. They had no children and Annalise yearned for a child. Grace assumed it was Annalise who couldn't have children because God knows she had enough male partners to populate the borough of Dun Laoghaire. But the matter of children was never discussed. As far as Grace knew, there were no tests done, no talk of adoption. They simply closed the chapter. Sometimes it's better not to face things. In a world full of the need to 'confront' one's anger, one's pain, one's past, Mike and Grace shared a desire to let things be.

They drove around the corner to a pub for a sandwich.

'Aren't these the absolute best?' said Mike, grabbing his doorstep ham sandwich and taking a huge bite, 'none of your poncey sliced pan here!'

'No,' Grace agreed, taking a small sip of her bowl of packet minestrone.

'Why does packet minestrone taste exactly like vomit?'

'You've got me there.' Mike smeared more mustard on his chunk of ham.

'Grace?'

Both Grace and Mike looked up. They noticed one of two men who'd been sitting at the bar rise and come towards them.

'It is Grace, isn't it?'

The man leaned forward warmly and took her hand, shook it once or twice and then pulled her forward awkwardly and kissed her on the cheek. On the ear actually.

'I … ?' Grace said, playing for time.

'It's Travis.'

'Travis!' Grace said, astonished. Mike looked on curiously, his sandwich forgotten on the plate.

'Mike, I'd like you to meet Travis. He was in the first Javelin commercial. Isn't that the strangest thing? We're just editing the latest round the corner,' she explained to Travis.

'Hope it's going easier than ours did.'

'We've the opposite problem this time. They wouldn't drink.'

'Ah,' said Travis, smiling and immediately becoming more like the boy she'd cast fifteen years ago. 'So,' he said, backing away a step, 'we should have a drink or – you don't do you? Lunch then. To catch up.'

'Yeah,' said Grace, 'that'd be really great.'

'Are you still in the same agency?'

'Well, for a couple of weeks anyway.'

Travis smiled again.

'OK then. I'll ring you. Cheers,' and he went to rejoin his friend.

'Isn't that wild?' Grace said when she and Mike were driving back to the editing suite.

'That was the shoot you were talking about – worst one of your life?'

'Ah it was a laugh really. Looking back.' Grace smiled to herself, feeling better for some reason.

It had been fifteen years ago that the agency had got the Javelin account – right after Myles Kitchen took over as Managing Director. It was his validation. For days he went round with a Cheshire cat smile bathing everyone, and especially the two creators of the concept, in the sunlight of his charm. Grace, with the same good luck that had marked Lionel's career, had become head of TV after her predecessor had finally succumbed to the manic depression to which he was prey. Not, however, before he had spent two hundred thousand of the agency's money during one of his manic phases – a spree that meant his departure was quite sudden in the end.

The creatives involved were an intimidating woman called Annie, some years older than Grace, and the then creative director, Nicholas. Nick was a man who was merely marking time with advertising until he followed his true calling – that of a painter – although, as the years passed, this ambition seemed less and less likely to be fulfilled.

The two had worked together for years and spoke in a sort of patois. They were overly influenced by avant-garde cinema, which they plundered regularly for their work – the present Javelin commercial owed much to a spate of Indie movies set in blue-collar America – and they were fond of 'challenging' the viewer, which meant they produced work no one fully understood.

The commercial was cast in London because, Grace suspected, Nick and Annie had an urgent need to shop. They stayed in a small hotel in an area skirting Soho. The casting went well enough although Grace didn't entirely agree with the final result. She wanted an actor whose career was about to take off while Nick and Annie – and the client – all wanted Travis. There was something about him that made Grace nervous. True, he was good. Actually he was too good. The actor who failed to get cast put her fears into words.

'Look,' he explained to Grace, 'I can just act dangerous and Travis – well Travis *is* dangerous.'

Four weeks later, Travis and the two other actors who'd been cast flew into Dublin for the shoot. There was to be a day of rehearsals, a day when the three actors could 'bond' as Nick and Annie explained with a great deal of arm-waving and persuasive smiles. The director, hand-picked by Nick and Annie on account of his complete inability to stand his ground on any issue, was called Simon. Or Simple Simon, as he came to be known almost immediately.

The bonding process started in a restaurant over an elaborate lunch that included a great deal of wine and much taking up of Nick's expansive offers of 'Another digestif anyone?' During the five years Grace hadn't been drinking, she'd almost forgotten what drinking did to people. Actually, even when she was drinking, she'd assumed everyone else was sober and, if someone fell over, well, they'd tripped, hadn't they?

Toying with her fourth mineral water, Grace looked around the table. The other two actors, Michael and Robert, were cut from the same cloth as Travis. Lads, wide boys. Sorry, 'real people'. They were all three shouting now, swapping theatrical anecdotes while Annie and Nick listened with rapt attention. Grace laughed dutifully as Travis recounted how he got back at an uppity second assistant director on some costume drama by insisting on frequent visits to the lavatory. Since he was wearing full armour at the time, this necessitated the second assistant reaching delicately into his groin and pointing his penis in the right direction. There was a great yelp of laughter and the other diners turned around disapprovingly. Grace made a little face at the head waiter which she hoped encompassed a wealth of meaning: I'm only here because I have to be, I hate it as much as you, I'm actually a really nice person and I want to come back because this is my favourite restaurant in the whole world. But the head waiter ignored her and, when Nick ordered yet another round of drinks, murmured contemptuously, 'Anozzer?'

They left and repaired to Cassidy's where everyone ordered pints of Guinness.

'Shouldn't you be drinking Javelin,' Grace asked, 'seeing as that's what you're advertising?'

'That shite?' said Travis, and Nick and Annie laughed as though this were the wittiest thing they'd heard all year.

The actors stumbled through their lines. 'Brilliant,' enthused Nick.

'I'm glad to see you're not precious about your work,' Grace said dryly. Half an hour later, Simon dispatched the actors into the night to 'really get to know each other'. Grace got a taxi home, conversing on autopilot with the driver. 'Awful.' 'Ridiculous.' 'I totally agree with you,' she murmured at intervals in response to the usual stew of racism, misogyny and political extremism.

She arrived at the shoot just before seven. Simon was already there, fumbling through his shooting script, occasionally going into a huddle with his lighting cameraman. At seven-fifteen, there was still no sign of the actors. Grace wasn't too concerned. One thing she'd learnt in her five years was that the actors always turn up. The second assistant would force them into a car, at gunpoint if necessary, and they would be there. What Grace had not considered was their condition when they did arrive, and Travis, Michael and Robert were in a terrible state.

The actors were trapped in that limbo between extreme drunkenness and a monumental hangover. Their eyes were bloodshot, their hands shook and a fine layer of grey sweat covered their faces. Adding a certain surreal touch to the situation, all three were covered in what looked like tattoos but were in fact little drawings in biro. None of the three could account for how they came by them. Nobody spoke for a moment and then Simon screamed:

'Doctor, we need a doctor.'

The doctor arrived about five minutes later, as if he'd been waiting in the corridor for weeks in anticipation of just such an emergency. He was small and fat, and his eyes darted around as though he feared he was being followed. He was the sort of doctor who'd be good for a gram if you were stuck, the kind of doctor with experience of mysterious stab wounds and the removal of bullets.

He gave the three actors an injection and for quite a long while afterwards, Grace kicked herself for not discovering what the injection was because it had a totally magical effect. It instantly rendered the actors simultaneously completely alert ('Dear Christ, I'm covered in biro!') and wonderfully sanguine ('Oh … whatever …').

'Well I think we can rest assured that they've bonded,' Grace couldn't resist saying to Nick.

'Sweet mother of Jesus!'

'That's me all right,' Grace said.

An hour later, the actors were lounging on bar stools waiting for a lighting check.

'So what do you think?' asked Annie.

'It's improved dramatically since they've had a drink,' Grace told her, 'the difficulty is preventing them from drinking any more.'

'The Code, right,' said Annie, uncharacteristically looking to Grace for guidance. The Drink Advertising Code dictated that only one swallow is seen on screen. It was OK if people looked as though they'd just been drinking or were just about to drink but the drinking shot was the only on-screen swallow allowed.

Grace frowned at the actors as Travis reached over the bar for a pint.

'Oh for God's sake.' She strode across the floor to where the brewery product man was pulling two more pints.

'Put those down,' she said to the actors, meanwhile smiling at Jack, the product expert who was blowing into a pint with a straw to bring up the head.

'Jack, you know you shouldn't be giving them anything – they'll be good for nothing by lunchtime. Apart from anything else we can't spare it. Spit in the pints if necessary.'

The day crept by giving truth to the cliché about filming – that it was rather like war: long periods of stultifying boredom enlivened by brief moments of frenetic activity.

'Have a cup of tea,' Brendan, the sparks, said to her at midnight and, persuasively, 'they've got snake-cake.'

'Ah,' Grace grinned, 'my favourite,' and she allowed the Swiss roll to unravel into a jammy snake, which she threaded into her mouth, wrinkling her nose as the sugar hit her.

'How are we doing?' she asked Simon.

'Two shots to go.'

Grace watched the three actors lined up at the bar for the penultimate shot.

'They look remarkably fresh. I thought they'd fade once that injection wore off.'

'Well they've been going to the loo a lot. An awful lot.'

Simon held one nostril closed and sniffed deeply through the other, all the while looking at Grace meaningfully.

'You've lost me,' she said eventually.

'Cocaine,' Simon explained patiently.

'Oh,' Grace nodded slowly, 'I see. Yes. Well at least they're awake,' she said finally, looking on the bright side. She went over to Simon's producer.   'What are you going to do about the actors?' she asked.

'In what way?'

'In the way of getting them on set tomorrow half-alive and free of illustrations.'

'That wasn't our fault,' said the producer defensively.

'Oh who cares whose fault it was?' Grace said. 'Just make sure they get a few hours' sleep.'

The next day it was colder and they were shooting exteriors. Grace looked down at her ugly, plastic, fur-lined boots with some affection. Travis was coming towards her, shivering in a shirt.

'Any chance of that doctor from yesterday?'

'I hear you're pretty good at self-medication.'

Travis laughed. She couldn't help laughing back.

'Tell you what Gracie,' he said, 'when this is all over, I'll bring you out partying. How'd you like that?'

'Oh, my party days are long over.'

'You're as young as you feel. What age are you? Thirty?'

'Actually I feel a hundred and four or so.' Grace grinned at him, then turned and made her way over to where Simon was deep in conversation with his lighting cameraman.

'Hiya pet,' Simon said, not looking at her.

'I'm fine, thanks for asking,' Grace said evenly, 'and don't call me pet.'

'Whatever you say,' Simon gave her a smile that didn't reach his eyes. 'Are we lit, Sunshine?' Simon enquired of the camera-man.

They moved fast, making up for lost time; it was good, Grace had to admit, grudgingly. The actors instinctively played to each other and you could almost believe they'd been mates for years. The next day started smoothly. Travis, Michael and Robert seemed alert enough; Nick and Annie were less arrogant and more inclined to ask her advice.

'It's going fine,' she told them, 'you were right about Travis.'

'He's got a quality, hasn't he?' Nick said eagerly.

'Well he's got something,' Grace muttered.

By eleven they'd gotten through two set-ups. Simon, delighted with himself, was bopping to the music playing at full decibel in the background, shouting 'Love it!' at the actors after every take.

'If you love it, why don't you print it?' Grace said under her breath.

During the lunch-break, things started to go downhill. First it was a call from a tabloid newspaper. 'Was it true that one of the actors in the commercial had been to prison?'

'What are you talking about? Who gave you this number?' Grace said, simultaneously waving wildly at Nick. 'I don't know what you're talking about,' she said finally, slamming the phone down.

'What was that?' Nick scrunched his paper cup and threw it in the bin.

Grace told him.

'Jesus!'

'Better talk to Travis I suppose,' Grace sat down on a roll of linoleum. 'It has to be Travis. I just knew it.' The phone rang again. It was Myles Kitchen.

'Of course I didn't know,' Grace said, 'I don't even know now. I am going to check. I do see the ramifications. No I don't have any ideas. I don't even have any information at the moment. Don't hang up on me you complete bastard.' Grace looked up at Nick.

'He hung up on me.'

'Bastard,' said Nick, showing rare sympathy. Now they were in it together. Grace got up slowly.

'Better check it out,' she said, making her way to the back of the set where Travis and the others were waiting for a camera rehearsal.

'Travis, I need to talk to you.'

He followed her out through the big double doors to the car park.

'So what's the story, Gracie?'

'Don't call me Gracie,' she said, then, turning to him, 'We've got a problem.'

He looked at her.

'I've had a paper on and ...' Grace looked away, 'Travis, were you ever in prison?'

Travis didn't reply for a while.

'Well?'

'It was in England. No way anyone could find out.'

'Well I'm afraid they have found out. May I ask what it was for?'

'Armed robbery.'

'Ah Christ!' Grace turned away for a moment. 'I thought it might be something ... ?'

'A bit more white-collar? Drugs, fraud?'

'Don't take that attitude with me Travis.'

Grace smiled blankly at a passing grip. Travis threw his still-lit cigarette into the street.

'I was eighteen,' he said finally. 'I was stupid. I didn't know anyone had a gun.' He paused. 'I did the time – you know?'

'OK,' Grace thrust her hands more deeply into her pockets.

'Anyway,' Travis said, 'what's it to you?'

'We've just spent a quarter of a million pounds filming an armed robber for a beer company who like to be seen as squeaky clean and it is a problem.'

'I'm sorry, I needed the work.'

Grace half-smiled.

'I know. I know you did. Don't worry about it. It's done now.'

'So?' Nick, now joined by Annie, asked on her return.

'So we soldier on,' Grace said, 'too late to do anything now.'

They wrapped at seven and crew and cast repaired to the pub, but Grace phoned a taxi and went home. She felt that tomorrow might be a day when she needed to be at her best. She got to the office at eight o'clock but Myles Kitchen had beaten her to it. There were two sticky notes instructing her to contact him immediately – the second one ending mysteriously with the warning, 'this is not a joke'. Grace went over to his office and walked in, unannounced.

'Why would I think it was a joke?' she asked.

Myles picked up a pen and held it lightly in both hands as though he intended doing a trick of some sort.

'Somebody has been imitating my writing and leaving messages for people. On their desks.'

Had to be Ian, Grace decided. He was the house forger. Need a concert ticket, seats for the rugby? Well Ian was your man.

'So, what are you going to do about this … this … ?' Myles was momentarily at a loss for words.

'Do what we always do,' Grace said, 'blame someone else.'

'I'm sorry?' Myles said dangerously.

But Grace moved smoothly on, 'It was the client who really wanted the particular actor, not us. I made my feelings clear at the time and the two creatives, well they weren't convinced at all about casting Travis. They went with the client. The director on the other hand was with me,' Grace lied.

'But then the client will feel we're dumping on him and we'll be in worse trouble. Christ, we've only just got this account.'

'Not if you make a plus of it,' Grace suggested, thinking on her feet. 'Before he has time to say anything, congratulate him on his courage in casting this person who has, after all, paid his debt to society. Tell him what a great leap forward it is for a brand that is seen as bland and boring to come up with a really gritty, hard-edged casting decision.'

Myles looked at her sharply trying to see if he could trust her. It was no secret that they didn't get on. If Grace had still been drinking, she would have told him at length just why she disliked him, but their mutual distrust remained something unspoken – something each carried around like a sharp-edged stone they occasionally ran their fingers over.

'It's actually a bloody good idea,' Myles said finally, 'bloody good.'

'Thank you.' Grace allowed a draft of cold air to enter the phrase so that they would each know where they stood.

The reason Grace disliked Myles was that she'd been so smitten by him when he'd first taken over as MD. The industry, and their agency in particular, was reeling under the effects of a recession. Myles took over a kingdom divided by petty jealousies, rent with bitterness and on the verge of bankruptcy. He needed to unite all his subjects in as short a time as possible. His method of doing this was to visit them individually in their offices. From a vast fund of personal anecdotes, he selected something of himself, and this act of self-revelation immediately encouraged the person to whom he was speaking to open up personally.

The story he chose to tell Grace had to do with animals. She loved animals – or rather the idea of them. It was about a gun-dog he had owned as a child. He told the story well, occasionally pausing to laugh in a collusive, intimate way that made Grace feel singled out, special. The dog was a present to Myles from an indulgent grandfather and, aside from costing a great deal of money as a pup, its training had involved further investment. Unfortunately, even the most rigorous training couldn't make up for the dog's limitations. Not only had it no sense of smell, it had no sense of direction. So, far from raising a pheasant, or charging off to collect the odd successfully downed pigeon, the dog couldn't even find his way back to the house from the garden.

Grace had been so charmed by this that she couldn't speak. The story played to all her weaknesses – the idea of a gun-dog that got lost in its own back garden both amused and touched her. She saw Myles in a whole new light – saw the bewildered child behind the suit and the briefcase and could picture the equally bewildered dog running hither and thither in the garden. Afterwards she grew bitter about the story and its effect on her. Out of all the stories in his considerable repertoire, how had Myles known that this was the one for her? How had he known?

Years later, in a rare moment of self-knowledge, she realized that, had the situation been reversed, she would have known exactly the right anecdote to tell Myles, but by then it was too late. By then she'd forgotten why she disliked him and only remembered that she did.

'So that was the first Javelin shoot?' said Mike. They'd been parked for some time while Grace finished her story. 'Well, well, well, how the mighty have crumbled.'

'Travis?'

'No – Nick and Annie. They left years ago, didn't they?'

'Myles is still here though.'

'Mmmh,' Mike opened the car door and spoke in at her, the wind whipping at his hair. 'Well a badly-cut commercial is going to be small potatoes after that debacle.'

'I suppose.' Grace opened her bag and searched for her purse. Mike never had parking money.

'So are you going to have lunch with him?'

'Travis? Yeah. Yeah I might.'

As they went up the steps to the editing suite Mike sniggered.

'What?'

'He must be nearly forty now – too old for you.'

'That wasn't what I had in mind at all.'

'At all at all?' She could hear Mike's laughter as he bounded up the stairs ahead of her.

SIX

THE TV PRODUCTION DEPARTMENT looked out over waste ground, a hummocky half acre of weed and burnt tyres with the occasional rusted car bumper rearing out of the ground like some ancient artefact. Grace had grown rather fond of this derelict garden that was holding out against the march of progress in a country overcome and over-run by its own good fortune. Through the thick glass, she could hear the hard cries of children playing – tiny thugs, tottering through the thistles punctuating their game with shouts of 'fuck' and 'yah bollix'.

'Gives a whole new meaning to "Blue Peter",' she said to Mike, who had just arrived.

'Before my time,' Mike said, sitting down heavily and staring at the pile of folders on his desk. 'Oh well, another day another dollar,' he sighed, opening the first and grimacing at what it revealed. Grace's phone rang.

'Hiya Gracie.'

'Travis?' Grace looked over at Mike, rolling her eyes but smiling.

'So how about that lunch?'

'When?'

'Today suit you?'

'Today?' Grace looked over at Mike who shrugged and mouthed, 'Go for it.'

'So eh ... what are you wearing?' Travis asked.

'Is this an obscene phone call?'

'It could be. But what I really need to know is, are you wearing a dress?'

'I'm wearing leather trousers actually.'

'Great! See you at one.'

Grace put down the phone and looked over at Mike.

'What was all that about?' he asked.

'God knows.' Grace clicked on her Café Pur file and opened 'Casting'.

'I thought you'd be downtown getting hubby his novel,' Mike said.

'Let him get his own bloody novel – or get the Child Bride to do it.'

'Well done Grace!' Mike got up. 'I'm going to make you a celebratory cup of coffee to mark the occasion, and next you'll be telling me your plan of how to shaft the agency.'

'I'm working on it,' Grace said, lighting a cigarette and leaning back in her chair.

Actually she didn't have a plan – not as such – but she had an idea. She opened her file on Javelin and started going through the costs going back fifteen years. It was slow work and brought her close to lunchtime but, in the end, she had six pages of notes, a sore back and the beginning of a feeling of triumph. This might just work. She was interrupted by a call from reception.

'Who's this?' said the plaintive voice of Maria.

'It's Grace,' she said, trying to keep her temper.

'Oh right,' said Maria, who in ten years had yet to come to grips with the complexities of the switch. 'There's someone here for you,' she tittered.

'I'll be right down,' Grace said as Maria gave a shriek of laughter.

Mike was standing at the window from where he could just glimpse the street. 'I might come down with you,' he murmured, 'I need a bit of cheering up.'

'Should I call a taxi?' Grace said, her hand hovering over the phone.

'Oh he's got transport,' Mike said levelly, 'no worries on that score.'

He followed Grace down to reception and out the front door. Travis was indeed there, lolling against a large black motorbike. Two helmets were looped onto his arm.

'Thought you could do with the fresh air.'

'You don't think …' Grace began but, hearing a snort of laughter from Mike, she strode over to Travis and put out her hand for a helmet. Travis eased it over her head. She felt like an old-fashioned deep-sea diver. Immediately her head, obeying the laws of gravity, fell heavily against her chest. From a long way off, she heard Mike's voice.

'Very fetching.'

A sound escaped from Grace somewhere between a whimper and a laugh. Travis threw his leg over the saddle of the bike. It looked incredibly large, more like a horse than a bike. Grace placed her foot on the chrome-plated footrest and clumsily climbed astride behind him. Afterwards she thought she might have fainted briefly at this point because she had no memory of the bike taking off, just a sudden sensation of wind cutting her face and cars receding away from her at speed – a blur of metal and sunlight. Then she concentrated on trying to keep her head upright although, more often than not, her helmet bounced off Travis's. From some forgotten part of her a message came through, 'go with the bike'. So when Travis leaned into a corner, so did she, and soon they were on the dual carriageway heading for Blackrock and her hands clung to the leather of Travis's jacket suggesting that their removal might require surgery.

When they came to a stop outside a bar in Dun Laoghaire, she was almost afraid to alight lest her legs collapse. She stood for a second noticing the startled glances of a group of people beyond the plate glass window and removed her helmet. She felt … amazing.

'That was …' she grinned at Travis.

'Wasn't it though?'

They went into the pub. Grace remembered it from years before when it was a series of snugs, the walls and ceiling greasy with smoke and bitterness. Its new owners had gone to considerable expense to replicate the yellowed ceiling but now the bar was an open space full of light, its blond wood etched with the black-clad drinkers who stood at the bar or sat at alcove tables as though waiting for a photograph.

'Very rocket and panini,' said Grace, not altogether approvingly.

'Do you remember the old place?' Travis asked her.

'Mmh. Used to drink here when I was a student.'

'I keep forgetting you're a hundred and three.'

Travis was leaning in over the bar trying to catch the eye of one of the three waiting staff who were discussing the merits of a 'Brazil' over mere bikini waxing. Finally one reluctantly peeled free of her colleagues and took their order.

'So …' said Travis when they were sitting at a corner table with their ciabatta sandwiches, 'what's been happening?'

Grace thought for a moment and then said, 'Nothing.'

Travis looked at her quizzically. Grace peered into her sandwich where a coil of prosciutto tried unsuccessfully to cover its base of bread.

'Nothing. Truly. Get up, go to work, go home, watch TV, go to bed, get up.'

Travis took a bite of his sandwich.

'But now,' Grace continued, 'all that's going to change. I'm going to get up, stay home, watch TV and go to bed. I've just been "let go" as they say.'

'Well that's good news.'

'Is it?'

'Well now you can start doing something that's a bit more interesting. I don't know, hire a car and drive across America.'

'I can't drive.'

Travis looked astonished.

'Really?'

'I had a bad experience.'

'Well you need to get back on the horse, look at me. I've come off that bike more times than I can remember but I just climb back on her.'

'Good for you. Anyway, I don't want to drive.'

'Yes you do.'

'No I don't. I don't want to be a bloody housewife creeping along in a Ford Fiesta getting the finger from some little shit every time I stall.'

Grace didn't tell him that one of her fantasies was acquiring the driving skills that made her first choice for anyone arranging a bank robbery, but Travis seemed to read her mind.

'It's just you don't want to drive like an amateur.'

Grace smiled into her uneaten sandwich.

'And I,' he went on, 'know exactly the person to teach you.'

'You I suppose.'

'Nah,' Travis called for the bill, 'cousin of mine. Ideal he'd be. He could start you next week.'

'Why not immediately?' Grace said ironically.

'He doesn't get out till Saturday.'

Grace smiled tightly, 'We'll see … what about you?' she asked finally, 'still acting?'

Travis pushed his plate away. 'Nah. Got bored.'

'It's a hard old haul,' Grace sympathized.

'I just couldn't be arsed really, doing shit in shit-holes for dole money.'

'So what do you do now?'

'Bit of this …'

'… Bit of that,' Grace supplied.

'Actually,' Travis leaned forward, 'I'm in security.'

'You're a bouncer.'

'Don't knock it. I'm a good person to know if you want to get into –' and he named a club frequented by fifteen-year-olds.

'I'll remember that.'

She arrived back at the office, breathless, her face pink, her hair squashed flat, her leather trousers flecked with mud. She ignored the large question mark of Maria's face. Mike was at a recording, so she was alone. She rifled through the notes he had left on her desk. One note explained the necessity of his presence at the recording. She or Mike always had to be there when Dermot was doing a radio commercial because of his inability to write within the time. He claimed that the script was exactly twenty-nine seconds when he read it, but midway through the recording there was always a frantic call to say it was coming out at forty seconds. Under questioning, this figure would be revised up to fifty – or even sixty. Unable to cut his own pearls, Grace or Mike needed to be there to wield the scalpel. Grace dialled the number of the studio.

'So,' she said, 'what are we coming out at?'

'About a minute and a half,' Mike said, 'wanker!'

'Don't cut it – let it go.'

'What?'

'You heard me – let it go.'

'But we won't have time to re-record. The airdate's tomorrow.'

'Well the agency will just have to cover the shortfall, won't it?'

Grace hung up the phone and went back to her notes of the morning. She was concentrating on the figures pertaining to travel, actors' fees and exigencies. Mike came back at four, looking mutinous.

'So how's *Girl on a Motorcycle*?'

'Who peed on your shoe?' Grace put aside her notes and turned to him.

'Here's your mini-series – I got it in at 60 seconds and it's still tight – the VO nearly had a heart attack doing it.' Mike threw a tape of the radio commercial on her desk and then turned to his computer. 'I've still got to work here you know.'

Grace, who had been about to show him what she'd discovered, hesitated.

'Jesus, you were the one who said I should shaft them.'

The phone rang. It was her father.

'Hi Dad,' she said, arranging her face into a mask of calm. 'Mum?' Her mother didn't reply but she could tell she was on the other line. They liked a 'party line' dimension to their phone calls to her. She held the phone a little way from her ear as her father launched into one of his tirades. Her mother had Alzheimer's –

she needed putting down, putting out of her misery. She had lost all her faculties. It was like living with a dog. He couldn't cope.

There was a screech from her mother. Alzheimer's? He was the demented one. Did this sound like Alzheimer's? Her mother started reciting random sentences, which, after a bit, Grace realized were clues from the Crosaire crossword. Her mother had, apparently, solved it in fifteen minutes. Her father, her mother hissed, couldn't even do the Simplex any more. His brain had been eaten away by syphilis. It was like living with a pig – a filthy, incontinent pig. She'd hang for him. She had been poisoning him slowly with weedkiller so it wouldn't be long now. There was a great shout from her father and the sound of crashing cutlery and breaking glass followed by the sweet tones of her mother saying, 'Didn't we like our shepherd's pie then?' Grace grimaced at Mike, who seemed to have thawed out somewhat, and managed to get in an 'I'll call round at the weekend … bye, bye, see you.'

And she hung up with her father in mid-spate. She had meant to tell them she no longer had a job but her parents were so totally self-absorbed that her news would have little impact on them. They never asked about her work – or indeed their grandchildren. On those rare occasions when they did enquire, neither Grace's mother nor her father was entirely sure of the children's names. 'And how's young eh – hmmh – the boy?' her father would say, his voice grey with indifference. 'He must be – older now?', at which point both Grace and her parents would tacitly agree to abandon the whole discussion and get back to more important matters like what it was like to be saddled to an ancient crone (Grace's mother) who'd turn the stomach of a saint.

'It's almost impressive really, isn't it?' Mike said. 'To live life at that pitch for what – over fifty years? It brings hate to an art form.'

Or love, Grace thought, remembering her bright idea of placing them in separate old people's homes. Her parents handcuffed themselves together and only revealed the whereabouts of the key when she agreed to forget the whole notion. When she told Lionel, all he wanted to know was where they'd got the handcuffs.

Grace spent the remainder of the afternoon dozing through a treatment presentation for a commercial that would be shot long after she left. It was a commercial for the government – either 'Get out and vote' or 'Get out and buy these government-backed shares', Grace couldn't be sure. Her contributions were limited to occasional comments of 'Too expensive' – 'Too much post-production' – and finally, kindly, 'Listen I don't think they're going to buy our shooting in the Caribbean, pleasant as it would be for all of us.'

Afterwards, it occurred to her that a week in the Caribbean might be just what the clients would like. She looked sourly at the young director who was clearly marking time in the commercial world prior to being whisked off to America to direct a big budget war movie with the opportunity to tell Robert de Niro that he needed to bring his performance down a bit. ('Smaller, Bob, smaller.')

Before she left, she picked up her messages. One was from Travis telling her that his cousin had got early release and would pick her up outside the National Concert Hall at noon the next day. When she tried to phone back, the number was unobtainable. Mike was just packing up.

'I'm starting driving lessons tomorrow,' she told him brightly.

'Good for you.'

SEVEN

IT WAS COLD FOR JUNE and Grace shivered in her linen suit as she waited at the gates of the National Concert Hall. A battered Honda Civic, approaching at speed and seemingly driverless, caught her attention. As it slewed to a halt right beside her, she made out the driver whose shiny head just cleared the steering wheel. The driver's door flew open revealing a boy of about twelve.

'Grace?'

Grace looked at him for a moment.

'Are you Travis's cousin?'

'Yeah – hop in.'

He slid into the passenger seat and pointed to the driving seat. Grace made a sound like a whale expelling air. She sighed and got into the car. 'Is it an automatic?' she whispered in a voice that seemed to come from someone else. The child winced. 'No,' he said as if she'd suggested sex, 'yah hafta have a stick shift for real driving. Dat's what you want isn't it?'

'I suppose so.'

'Right, ignition on, foot on clutch – dat's the one on de left – middle one's de brake, right-hand's de accelerator. So foot on clutch, into first gear and – ease your foot off de clutch as you press de accelerator.'

Grace did what she was told, fudging the gears so that when she pressed the accelerator the car leaped forward.

'Very good,' said her teacher, 'but remember,' because by this time the engine had cut out, 'de idea is to keep movin'.'

Somehow, under his tutelage, Grace managed to drive twice around St Stephen's Green with only a few shouted expletives from other drivers to mark her ineptitude. During the drive, the child kept up a steady stream of anecdote interspersed with instruction so that a comment like 'complete shite' could refer to another driver or the food in his last place of abode. Finally, when Grace felt the moment was right, she asked him what he'd been 'in' for. He gave a staccato laugh.

'Cars, didn't Travis tell yah? Right, pull her in here and I'll take over till we get somewhere quieter.'

They drove down Dawson Street, round by Pearse Street and then headed north of the city to where factories gave way to scrubland interspersed with new housing. Eventually they reached a half-built industrial estate where glass-fronted buildings with windows criss-crossed with tape reared up against the clouds.

'Why here?' Grace said, beginning to feel frightened.

'Parkin'.'

With that they turned sharply into a vast car park attached to a scaffold-encased office block and with a slew of gravel and mud, came to a halt. In the distance, a dog barked – low and threatening.

A man in uniform ambled round from the back of the building with an Alsatian straining on its leash ahead of him.

'Now what?' said Grace but the driver, ignoring her, thrust his head out the car window.

'Whaley – yah cunt!'

The man in uniform grinned.

'Red, yah bollix. When did you get out?'

'Yesterday man. Anyway,' and he indicated Grace, 'dis is Grace.'

The uniformed man stretched out his hand across Red and shook Grace's hand warmly.

'Are you his mudder?'

'No I'm not his mother,' Grace said crossly.

'She's a mate o' me cousin's. I'm teaching her to drive.'

'No better man,' Whaley told Grace.

'So lizzen, head, can we use de car park here? Get her a bit a confidence like 'fore she hits de traffic.' Red had by this time stepped out of the car and was standing at the passenger side.

'No sweat, be my guest,' Whaley said, gesturing grandly at the expanse of tarmac as though he held the shooting and fishing rights.

'Right Grace, slide across,' Red said, and Grace climbed awkwardly over the gear-stick until she was seated at the steering wheel staring out at the dark acres of her schoolroom.

They swept around the car park a number of times, the car emitting a high shriek each time Grace changed gear. Red liked a lot of gear changes and as much noise as possible. Occasionally, she glimpsed Whaley and his dog looking on with the incurious gaze of people at an insignificant, poorly attended football match.

'Oh sweet Jesus,' muttered Grace and gave all her attention to learning how to reverse at seventy miles an hour. 'Because,' Red explained patiently, 'if you're goin' backwards, it's because you're in a hurry – righ'?'

'But what about if you're reversing into a parking space?' Grace felt bound to enquire.

'It's best to keep movin' all de time,' Red was suddenly serious. 'If you hafta stop, nick another car's de best ting really.'

'Right.'

He got the name Red – 'On account of I have dis ting about red cars,' and, amongst other skills learnt that morning, he taught her how to hotwire a car.

'This is for when I lose my keys,' Grace said, rhetorically.

'Abso-fuckin'-lootly.'

He took the wheel on their return to the city. They made the trip in less than ten minutes, thanks to Red's indifference to red lights or one-way signs. When Grace reached into her purse to offer him money he said shyly, 'Ah you're arigh'. Have dis one on de house. It'll be twenty next time.'

'Should I get a provisional licence?' Grace asked. She could hear Red's laughter bubbling out the open window as he accelerated up the street. Then he turned into Hume Street and the squeal of his brakes drowned out all other sounds.

Grace stumbled across the road to the hotel and went straight to the bar where she ordered a large vodka and soda. After the second of these, she felt sufficiently relaxed to cope with a taxi. The cumulative effect of the vodka and the bottle of wine she drank when she got home meant that she woke up on her couch at four in the morning with a thundering headache and the feeling that at some time during the last few days she had taken a side-road off the motorway of her life and that there was no turning back.

It seemed pointless to go to bed so she dozed till seven, had a coffee, showered and dressed. Her trousers were loose on her. If this level of adrenaline overload kept up she'd be a size eight by Christmas.

She climbed the stairs in the agency to the first floor, a huge open-plan expanse that housed the creative department and TV production. TV production had an office of its own with a glass wall looking out on the workstations of creative. She didn't bother closing the door and the sounds of the agency drifted in – a casual, expletive-peppered backdrop to her day. Two young creatives strode past brandishing 'rejected by client' scripts like petrol bombs. 'Stupid fucking cunt. Wouldn't know a good idea if he ran over it in his fucking Mercedes.'

Across one of the partitions, she could hear the voice of a senior account executive, a man so disorganized that while he'd managed to be exactly on time for his own wedding, he had contrived to arrive at the wrong church. His white-knuckled hand was clutching the top of the partition and he punctuated each word with a violent shake to the flimsy, baize-covered wood. 'Jesus Christ! All I want is a big, fuck-off bottle and a line – preferably funny – that includes the word 'refreshing'. Is that asking too much?'

'Yes asshole,' Grace said under her breath. Along with the other bad habits acquired over the last days, she now swore as effortlessly as the characters in a Scorsese movie. She gazed out over the office. It felt strange, foreign, as though she'd been beamed down from some alien spacecraft. But this was a familiar feeling and one shared by all her colleagues because the offices were completely redone every couple of months, although the phrase used was not 'redo' but rather 'rethink'.

'We're rethinking the entire office,' Myles would say, stroking his stomach with satisfaction. Plans would be drawn up, the creative director would write the names of his staff on tiny, yellow pieces of paper and then he'd juggle the bits of paper from white space to white space on the office floor plan. Meanwhile, samples of paint and carpet swatches littered the floor. Finally, the work was completed. The tree-size plants were replaced by wooden 'sculptures'; the twelve huge, garish primitives by one up-and-coming artist were switched for the cool geometry of another; the grey floor became a brown floor and life went on as before.

'Sorry Grace but I'm going to have to hurry you on that Café Pur casting.' It was the diffident voice of James, account director on Café Pur, someone who clearly wasn't made for the cut-and-thrust of advertising and would have been more comfortable as an airline steward or a terribly, terribly kind GP in some rural backwater where no one ever got sick.

'I'm going to wrap it up today,' Grace told him nicely, sifting through her in-tray for the shortlist of actors destined to appear in the Café Pur ad. Three had asterisks beside their names. She showed the list to James. 'So these three are your first choices – any ceiling when I call their agents?' James thought for a moment. 'Cheap,' he said finally.

'Cheap? That's the ceiling is it? You wouldn't like to put that in real money so I don't actually have to say the word 'cheap' when I'm negotiating with Sarah Weiss who, last time I attempted to bring one of her client's price down, sent me a solicitor's letter?'

'Sorry Grace,' said James forlornly. Grace looked at the list again.

'Are you totally stuck on Mike Good? 'Cos he's going to cost! He's done a few cameos in various TV series and he's up for the new Michael Ritchie.'

James frowned as though thinking. 'You haven't a clue which one I'm talking about,' Grace said, taking pity on him. She pulled a Polaroid from a file. 'Him,' she said pointing at a sulky skinhead with bad skin. 'Oh my God,' said James after a while, 'but the creatives said …'

'… That he was pure sex? I know. Well actually,' Grace looked at the Polaroid, 'he cleans up well. His hair is longer now too. It was like that for some prison thing. Here's your second choice.' Grace took out a picture of a good-looking blond boy gazing into middle distance.

'Well he's … he's perfect. Is he? I mean he looks much nicer,' James looked helplessly at Grace.

'He's too modelly – the creatives will slay you.'

'The client likes modelly. Well clean anyway. With no spots – and some hair. And a good dentist.'

'He's not bad – I saw him in a play in the Bush and he was bloody good. I'll see what I can do,' Grace told him. 'I'll tell them he's just out of rehab. They love that.'

She rang Sarah Weiss, who handled two of the actors. Grace had been a bit disingenuous with James because Sarah and she got on very well. Not well enough to get a cut-price Mike Good but well enough to talk straight to each other. When she was finally put through to Sarah, who always talked as if you'd caught her tuning up on the starting grid at the Monaco Grand Prix, Sarah shouted breathlessly, 'My darling I have one second at most to talk to you. Speak.'

Grace told her what she had available – under-quoting by fifty per cent. Sarah laughed hugely and quoted a sum twice the size of the one she was prepared to accept. After ten minutes they arrived at a mutually acceptable sum, both assuring the other that the arrangement would ruin them. Grace told her about her impending retirement. Sarah was delighted. 'Buy a nice house in the south of France,' she advised. 'With what?' Grace asked before explaining that she'd be leaving with nothing.

'Remind me to be very cross with you when I see you,' Sarah told her and they agreed to meet for lunch when Grace was next in London. During the afternoon, there was a call from Lionel. He sounded ominously close.

'Where are you?' Grace enquired carefully.

'I'm in the Clarence – in Dublin,' he finished unnecessarily. 'I hope you didn't post that book yet.'

'No.'

'Good girl.'

Grace felt the rage that always accompanied any conversation with Lionel spread through her stomach like an old friend.

'So listen old thing, I thought I'd stay with you 'cos I'm only here for a couple of days and I'm … badly shook. Shell-shocked – post-traumatic war-zone whatchamacallit.'

'Oh shut up! Just shut up. The only time you heard a shell explode was on Sky-fuckin'-news.'

'Ah Grace. Don't be like that.'

'You've got a wife and children. That's whom you stay with. Bastard.'

'God, Grace. You're turning into your parents. What's the matter with you? All I want is a bed and a bit of peace and quiet. I'm too … distressed to be with young children.'

'You should have thought of that before you had your vasectomy reversed.'

'So is the key still in the usual place?'

'No, Lionel. No, no and again no.'

'So what time will you be home at, sweets? I'll do dinner.'

And he hung up.

Grace screamed once, quite loudly. Seconds later, Andrew came to her door.

'I hope you're not taking this badly, Grace,' he said severely, 'nothing's forever you know. And you were the one who resigned after all.'

'Oh go fuck yourself,' said Grace just as the phone rang again. She answered it and glared at Andrew who was making asthmatic noises and mumbling 'menopausal'. It was Travis on the line wanting to know how the driving lesson had gone.

'Excellently well,' Grace told him. 'I can now both steal cars and reverse out of a police roadblock. As to tootling down to Superquinn for the weekly shop – well I'm not so sure. Have to go now. I'll call you.' She replaced the phone and smiled hugely at Andrew who was still standing in her doorway.

'Was there anything else?'

'Well actually, I wanted to know how you felt about a surprise party for your leaving.'

'A surprise party for whom?'

'You, of course.'

Andrew had become creative director by default. When Nick left, the two obvious choices to replace him became so thoroughly embroiled in smear politics against each other, they failed to notice the amount of time Andrew spent in Myles Kitchen's office. And of course, they weren't to know that he had a permanent table booked in Restaurant Patrick Guilbaud, over a three-week period, where he wined and dined each of the agency clients – using, unusually, his own money. When it came time to make the appointment, there was no contest really.

'Does it bother you that it won't be a surprise seeing as how you've now told me about it?'

'Well I know you don't like surprises Grace so …'

'Most thoughtful, and no, I don't want a leaving party – surprise or otherwise.'

'I see,' Andrew said huffily.

'Are you surprised?'

Andrew stared out over the waste ground, fidgeting with something in his pocket so that a jangling sound punctuated his next words.

'What about a lunch then? For your friends. You and some friends.'

'I don't have any friends,' said Grace, suddenly realizing that this was true.

Andrew didn't contradict her but continued to look out over the tussocky green space beyond the window. Grace felt compelled to add something to her confession.

'I don't like sitting around in restaurants drinking Chardonnay and chatting about my clitoris thank you very much.'

'I know,' Andrew said, who hadn't been listening but, from the porch of his ear, extracted the word 'clitoris'.

'What did you say?' he said, turning towards her, his frame haloed with light from the window.

'Nothing,' said Grace, reaching for the phone that had started to ring.

'Grace darling!' It was Lionel. His voice was breaking up and all she could make out was the name Olga and 'tonight' – then very clearly, 'You're a sweetheart. See you later.'

'My ex,' she explained to Andrew.

'Really!' Andrew drew himself up, affronted, 'I didn't know you were married.'

'Well I'm not – not any more.'

'I see.' Andrew left the office, turning once to look over his shoulder, his expression one of someone who's been lied to.

Grace got the taxi to stop at an off-licence on the way home and bought half a case of wine and a bottle of vodka. Just in case. The taxi man grinned at her.

'Am I invited?'

'Absolutely,' she said and then, lest he think she were serious, 'it's for my husband. He's been away.'

As she hefted the case of wine from the boot, she was conscious of people lolling on their steps, stealing the last of the wintry sun. Young people, full of opinions and beer – the women smug in their plumpness, bellies bared, pierced navels glinting. The house smelt of dust and the perfume she wore. She put the wine in the rack that had recently held just mineral water. She put the vodka in a drawer with the saucepans. The doorbell rang. She opened the door. On the step, a tall woman was rifling through a bag. She looked up when Grace opened the door.

'Grace?' said the woman in heavily accented English, 'I'm Olga.' The woman upended her capacious bag on the step. Lipsticks, a Tampax, a purse and some small coins bounced on the granite.

'Focking cigarette gone. Can you beleef? Fock.'

Grace looked first at the step with its sad little scattering of belongings and then up the long, long legs of her visitor. She was wearing black stockings and a very small denim skirt. On top, she wore a gypsy blouse – and through its diaphanous swathes, her breasts tumbled and fought with the lazy intent of a slow-motion film. Her hair was red and there was a great deal of it. Her mouth was a purple scream – perfectly matching her fingernails and, Grace noted through the hole in one of the black stockings, her toes.

'Lionel tell you anyway,' the woman said, elbowing her way into the house so that suddenly Grace found herself in the hallway with the woman who was now looking around.

'So,' said the woman, 'where am I?'

'I … look … who are you?' Grace leant against the telephone table for support, conscious of a smell of sweat that came in waves from the woman.

'He diden call? Lionel?'

The woman sat down on the stairs and her purple mouth yawned wide before it emitted a deep shout of laughter.

'He soch a prick that Lionel.' Wearily, she got to her feet and began to climb the stairs.

'Jus show me the room Grace and I lie down for a while. I'm total focked – you know?'

Grace was lost for words as Olga's legs in the black hold-up stockings receded up the stairs. She quickly looked away as she noted the absence of knickers.

'I don't think …' Grace essayed, but Olga had already gone into the first room at the top of the landing. There was a thump as the sausage-shaped holdall she was carrying hit the floor. Grace stood for a moment undecided then hurried up the stairs after her. Olga was sitting on what used to be Emily's bed. The room was largely unchanged from that time and contained a selection of artefacts that led one in layers through Emily's life, like the different levels of an archaeological dig. The walls, what bits of them were visible between the posters of pouting Spice Girls and

Michael Hutchence, were painted pink. Over the bed hung a heavy, gold-framed portrait of a horse, gazing beatifically at the spotted duvet. The dressing-table held an assortment of ornaments and toys interspersed with suntan oil, tubes of make-up and lipsticks. Olga surveyed the room with the philosophical disgust of a train passenger obliged to spend an hour or two in an unheated railway carriage the cleaners had missed. From the bedside table, she lifted up a plastic toy.

'What's this?'

'My Little Pony,' Grace replied shortly.

'Your little pony?' She paused, her big lips curving in a smile. 'Really?'

And she picked up the little plastic toy and tossed it to Grace, who caught it clumsily. 'You'd better have it then,' said Olga, stretching out on the spotted quilt.

'It is,' Grace explained, 'a toy – a toy called My Little Pony. Young girls buy them – the ponies – and then they buy accessories for them like – eh – stables and jumps and things.' Grace was warming to her theme, 'Just like a Barbie doll – except of course it's a pony.'

Olga gathered the pillows more comfortably behind her head and regarded Grace seriously.

'You're very funny people, you know, you Irish, you British. Anyway,' she yawned, 'take it away, it give me the creep.'

'It's plural,' Grace said, holding the toy at arm's length like a mouse, 'it's "creeps" – not "creep".'

'Thank you,' Olga said with some warmth, 'I want to speak better – always correct me – you know? I don't mind. I prefer it actually.'

'Good. Fine.' Grace stood at the doorway for a moment. Olga rolled on her side with an air of finality. Grace closed the door softly. When she was halfway down the stairs, the phone rang.

Grace tumbled down the last few steps, grabbed the phone on the second ring and answered it in a whisper.

It was Josh.

'What's wrong? Why are you whispering?'

'I don't want to wake Olga.'

'Who's Olga?'

Still whispering, Grace explained that Olga was a friend of Lionel's and that incidentally, he was home. Josh snorted and said he was dropping round to discuss things.

'Oh that's nice,' Grace said insincerely, 'you'll have a chance to meet Olga – and your father come to that. Apparently he's staying here.'

'Why isn't he staying in his own house?'

'Well this is his house, in a way.'

Actually it was Grace's house, as Lionel had given it to her – a grand gesture she knew he regretted. She went into a sort of daydream as Josh talked on, his sentences punctuated by words he underlined: 'compensated', 'determined', 'legally', 'lax' and 'passive' – the last two words referring to her, she supposed.

'You're right, you're right,' she murmured at intervals, using the time to gather up the tulip petals that had fallen from the flower arrangement on the hall table. Behind the vase, she could see her face reflected in the mirror – two little dark nips of worry played above her nose.

'Goodbye then,' she heard Josh say.

Grace replaced the phone in its cradle and then took it off the hook before going down to the kitchen and pouring herself a drink. The kitchen smelt of cleaning agents and the sour yeast of mouldy bread. She emptied the contents of the bread basket into the bin, took a large swallow of neat vodka and waited for the alcohol to take hold.

When Josh was about seven, a while after the incident when she'd lost himself and Emily, they'd taken a house for a month in Connemara – near Ballyconneely, ten minutes or so from the Coral Strand. It was a square, white cottage standing on a hill overlooking the sea. It was sparsely furnished and smelt of damp and old people. A fine cloak of dust lay on every surface and the floor scrunched underfoot when you walked where generations of sand-caked feet had walked before you. It occurred to Grace that she might sweep a bit and dust, but she thrust the temptation aside and after a half-hearted attempt on the first day, left the house to itself. It had been a very un-Irish summer. Each morning dawned bright and clear, the blue skies dappled now and then by the smallest of clouds, which floated by only to disappear into the grey-green mountains behind. It was a perfect summer. The three of them – Emily, Josh and Grace – fell into a blurry rhythm of sand and sea and gorse-packed hillsides. They rose early, barely speaking, foraging for food, and then Grace made sandwiches of whatever she found lying about – ham, banana, peanut butter or bits of cold sausage. She filled a flask with milky coffee, a bottle of water from the tap and they'd wander down to the beach where the water had a Caribbean blue as it washed over the fine coral of the strand. The children collected shells tirelessly and arranged them into complicated piles to denote groceries in a shop or, when they were feeling more creative, described elaborate mosaics of yellow, cream and blue from the abandoned homes of the peri-winkles. Grace read uncritically, greedily – finishing a history of World War II to move effortlessly on to a romance set in Cornwall, or a thriller.

The days sank by them, interspersed with swims: the first grip of steel as the water clung to warm thigh and stomach, the heart-stopping moment as they lowered their shoulders and faces into the blue, the screeches of laughter and shock until, acclimatizing to the cold, the sea claimed them and they swam and played for hours at a time.

They lingered on the beach until the sun was low and they grew hungry. They walked up to the village to buy whatever the small shop had to offer because, of course, Grace didn't drive then. They walked back in the balmy evening air with the smell of cows and salt all around them and Grace cooked dinner. She made pasta because the oven was erratic and she was too lazy to peel potatoes.

The thing of it was, during that summer, for the first time, she felt a fierce love welling up in her that hadn't been there before. Often, as she lay on the sand, stretched out on the green plaid rug, lost in whatever book she was reading, she'd suddenly catch a glimpse of Josh through the corner of her eye, his skinny brown limbs cartwheeling towards the sea, his scream lost on the wind, and she'd feel a knife of love pierce through the torpor of the day. You try not to love one child above another, but sometimes you can't help it.

So what had happened then? At what point in Josh's growing up had he slipped away from her into this pompous, querulous, self-righteous adult who sighed about his mother as though she were one of his less satisfactory investments? He left school at eighteen, mutinous and irascible but still loveable. Or rather, loved by Grace. And both Lionel and she had been pleased that he'd taken a year out to mooch around Asia, finishing up in Australia where he worked in a bar. But then he'd come back and, while Grace knew this was impossible, her memory of his return was that he had arrived wearing a pinstriped suit. He wanted to work in a bank, he said. Grace couldn't have been more surprised if he'd expressed the desire to join a circus.

He moved out of home a week after his return. He came for dinner occasionally, trailing a succession of drab girls that he seemed to have plucked from some old black and white movie; girls with names that blurred together, like species of plants – Zoe and Chloe – Sarah and Lara and Zara – Jane, Elaine, Blayne. None of them impacted on Grace at all. She called them all 'darling' or 'dear' and was never sure when one had been replaced. They were all blondes.

Josh seemed as confused as she was. For instance, he called both Emily and Emma, 'Em'. This, Grace surmised, was because he wasn't certain either. Sometimes, when she tired of the effort of making conversation at the dinner table, she listened to their voices. But the voices too came from the same sheet of music; voices honed and toned by the schools they all went to – Mount Anville, Alexandra, Sion Hill. They worked in magazines and for design companies or did research for independent TV firms. They wore clothes that while fashionable were self-effacing, almost like a uniform. Josh treated them all with the cool sense of ownership you might feel for a briefcase or a particularly nice pen. Perhaps he was gay.

'You drink like Russian.'

Grace had been pouring herself another drink, splashing the neat vodka into a tumbler. She turned to see Olga standing in the kitchen doorway. She was wearing a pair of Grace's jeans and a freshly laundered shirt that Grace was saving for a meeting later in the week.

'You don't mind do you?' said Olga, thrusting up the starched white cuffs of the shirt with a proprietorial flourish.

'Well actually …' Grace started and then trailed off and reached for another glass. Olga took the bottle of Absolut from her and poured a hefty measure, took a swallow and made a moue of disgust. From the hallway came the rattle of keys in the hall door followed by the appearance of Lionel, who was carrying two brown bags smelling of curry and a plastic bag containing two bottles.

'Darling!' he said, making straight for Grace and kissing her soundly on the mouth. He put down his bags and enclosed Olga in a hug until she punched him quite hard in the shoulder.

'Well,' said Lionel, not in the least put out, 'is the oven on?' and he proceeded to unload his tin-foil boxes from the takeaway.

'I thought you were going to make dinner,' was all Grace could think of to say.

'"Do" – I said I would "do" dinner.'

Lionel clicked on the oven, simultaneously reaching into the drawer for cutlery.

'I think I've done us proud. Lamb Saag, Prawn Jalfrezi, Chicken Bhuni, a couple of dhal and naan bread.'

He opened the fridge without looking and reached in for a pot of yoghurt – his hand automatically going to the right shelf, as though he'd never left. As though he'd never left. There didn't seem to be anything for it but to row in, so Grace set up the table for four and, after a moment's indecision, lit two candles. Lionel took in the fourth table setting.

'Josh said he'd drop by,' Grace said. Lionel took this news on the chin. For someone who lived a somewhat chaotic life, he hated surprises. Grace looked at him properly for the first time since he'd arrived. He was tanned; his face was lined with rivulets of crow's feet spilling white from either eye – tired tributaries of a life spent squinting into the sun. He was thin and muscled. All those gyms in all those hotels had made him seem toned and vital – the sort of man you might expect to find dodging shells in some desert battlefield, selflessly bringing the news to lesser mortals as they ate their toast and drank their coffee on the other side of the world.

'Lionel?' said Grace, eyeing the door meaningfully.

'What?' said Lionel, who was opening a bottle of wine.

'I think she want to talk to you – say, "what the fock you bring Olga here for?"' Olga poured herself another drink. Grace smiled tightly at her and went out the door up to the living room. A few seconds later, Lionel followed. He was already talking as he came into the room.

'I've known Olga for yonks. Interpreter – eh – Albania, in Tirana actually – about six years ago? Then I ran into her in London of all places and she's in a bit of bother so I thought why not it's only for a few days after all? And Grace won't mind.'

Grace looked at him without saying anything for a while and then lit a cigarette.

'She looks to me like a whore of some sort, Lionel.'

Lionel opened his mouth as though to speak and then arranged his face into an expression of astonished outrage.

'She's a linguist ... of enormous talent actually.'

'I can imagine,' Grace murmured, smiling in spite of herself. 'And when did you start smoking?'

They both looked up at the sound of Josh arriving, accompanied by small explosions of the expletives from the comic books of his youth ('Oh dash, bother, darn, darn, darn it.')

'We're in here,' Grace carolled.

Josh hovered in the doorway.

'Hello Lionel – eh Dad,' he muttered all the while looking at Grace. Olga appeared, her glass dangling at the end of one creamy wrist, the purple nails arranged around the rim like some barbaric design. Josh's mouth dropped open in a way that Grace found amusing and Olga ignored.

'I'm Olga,' she said smokily, not bothering to look in Josh's direction but rather taking in the furnishings of the room as though she were doing an inventory.

'Well Josh – eh – son,' Lionel said with great heartiness, 'you're just in time for dinner. Takeaway all right with you?' he asked, leading the way towards the kitchen. Dinner passed pleasantly enough, carried along on the tide of Lionel's anecdotes.: the time he was kidnapped by Chechen gangsters, the mad night with Marko Milosevic in Club Jazz when Marko had speeded up the service with sprays of bullets from his Heckler, that great chat he had with Saddam Hussein who was really splendid company once you got to know him. With the collaboration of his audience, Lionel led them through his fantasy life in a most agreeable way so that in no time, it seemed, Grace was loading the dishes into the dishwasher. Olga's contribution to tidying up was to remove her elbow from the table briefly so that Grace could gather up her plate.

There was, of course, the occasional awkward moment. Josh, who now worked for one of the larger financial institutions, mentioned Goodbody's. Olga nodded approvingly.

'Good body? That's good. You should go to gym more,' she paused to spear a piece of lamb, 'you look like a refugee.'

Josh had many strong feelings about refugees and empathy wasn't one of them. He followed Grace out of the room when she was going to the lavatory and spoke to her through the door – another relic of childhood. Grace sat staring at the door as his irate whispers rasped through the panelling.

'What's that tart doing here? You know she's a whore don't you? God almighty Mum, she's probably stealing everything in sight.'

Grace stopped peeing, mid-stream, in order to answer.

'There's nothing to steal,' she said, thinking that it was thanks to Josh that she had such an excellent pelvic floor. When she came out, Josh was still standing there.

'And this business about your job. It's just – irresponsible. Mum? Grace?'

Grace ignored him and went down the stairs, blocking out Josh's assurances that he would go over her finances. Experience had taught her that Josh would do no such thing. His eyes glazed over with boredom when he encountered any sum of less than six figures, so Grace's puny salary and savings were safe from his scrutiny. Actually, she didn't have any savings. She felt a momentary stab of fear but then relaxed. She had the house and it was far too big for her, well, usually, she corrected herself as a shout of laughter from Olga came from the kitchen, followed by Lionel's manic bray.

Over coffee, she managed to steer the conversation away from dangerous waters. The various tribunals, for example, threw Lionel into a frenzy of rage as he recited the barristers involved like a list of war criminals. These were his fellow classmates, cleaning up in the comfort of the courts while he lay trapped in bombed-out buildings eating boil-in-the-bag chili con carne and drawing lots with his colleagues for who would dodge the bullets to get water from the well.

'Oh Christ!' Grace jumped up from the table, 'I forgot to go over to Mum and Dad's.'

'They're hanging in there, aren't they? You'd think they'd have the decency to die. I thought your pop had cancer.'

'He got the all clear months ago.' Grace was putting on her coat.

'I'd pity the cancer that got anywhere near him, the old bastard,' said Lionel.

'He thinks a great deal of you too,' said Grace and then to Josh, 'Be a sweetheart and drop me, would you? I don't want to hang around for a taxi.'

'You could learn to drive.' Lionel was pillaging the freezer in search of chocolate.

'I might surprise you yet.'

Once in the car, Josh became more relaxed, easily negotiating the traffic in Grace's narrow street with its well-bred landscaped gardens, all pebbles and potted box trees – spurting away from the lights at the junction of the main road with a pleased smile on his face at the Mercedes's acceleration.

'So, anyone new in your life that I should know about?' Grace spoke lightly, the question designed to take Josh's mind off Olga. She didn't want the journey's background music to be the discordant melody of Josh's disapproval.

'Well you know Tanya and I split up.'

'Ooooh,' Grace's sympathetic tone masked her inability to remember anything about Tanya apart from her name which was vaguely familiar.

'No big deal.'

'Well that's …' Grace paused, unsure. Was it sad that it was so little a thing or was it good? What was the point of all these girls – girls who seemed to have as little impact on Josh himself as they did on Grace?

'What did you think of her?' Josh's voice sounded boyish, vulnerable. Grace wanted to capitalize on the moment but could think of no response so instead she said, 'Do you know who I really liked? That girl – the waitress – Josie?'

Josh laughed out loud.

'That was when I was seventeen, for Christ's sake.' He sighed, 'Josie! God I'd forgotten her – complete slapper.'

'Well I liked her,' Grace said in a small cold voice.

Josh dropped her at the top of the road where her parents lived to avoid being caught in a one-way system. He always spoilt any generous gesture with some small meanness that took the good out of it.

'You need to get that woman out of the house,' he told her as he made to drive away. 'And don't bang the door.' He was inordinately proud of his Mercedes – which, being bright red, was the only colourful thing about him. Grace didn't bother answering.

She made her way down the ill-lit, tree-lined street, almost falling over a discarded skateboard that lay across her path. Grace smiled, imagining her father's reaction if he had been there. She turned into the gate where the bow window of the living room spilled light onto the rosebushes. She paused for a second to look through the uncurtained window. Her mother and father sat on their usual chairs, either side of the fireplace. They were talking animatedly to Emily who was sprawled on the couch, her booted feet resting on a cushion. Emily was laughing, an occurrence so unusual that Grace almost hadn't recognized her. And her parents – her vitriol-filled, quarrelsome parents – had an air of complicity, of cosiness. She used her key to get in, singing through the doorway,

'It's me – sorry I'm so late.'

By the time she got to the living room, Emily's expression had reverted to the one Grace was more familiar with – that is, she was expressionless – while her parents had stiffened and were darting accusing looks at each other, spoiling for a fight.

'Hi,' said Emily, in a flat tone.

'Emily, what a surprise.' Grace couldn't think of anything else to say.

'How's work?' Emily looked away, not waiting for an answer.

'Fine,' Grace said and, after a moment, sat in a small bucket-shaped chair near the couch. There was an uneasy silence broken occasionally by her father's irritable drumming on the side of his chair. Emily got up.

'I'm going to bed. 'Night Pops, 'night Grams,' and she kissed them both on the cheek and went out, closing the door behind her.

'She stays here?' Grace said finally.

'Oh yes,' said her mother comfortably, 'often. She often stays.'

'But …' Grace was lost for words.

'She gets lonely in that flat, that apartment,' said Grace's father, giving the word 'apartment' a curl as though it had been translated from the Greek.

'But I thought, well you never seemed to have much time for them – half the time you couldn't even remember their names,' Grace laughed a little wildly to take the sting out of what she had just said.

Her father spoke leaning forward in a kindly way. 'We don't like children,' he said, and he sat back satisfied, as though that explained everything.

'I've always wondered why I was an only child,' Grace said with a wintry amusement.

'There you are then,' said her mother and then hastily, 'but we're very fond of grown-ups. Like Emily and, of course, you.'

'Thank you,' Grace said but the irony was lost on her mother.

'So,' said her father, 'how's the big world of …' he thrashed around for a while and then decided to give up, 'the big world of work – your work?' he finished, triumphantly.

'I've resigned.'

'Sacked you did they?'

'No,' Grace said, 'no. I just … resigned.'

Her mother and father looked at each other, a little lost. Floundering. Just as Grace was floundering in this new image of her parents, sitting by the fire, safe in the conspiracy of old age and companionship. She rather preferred them at each other's throats.

'So when did this thing start – this thing with Emily?'

Her parents bridled.

'It's not a thing. She's our granddaughter,' scolded her father, 'and she's been through a very rough time and she's come out the other side.'

'A dear girl – and so agreeable, so pleasant to have about,' added her mother.

'Right,' said Grace whose conversations with Emily over the last four years had been monosyllabic.

'Would you like anything?' her mother said in a high, social voice, 'Tea? Cocoa?'

'Cocoa would be nice,' Grace agreed, wondering idly how it would mix with the Prawn Jalfrezi. But it didn't matter in the end.

'We've run out,' her mother said regretfully and didn't offer an alternative. Come to think of it, her parents were not great entertainers. Her father's practice – he was a GP – had been in the house and perhaps they felt they had enough people trailing through the front door without encouraging visitors. He'd retired now, but the surgery remained exactly as it had been with the leather couch and the antique instruments, looking like the set from a BBC costume drama.

He had been much liked as a GP – even though he was of the 'pull yourself together' school of medicine and wrote prescriptions sparingly as if a levy were exacted on every stroke of his pen. The sample drugs he received from pharmaceutical companies he kept for his own family. These he doled out like treats. For three months, when Grace was eleven, she was on HRT.

Grace made an effort and said brightly, 'So how are things with you?' Her parents looked at each other as though it was a trick question.

'Very good,' they said in unison. There was silence for a moment until her mother said, 'I think the roses should be good this year.'

'Unless you've killed them, blind old bat,' snapped her father.

'*I* didn't put a treble dose of weedkiller on them. I'm not senile,' said her mother.

Grace closed her eyes, lulled by the familiar rhythm of their bile. It'd be easy enough to get a taxi at this hour.

EIGHT

GRACE SAT on a collapsible canvas stool in the middle of a large field. It was raining. Somewhere, underneath the oilskin coat, the anorak, the padded jerkin, the jumper, the two T-shirts and the silk thermals she was wearing, she felt an itch. She would have liked to scratch it but that was impossible. She would have liked a cigarette but even that small movement was out of the question. She felt like a child again, tightly packed into too many coats, as if her body had been extruded like sausage-meat into its woolly casing. In the distance she heard the religion of film being played out – the bored litany and its responses:

'Turnover.'

'Rolling.'

'Camera?'

'Speed.'

'Slate.'

'And … action!'

Grace looked across the field towards the cluster of people around the camera, its lens protected by an umbrella. An arc light shorted in the wet and sparks flew into the grey sky lending a brief moment of gaiety to the drabness of the scene. In the distance, she glimpsed the flame of Olga's hair as she walked towards the camera. Her hips swayed slowly and, although Grace couldn't see the detail of her face, she knew she was smiling, her big mouth curved, her cheek-bones sharp against the cream of her skin. Grace laughed out loud.

What had happened was this. The morning after the dinner with Lionel, Olga and Josh, Grace had gone into work. She was looking through her Filofax, trying to remember the faces of all the actors noted there. She was looking for someone who would get the thumbs up from Bruce, the art director. He was devising a poster campaign for the only multi-national client the agency held and there was, as Andrew pointed out at thirty-second intervals, 'a lot riding on it'.

Bruce was looking for a face to front the campaign. A face and a body. He was very particular. He'd gone through sheaves of portfolios of models from Ireland and Britain. But he wasn't happy. Normally Grace would not be involved in posters but, having failed in his trawl through models, Bruce was now looking at actors.

Grace was trying to visualize a girl called Marie – or was it Mary? – a very beautiful girl she had seen once in the Abbey, when a shadow fell over her. It was Bruce. Unusually for someone in the business, Bruce said very little. He was a stocky, unremarkable young man – someone you'd associate more with long-distance lorry driving than advertising. He had calm, blue eyes which, even when they were staring directly at you, always seemed focused on a point several miles behind your head.

'I'm looking through names for your shoot,' she explained, swivelling round to face him. 'So what are you looking for exactly?' Grace pressed gently as it became clear that Bruce was not going to answer. 'I really need a hint here Bruce because otherwise I'll be getting you Cameron Diaz when you really want Nicole Kidman.'

'They're both wrong,' Bruce said, shaking his head rather violently.

Grace laughed lightly. 'What I meant of course were people who were that type. Not the actual people. Not actually Cameron Diaz or Nicole Kidman.'

Bruce was wrinkling his forehead suspiciously. Grace was losing patience.

'Bruce, what do you want? Describe this woman to me.'

'She's a warrior,' he mumbled. 'She's tall, red hair – very strong, sexy. She looks as though she's – lived.'

'Oh.'

Grace picked up her Filofax with a sigh. And then she had – well a sort of epiphany.

'Bruce,' she said, 'I think I've got exactly the woman you want,' and before reason could intervene, Grace had dialled the number of her house and, after what seemed a long time, Olga answered with a truculent, 'Yes?'

Grace explained that she was sending a taxi to pick her up. That Olga was to shower, get dressed and look gorgeous in the space of twenty minutes.

'No problem,' Olga agreed lazily, 'I'll wear that black dress you have, Dolce & Gabbana. That look good on me.'

Grace started to hyperventilate at the thought of Olga plundering her wardrobe and instead said, 'The taxi knows where to come.'

An hour later reception rang to say Olga had arrived. Grace told them to send her up to the creative department. It was a particularly busy day and the noise level in the department was even more strident than usual but suddenly a silence fell. Grace got up and looked through the glass of her office to where Olga stood, all six feet of her, Grace's black dress curving around her body like a hand, her hair tumbling down in a mass of auburn curls. She glimpsed Grace and gave her a half-smile before describing a slow, undulating walk over to her office. You could hear the air-conditioning against the silence – it sounded like a jet taking off. Olga came in and placed herself on the edge of Grace's desk. 'Very small office,' she remarked, 'you need big office if you want to get ahead.'

'Thank you for coming,' Grace said. Olga reached over to Grace's bag, took a cigarette, lit it and blew a long plume of smoke into the air.

'No problem, I wasn't doing anything.'

Grace beckoned to Bruce and when he came to the door, indicated Olga.

'Am I getting close?'

For the first time since she'd known him, Bruce looked directly at Grace. He took her hand and squeezed it hard. For a while he didn't say anything at all and then, 'She is so … she is so, so right,' he managed. 'Thank you. Thank you Grace.'

'Well great!' Grace reached over for her bag. 'Lunch?' she said to Olga.

She asked reception to call a taxi while they waited on one of the two very clean, new cream couches that sat in reception. Myles changed the couches on average every two weeks. These were unusually handsome specimens. Grace was amused to discover that the wool of her coat came off on the fabric so that when she stood up, the pristine cream was smeared with a crescent of grey. As she and Olga walked out to the taxi, Grace wondered what happened to all the discarded couches. Maybe Myles had a country seat somewhere whose vast, cavernous halls held banks and banks of couches waiting for guests who would never arrive. Grace gave the taxi man the name of a restaurant she knew on the canal. 'You'll like it,' she told Olga, 'they have red cabbage.'

'I hate cabbage. Cabbage of any colour,' Olga said, staring out the window at the grey day and the grey terraced houses that lay on either side of them.

In the restaurant, they were shown to a table overlooking the canal. Some swans floated by but Olga remained unimpressed.

'Are there many swans in Russia?' Grace asked, having already rehearsed several other questions in her head and discarding them.

'It's a long time since I am in Russia – how the fock would I know?'

'God almighty,' Grace said to no one in particular.

'Sorry,' said Olga, 'I get my period. Makes me like a pig,' and she smiled so nicely at Grace that she had to smile back.

When menus arrived, Olga cheered up. Even though she had trouble reading the handwritten items she was impressed by the size of the menu and the amount of dishes it seemed to contain.

'You order for me,' she instructed grandly.

'Well, what do you like – fish, beef, game?'

'Everything except cabbage and 'arse – no 'arse.'

'"Arse"?'

'I don't eat "your little pony".' Olga snorted with laughter.

Grace smiled coldly and ordered the same for both of them – tian of crab and pheasant. The waiter, whom Grace knew from previous visits, brought their starters.

'Lovely,' he murmured, as he always did when delivering a dish, so that it seemed churlish not to agree. Olga ate rapidly, with the occasional little grunt of satisfaction.

'Did you enjoy that?' Grace asked in a high voice. She was beginning to feel the onset of panic.

'Was OK.'

The two women sat without speaking for a while, looking out over the canal with its fringe of reeds and its elegant, long-necked tenants.

'That's a High Court judge over there,' Grace said finally to break the silence, indicating a craggy-faced man sitting with two companions, about to order a second bottle of claret.

'A judge? That's good,' said Olga, regarding the judge closely, as though weighing him.

The pheasant arrived accompanied by its fond introduction 'lovely' and Olga gave the waiter a brilliant smile. She attacked the pheasant with great concentration and the adroitness of a butcher. First she peeled off layers of meat, which she chewed thoroughly before hoisting the next forkful to her mouth. When she got to the carcass, she fell to ripping the bones apart and then pincered any residual meat between her strong, white teeth, running along the bone like an otter stripping bark. Finished, she pushed her plate away and leaned back in her chair. Grace laid down her knife and fork neatly having left most of her meal.

'Well?' Olga asked.

'Well what?'

'What this all about? Go to your work. Dress up. That man with cow eye.'

Grace explained the poster campaign – how it needed an unusual face – a face that wasn't known. She said there would be a bit of money in it – a couple of thousand at least. Olga nodded, suspicious. What was the advertisement for, she wanted to know. It was a line of cosmetics; Grace told her the name. Olga nodded again, impressed at last. Grace said it would be just a picture of Olga and a line of copy. Olga looked nonplussed.

'A line of words,' Grace elucidated.

'What words?' Olga asked.

'"Then I saw her face",' Grace said.

'What?'

'"Then I saw her face" is the line on the poster,' Grace said, articulating each word clearly and slowly. Olga sighed with exasperation.

'"Then I saw her face" what? Is not a sentence "then I saw her face". I speak eight languages you know.'

'It's a line from a song.'

'What song?'

'"I'm a Believer" by The Monkees.'

At this point Grace regretted getting into the conversation in the first place. Olga looked thunderstruck.

'Monkeys?'

Olga moved the word round in her mouth as though she intended spitting it out but then her face cleared and she gave one of her shouts of laughter. Across the room, the High Court judge turned and his look of censure rapidly changed to that expression all men wore when confronted with Olga. She glared over at him.

'So,' she said, leaning closer to Grace, 'what do we have to do?'

Grace studied the tablecloth, pristine white except in the area of Olga's plate where it was spattered with gravy. She had absolutely no idea what they had to do. She hadn't thought it through. The call to Olga had been an impulse and now she needed to think. Then her mobile rang. 'Shit,' she said looking around the room in an effort to embrace all its occupants with the sincerity of her penitence. 'Hang on,' she said into the mobile as she made her way to the foyer. It was Bruce. He was over the moon; he couldn't be more delighted. He and she must make this happen. Could she hold on for Andrew? Andrew's voice came down the line. How little could they get this woman for? Fifteen hundred say?

'Is this some sort of joke? Six thousand minimum.' Grace used the crisp tone she reserved for talking to outside producers.

'Grace, whose side are you on?'

'My side, Andrew. I'm on my side. Six thousand. Take it or leave it.'

'Five.'

'Thank you Andrew,' Grace said pleasantly and ended the call. She returned to the table, smiling to herself, and sat down.

'Well,' she said, after a moment, 'it looks like I'm your agent.'

Olga reached out one of her large, perfectly shaped hands and, clasping Grace's much smaller one, shook it vigorously.

'There — is bargain. We show them.'

'We certainly will,' said Grace as she envisioned the side-road of her life widening into a long, straight freeway thrusting into the sun.

NINE

GRACE WAITED as before outside the Concert Hall. This was her fourth driving lesson. Red arrived promptly, wreathed in smiles, in a red Mercedes Sports. He bounced over to the passenger side and Grace slid in.

'My son has a car exactly like this. Isn't that a coincidence?'

Red shrugged and, once Grace had started up the engine, enquired lightly where her son lived. When Grace told him the address, he looked briefly concerned.

'It's not his car is it? You didn't steal my son's car?'

'Pull in,' Red ordered and when Grace had done so, rounded on her, outraged.

'I did not steal annyting Grace. I "borrowed" dis car because, Grace, I thought you would like to drive a nice car. He won't miss it. He came home bombed out of his brain about five dis morning. I'll have it back before he wakes up – and in one piece, I hope,' he added as Grace moved out, narrowly missing driving into the back of a stalled van.

Red had grown quite schoolmasterish as Grace's preference

for the flashier elements of driving became apparent. Grace confessed she had a hankering to pass everything on the motorway, tucking neatly into line after each pass so that it would look pretty if shot from a helicopter.

'It's not fuckin' Scalextric Grace,' said Red.

The lessons had grown in length as they got to know each other. Grace told him about Emily and their estrangement. Red nodded sagely. Bound to happen, he said. Grace asked him if he thought she should make more of an effort. Try to bridge the gap.

'Do nothin',' he advised. This was his advice in most instances. For example, he explained, when he was trapped by police hiding out at the back of a warehouse in a stolen BMW ('an oul' green ting') he had a choice of ramming the cop car or giving himself up. And what did he do? Nothing! Eventually the cops got bored and buggered off. He sat back, satisfied, his point proven.

Grace was impressed, even though she knew that his father, who was a classic exponent of the 'do nothing' school of thought, had passed on Red's philosophy to him. He had done nothing all his life – even when the unemployment figures were so low it was almost impossible to avoid a job in Ireland. He was, Red explained proudly, one of a tiny minority who stuck to the dole through thick and thin and you'd have to admire him for that. Grace told him about Emily's former drug problem and how she'd now gone to the other extreme. Was she a vigilante? Red wanted to know.

'In a way, she goes to an awful lot of NA meetings.'

'Oh right,' said Red, quickly followed by, 'Watch your left, watch your left. Dere's a cunt on a bike who's goin' to clip your mirror. Bastard,' he continued, as the bike swept by them, its rider cool and fluent. Behind his back his hand gestured, one finger erect.

'I'd have flattened him wit de door 'cept it's your son's motor.'

On the subject of Olga, Red was ambivalent. He was casually racist and a lot better in an argument than Grace so that invariably she tied herself into well-meaning, liberal knots while Red triumphed.

'You've no answer to dat, have you Grace?'

And most of the time, she hadn't. By then she would have lost her place in the bible of her blurred beliefs which always contained phrases like 'on the other hand'. There was no 'other hand' in Red's thinking – everything was black and white. The list of things and people he hated was both myriad and random. In fact, so indiscriminate were his prejudices that you could hardly call them prejudices. Red hated cats, cyclists, cycle lanes and cops. He hated culchies, frogs, Eye-ties, Brits, anyone from Northern Ireland and most especially anyone from a county that gloried in Gaelic games. He hated all foods except burgers from a particular chain, wine gums and rasher sandwiches. He loathed buses and bus passengers ('Have you a death wish, yah fuckin' eejit?') but loved bus lanes, regarding them as his private highway. He hated weather of any kind. If it rained, it was 'dis cuntin' country – fuckin' *Waterworld*'. If the sun shone, 'God I'm roasted – sweatin' – I'll have de flu by de weekend.' He despised Indians, Chinese and black people. Having elicited the information that Olga was white, he still thought she was some kind of gangster.

'They all are,' he explained kindly to Grace. 'The blacks come here for the free medical and the Ruskies are here to fleece us. That's all they know.'

'Oh I give up,' Grace said crossly.

'Just start to turn de wheel de minute you clock dat you're parallel wit de odder car Grace.' Red had decided that parking was a necessary skill after all. Grace slipped into the parking space in two adroit movements.

'I wasn't talking about driving,' she said savagely. But she couldn't stay angry with him for long because, well, because he was so restful – so predictable.

'So you really think I should let things be with Emily?'

She had to shout over the considerable engine noise. Josh's car could accelerate from nought to sixty in seven seconds. With Red at the wheel, this was the first time the car had had the opportunity of living up to its advertising.

'What am I tellin' you? Do nothin',' he yelled back.

Red dropped her at the usual spot and disappeared down the road quickly. 'I wouldn't like Josh wakin' up and findin' it not dere – let him down like.'

Grace decided to walk home in order to think. She really ought to be formulating a plan for Olga. Maybe they could spin this thing out. One poster was good but – what if Olga took off? What if there were some real money in it? But instead she fell to thinking about Emily.

During adolescence, Emily changed from the neat, pretty, affectionate child she had been into – well, a black hole. She stayed in her room during the hours of daylight, although she must have gone to school occasionally, otherwise there would have been a letter. She had friends who seemed to enter the house through a secret route under the foundations because Grace never saw anyone at the front door. One moment there was silence and then, like some seismic disaster, the walls began to throb and shake with the vibration of music that wrenched at Grace's body like an explosion. Somewhere behind the screech and thump you could hear voices and shrieks of laughter but when Grace knocked at the door the laughter stopped and Emily's cold, clear voice cut through the music to say, 'Yes?'

When Grace asked her friends if they had the same problems, they laughed and threw their eyes up to heaven. They seemed to think it was funny – an amusing aspect of their life that gave birth to anecdotes to chuckle over at dinner parties. 'Oh they're ghastly at that age,' they said dismissively, 'they grow out of it.'

But Emily didn't grow out of it. She grew through it, her blackened eyes and pale face rearing up at intervals around the house to glare at Grace as though she were responsible. The only thing that changed was that fat Emily became thin Emily – her white face cadaverous, her shoulders sloping into shoulder blades that shot through her clothes like wire hangers. Grace tried to talk to Lionel about it but he was as useless as her friends.

'Oh stop making a fuss – all young people are like that.'

'You don't think she's on drugs?'

'Don't be such a housewife Grace,' said Lionel who still smoked the odd spliff and popped Valium like free peanuts in a pub.

Then Emily moved out. On her way in from work, Grace came upon her dragging the last of several bin bags stuffed with clothes down the stairs. A girl who might have been Emily's twin, bones rattling around in a selection of black garments, sat on the bonnet of a waiting car.

'Hello,' said Grace carefully.

'Yeah,' said the girl, not looking at her.

'Will you leave a number? An address?' Grace said when Emily had placed the last bag in the boot and was sitting in the passenger seat.

Emily looked at her for a minute and then gave a short, dry laugh. 'Right.' She shook her head slowly in amusement.

She returned at intervals, sometimes to ask for money, sometimes just taking it. Grace got into the habit of hiding valuables while never admitting to herself why she did it. On two occasions, the police called up and she'd gone down to the garda station where Emily accepted the release without comment and without thanks. Each time Grace tried to drop Emily home but she'd insisted on being left in the centre of Rathmines, so Grace was no wiser as to her actual address. She watched her walking away, pounding the footpath angrily, her legs rising out of the heavy boots like needles from a ball of wool.

She hadn't heard from her for months until one day she called and said she was going into a treatment centre and Grace might have to come to 'confront' her. Grace would have preferred if she'd called looking for money.

When Grace got home, Lionel and Olga were in the kitchen looking like a couple about to be photographed for *Hello!* magazine. Lionel was raffish in combats and sunglasses. Olga was wearing trousers and a shirt belonging to Grace. On Grace they looked safe and evident of a certain quiet good taste – on Olga they looked glamorous and a little *louche*. Olga was painting her nails. Lionel was making phone calls on Grace's mobile. He was in mid-call.

'He's a what? The Supreme Court? But he's the same age I am – yes, well. Plus he was the stupidest person I've ever met. In my life. And I've met many stupid people believe me.' Lionel paused to beam up at Grace, 'Hi sweets, nice lesson?' and then returned to the call, listening with growing rage. 'Not Farty Flynn – not that fat fuck who failed everything including every breathalyser test he took.'

Grace got herself a glass of water.

'Any calls?' she asked Olga.

'No.' Olga tsked with exasperation as the brush failed to make contact with the nail varnish in the bottle. 'You need new,' she indicated the almost empty container and then added, 'I forget. Your daughter here.'

'Here? Emily's here?'

'No. Is gone. Was here.'

Lionel finished his call. 'Yes. She was sorry she missed you.'

'I'll say,' Grace took a mouthful of water and a cigarette from the pack in front of Olga, 'What did she want?'

'To see me I think,' Olga smiled, 'Josh tell her. She come see.'

'Excellent.' Grace took a throat-burning drag of her cigarette.

'Nice girl,' Olga said, blowing on her nails.

'She was in great form,' Lionel said, 'quite cheery really. A breath of fresh air, wasn't she Olga?'

Olga laughed and Lionel joined in. Grace felt a moment of loneliness, of exclusion.

'I can think of many words that describe Emily and "cheery" isn't one of them. Neither is "a breath of fresh air", come to that.' Grace got up and went upstairs. The wardrobe was open but otherwise everything was as she'd left it. She kicked off her shoes and lay down on the bed. It felt as though she'd only closed her eyes for a moment but when she opened them, the room was in darkness.

'I make pasta,' said Olga's voice from the end of the bed.

'You do that.'

'I do. Is done. Is ready.'

Grace got up on one elbow, and said, 'Then you made pasta. It is in the past. Made.'

'Yeah. OK. OK. You come?' Olga flounced out the door and

after a moment, Grace followed her down to the kitchen. The table was set for two.

'Where's Lionel?'

'I tell him go home to his wife. Come back tomorrow.'

'Oh.'

The pasta was rather good considering Grace had neglected to shop and Olga had made do with whatever she could find in the cupboard.

'Puttanesca,' Grace said.

'What?' Olga asked dangerously.

'My favourite sauce, Puttanesca, so-called because the Italian whores on the autostrada used to knock it together between customers.'

Olga looked at her for a moment, a twirl of pasta dangling from her fork. 'Don't talk to me about fockin autostrad.'

After that, the two women ate in a companionable silence. Lionel phoned when Grace was doing the washing-up. Olga had looked as if she might do it but her efforts only reached the point of lifting up a plate and then replacing it with a sigh. Lionel was shouting over the sound of crying children.

'Grace? I forgot. A fellow called Travis rang when you were out. Is that a makey-up name?'

'No,' Grace told him coldly after a pleased little shock at hearing he'd called.

'Well, I'd watch him if I were you. Travis? The character Robert de Niro plays in *Taxi Driver*?'

'Oh right,' Grace had wondered why it sounded familiar.

'Grace, this is hideous,' Lionel's voice had lowered to a whisper and the crying noises had ceased. He must have gone to another room. 'It's like a zoo here. They're ghastly. The noise! God, and it's seamless – a seamless white noise 'cos there's two of them and they're working together. They're working together to drive me mad. And she just sits there like a sphinx, smiling. I think she's actually gone mad and that's why she doesn't notice. I think I'll go to Zimbabwe,' he went on miserably, 'I mean I should be in Zimbabwe, shouldn't I?'

'Whatever you think,' Grace told him soothingly knowing that Lionel had no intention of going anywhere that didn't have a decent dry-cleaning service and a barman who knew his way around a martini.

'So who is this – this Dravis?' Olga had accepted a cup of coffee and was drinking it, accompanied by a large brandy.

'Oh he's just …'

Grace found herself telling her how she'd bumped into him, how she'd first met him. Olga nodded, eyes narrowed against the smoke from her cigarette.

'And you're focking him?'

'Dear God,' Grace became flustered, 'certainly not. Absolutely not. Not at all.'

'Oh,' Olga got up, her eyebrows arched a little in surprise. She got herself another drink and, when she'd resettled asked, 'Is he ugly? Poor?'

Grace laughed, 'Well he's certainly not rich but no – he's not ugly. He's quite attractive really.'

'So!' Olga exclaimed, as though something had been decided.

'No!' Grace put down her cup with a clatter.

Olga stretched, 'Why not? You need man.'

'No I don't. And anyway he's too young and I'm too old.'

'What age he?'

'Thirty-seven.'

'Pffhaw! I think you're going to tell me he sixteen. Thirty-seven is old. Plenty old. I think you should fock him – you know?'

Grace hadn't thought about Travis like that. Well maybe she had but just as fantasy – in the same way she might linger at the bank forecourt where the Rollerbladers gathered and think, that'd be fun. But it didn't mean she was going to go out and buy a pair of Rollerblades. She explained this with some difficulty to Olga who was tired of conversing in another language. Olga said that Grace didn't need to buy the Rollerblades – she just needed to try them on.

Later Olga asked to make a phone call. Grace handed her the mobile but Olga shook her head and went to the phone in the hall, closing the kitchen door behind her. Grace could hear Olga's voice through the door. She was speaking in Russian, her tone growing angrier – desperate even but, when she returned, her face was expressionless.

'Problem?' Grace asked.

'Just business,' Olga said and poured them both large vodkas. Grace took the glass thinking she'd better stop this before she started hiding bottles in the lavatory cistern again. Olga cheered up after the drink and, having looked at Grace for some minutes, said, 'You should do thing with hair before Travis.'

'What?'

Olga pointed at Grace's neat bob. 'It look ridiculous the hair.'

'Does it?' Grace took a tendril between her fingers. She was quite proud of her hair, which was always in good condition and was a pleasant, if unremarkable, shade of brown.

'You look like school mister.'

'Mistress,' said Grace automatically. 'So what do you think I should do?'

'Cut it don't give fock.'

'Sorry?'

'More colour. More short. Like don't give fock.'

Grace went to the hallway mirror. She took a handful of hair and yanked it to the top of her head. Immediately she looked ten years younger, but perhaps that was because she'd pulled up her face with the hair. When she washed her hair and tied it up in a towel, turban-style, she was amazed how young she looked. Then, of course, when the towel came off, down came the face and on came the years. Those forties film stars knew what they were about with their turbans.

'I'll do it,' she announced when she came back to the kitchen but Olga was reading a magazine and didn't respond.

'Do you want another drink?' Grace said finally.

Olga flipped over a page of the magazine.

'For someone who don't drink, you drink a hell of a lot.'

'I don't drink. I haven't drunk for years. I just … it's just a temporary thing.'

Olga put down her magazine.

'I see. Just for now you mean.'

'Yes. Anyway, who told you I don't drink?'

Olga yawned. 'I forget. Anyway, drink if you want. Is your house.'

Grace felt a prickle of anger.

'I don't want a drink as it happens.'

Olga didn't reply. She just smiled into the magazine as though its pages contained something that amused her.

TEN

THE NEXT DAY started with a flurry of activity. Some of the dialogue in the commercial was unclear. They were going to have to revoice to film.

The creatives listened to the taped voices over and over again. They were perfectly clear to them, they said. Grace sighed and booked time in the studio. She then rang the actors' agents and arranged for them to be in studio for eleven.

'Thank God they're all available,' she said over her shoulder to Mike.

'Do you want me to do it?'

'Would you?'

'No problem.'

'You'll make sure we can hear every single syllable?'

'Every last consonant.'

'You'll make sure the sync's right so it doesn't look like the original voices were Spanish?'

'Grace we only have to revoice two words and one of them is "pint".'

'Well.'

Mike started to gather his scripts and invoice slips.

'Mike?'

He turned round. Grace was leafing through a series of bills.

'I don't remember us having featured extras for that butter spread thing.'

'What butter spread thing?'

'Beginning of last year? There's a gi-normous bill here for extras.'

Mike shook his head slowly.

'Haven't the foggiest.'

'The thing is – there weren't any extras, featured or otherwise.' Grace looked at the bill again, 'Probably some mix-up.'

'Grace, I'm running late already.'

Mike paused at the door, 'It's some other commercial – forget about it,' he said.

Grace threw the bill into a drawer.

'Yeah,' she agreed, 'I've enough to do without worrying about something that happened two years ago.'

Just before lunch, Mike phoned to say the recording had gone OK but he was feeling a bit off and was going home. He said he'd bike up the tapes. The line went dead before Grace had a chance to be sympathetic. She decided she'd go into town for lunch.

Grace rolled her shoulders and stared at the screen of her computer. She'd had three drinks at lunchtime and her eyes felt gritty. Her phone rang. It was Myles. Grace was relieved that he was at the end of a phone rather than near enough to smell her breath. Then she got annoyed with herself for even thinking like that. What could he do after all, fire her?

'Grace?' his voice had a wheedling tone to it.

'Yes?'

'You wouldn't be free for dinner tonight?'

Grace thought fast. Dinner? A sort of going-away softener? The thought of three hours making smalltalk with Myles filled her with dread but before she could say anything he went on.

'It would be a huge favour. It's just that Gerry knows you and it would make things easier all round. Gerry Taylor?' he added when there was no response from Grace.

'Gerry Taylor?'

'Yes, there's a possibility he might be able to put some work our way now that he's in the you know ... ?'

'Oh right,' said Grace drily, remembering that Gerry was now a junior minister.

'He mentioned your name.'

'He was more a friend of Lionel's. My husband. Ex-husband.' Grace delivered the last phrase with a hint of apology – as though somehow having an ex-husband and an ex-job were symptomatic of some failure in her. In fact Gerry Taylor had been her friend first. She'd known him since first year in college but then he ceased to be her friend and became Lionel's. She hadn't seen him for years.

'Well that's all settled then?' She could hear Myles clicking his pen against the mouthpiece of his phone. 'Would you like a car?'

'A car would be nice.'

'Pick up at seven-thirty? Give you a chance to ... well ...' He floundered.

'Make myself beautiful?'

'Absolutely!'

Actually, when Grace thought about it, she realized that she'd never liked Gerry Taylor. He was big and florid and given to telling long involved jokes innocent of anything resembling a punchline. Lionel had liked him because Gerry had money and Lionel had none. They'd enjoyed many free dinners in return for Lionel's laughter. Nobody laughed like Lionel, particularly when he was at the receiving end of a decent claret and a very large steak.

'I'm going out for dinner,' Grace told Olga. It was close on seven-thirty and she was dressed and ready.

'Have you been drinking?'

'No!' Grace laughed lightly. Actually she had left work early and had had several drinks in a hotel close to the office before catching a taxi. She'd also had a large one in the shower.

'You just seem a little …'

'A little what?'

'A little drunk.'

'No I'm not.'

'You want my advice?'

'No.'

'Fine. Go then. Make idiot.'

'Oh fuck off.'

The doorbell sounded.

'My car,' Grace said grandly and then, pathetically, 'How do I look?'

'You look drunk,' Olga told her.

Gerry Taylor, who had looked middle-aged when he was twenty, hadn't changed a bit. He was sitting with Myles and Andrew in the well of the restaurant. Steps led down allowing for a dramatic entrance. And Grace's *was* dramatic.

Somewhere between the third and fourth step, she lost her

balance. She was wearing a silk stole. It seemed hugely important that she hold onto the stole rather than the banister and so it was that she met Gerry Taylor's feet rather than his face. His shoes were very shiny.

'Drunk again!' carolled Andrew but he looked at her strangely.

'Grace doesn't drink,' Myles explained to Gerry, reaching down to help her to her feet. Grace looked across the expanse of white floor tile. There was a smear of her lipstick on one of them. She gathered herself.

'Gerry!'

'You look exactly the same,' Gerry said. Grace, pleased by the comment, glanced at herself in one of the many mirrors that surrounded the walls of the restaurant. Her face looked frightened – wild even. There was lipstick on her chin. Exactly the same?

'Are you ill?' Andrew hissed at her as they went to the table.

They sat in an alcove, Gerry's thigh pressing against hers. The men argued over the wine list. Grace thought that a drink might sober her up but she couldn't drink here. Not in front of Andrew and Myles.

'Excuse me,' she smiled and squeezed her way out. She mounted the stairs carefully and then ran to the bar.

'Double vodka straight up.' She drank it in a swallow, conscious of the open mouth of the Spanish barman as she turned and ran up the stairs to the ladies' room. Her face was flushed; her eyes a little bloodshot. She grabbed some loo roll, spat on it and rubbed at the smear on her chin. She re-applied her lipstick and blinked several times in an effort to clear her eyes.

When she returned, the three men were laughing.

'Ha, ha, ha,' said Andrew. 'Very good. *Very* good. Ha, ha, ha.'

'Still the joker,' Grace said. The three men ended their laughter on a sighing note and fell to perusing the menu. Grace's eyes swam across the offerings. She decided she'd eat anything she didn't have to cut.

'Fish pâté and turbot,' she said and then, 'I'm sorry?'

Andrew was speaking to her.

'Tell us the one about the cat.'

'The cat?'

'Remember the cat in the commercial? Go on Grace. You'll love this Gerry,' he said, refilling Gerry's glass, splashily.

Grace couldn't remember the story or why it was funny in the first place. She tried to tell it but the words seemed to meld together. All three men looked alarmed.

Then she did remember the story – the anecdote. Remembered the evil marmalade cat with its halitosis and the unfortunate actor with cat food smeared through her hair so that the cat would appear affectionate towards her.

She remembered the cat's arrival on the set, spitting in its cat-box with little tufts of hair floating out of the apertures like dust motes.

'He's moulting.' The trainer, a jolly woman wearing men's trousers thrust into green wellingtons and, incongruously, a chiffon blouse, produced a hairbrush from her pocket.

'A good brush will soon see to that,' she said chattily, releasing the cat, which was huge with a long fat tail.

She placed the cat on top of the cat box and started to brush it, adroitly avoiding the angry swipes from the cat's claws. Clouds of orange hair rose in the air. The actor who was to hold the cat sneezed noisily. It had taken twenty-three takes to get the required shot by which time everyone on the set had grown to hate not just this cat, but all cats. She remembered the evil potpourri of cat hair, cat food and the heavy perfume the trainer wore. She remembered how, in the end, a sort of giddy hysteria had fallen over the shoot. What a funny day it had been.

And now Grace couldn't speak for laughter. She could half-see Andrew's horrified face and Myles reaching across the table to her just before she knocked over his glass of wine.

The last thing she remembered was Gerry Taylor's face through the taxi window.

'You'll be fine in the morning,' he said.

'Tea.' Olga banged a mug on the side table.

'Oh Olga.'

'Drink the tea.'

'Oh God.'

'It's not end of world.'

'Oh God.'

'Is hangover for God's sake. Get over it.'

'I've ruined my life.'

'No you haven't. You just need to stay in bed. And stop drinking.'

Grace sat up and had a sip of tea.

'Jesus!'

Olga looked round from where she was adjusting the curtains.

'I put shot of vodka in. You don't want to stop too sudden. But I mean it, stop.'

'Oh really? What about you? I've never know anyone who drinks so much.'

'I don't need it. You need it.'

'My drinking is perfectly under control thank you very much.'

'You think?'

'I haven't drunk for years and I've only drunk a couple of times in the last few weeks. I've just lost my job, I'm broke. Mother Theresa would drink under the circumstances.'

Grace drank the tea slowly. The alcohol was making her feel a bit better.

'You need stop. You ruin everything if you go on.'

Grace looked at her for a moment.

'Yeah. I know.' She took another sip of tea. Olga grinned.

'You'll be a bitch in an hour.'

'I will?'

'That's your last drink. Oh and I rang office. Said you'd mix up medication.'

'Thank you.'

'You won't thank me in an hour.'

'Were they able to understand you?' Grace asked, curious.

'Of course,' Olga said shortly, putting an end to the matter.

Grace finished the tea, feeling so well that she was able to have a cigarette. An hour later, as Olga had promised, it was a different story.

Grace begged Olga to go to the off-licence but Olga wouldn't go. Grace cried. Grace pleaded. Grace said she'd go herself but Olga had found internal keys so they were locked in.

'What if there's a fire?'

'We burn,' Olga said, lighting a cigarette.

By three o'clock, Grace wasn't feeling well at all.

'At least open the doors.'

'No.' Olga was sitting in the kitchen reading a magazine, her lips forming the words as she read.

'Olga, I need a doctor.'

'No you don't.'

'Olga, please.'

'Phone somebody. Phone Emily.'

'Why would I phone Emily? Emily of all people.'

'She's an addict. Maybe she can help you.'

'It's not the same thing at all. It's completely different. No. Absolutely no.'

'Don't then.' Olga turned a page in the magazine, licking her thumb to facilitate this action.

'Don't do that. It's so common.'

'I am common.'

'What are you doing in my house anyway?'

Olga didn't reply.

Grace curled up on a chair in the kitchen – the one with the cushion.

'I can't believe I got like this.'

'You'll be fine in an hour or two.'

And she was. Well she wasn't fine, but she was better. A bit shaky but OK. They watched television and at ten, Grace went to bed.

ELEVEN

'**Y**OU LOOK WRETCHED,' Grace told Mike. He'd been out sick for three days. She'd been out for the first of those three but she didn't mention this to him. At one point Andrew came in and told her a long involved story about the time he'd mixed warfarin and aspirin. Grace remembered just in time the cover story Olga had invented for her. She mumbled something about muscle relaxants and allergic reaction. Finally Andrew left.

Throughout the exchange, Mike sat staring at his computer. Grace scrolled through her messages and then swung round to face him. 'So, what was it – flu?'

Mike's skin had a yellowish tone with pockets of loose skin gathered in dark pouches under his eyes.

'Oh I'm OK. Feel better than I look probably.'

'Well,' said Grace, leaning back in her chair with the smug complacency of a parish priest, 'guess what I've found?'

'What?' Mike sat back looking, if anything, even sicker.

'Are you all right? Mike?'

'No tell me. Have you found something else? You know with the fiddling the books thing.'

'Well, I found some interesting hotel invoices.'

'Oh?'

'Two overseas actors, but eight hotel rooms? Probably a mistake.' Mike laughed, ending on a hacking cough.

Grace put her hand against his forehead, for a second catapulted back through the years to when Josh and Emily were toddlers.

'Anyway, I've stopped that for a while. This is something else. The silliest thing.' She leaned forward the better to tell the story, 'Well, Lionel invited this Russian woman Olga to stay. Amazing looking woman. Anyway – remember Bruce was looking for "the face"? It suddenly came to me that she'd be totally ideal. And he's crazy about her: she got the gig and I'm her agent.'

Mike reached shakily for a bottle of mineral water. 'That's great Grace, terrific.' He took a gulp of water and shook his head laughing quietly to himself. 'You're amazing. You really are.'

'Amazing Grace – that's me.' She put her hand to his forehead again to check. 'You don't have a temperature. Just a bit shook I expect.'

'Yeah, I'll be fine in a while.' He smiled at her with genuine affection, 'Thanks Grace.'

Outside their office, the agency was in turmoil. Running figures flashed past the window clutching sheaves of paper covered in gashes of black marker – roughs for the pitch everyone in the agency was working on. Trails of heated exchanges filtered through the glass. 'Because it's banal, it's boring, it's total bollix and – more importantly, it's been done. That's why I don't like it.' Andrew was clearly cracking under the pressure.

'What's the pitch?' Mike got up from his chair to have a better view.

Grace mentioned the name of one of the largest financial institutions. Mike whistled softly. 'Thought it must be serious. Melvin's in and it's only half-nine. Look at him – the man who invented *homage*.'

Grace was creating an 'Olga' file on her computer. She got up and joined Mike at the window. Melvin was leafing through a pile of *Design & Art Director* annuals, occasionally pausing to affix a yellow sticker to an award-winning ad that particularly appealed to him.

'He went into a pitch with the actual ad he was plagiarizing once. Said, "It'll be just like this except we'll change the product".' Grace chuckled. 'Andrew nearly had a heart attack.'

'Are we doing any radio demos for it?' Mike wanted to know. Grace sighed.

'Now Mike, you know they're not going to decide that till around five this evening so that we feel a proper sense of crisis. Nothing I like more than sitting around a studio at midnight recording demo commercials that'll never see the light of day.'

Mike tore himself away from the window and got on the phone to the recording studio to warn them that they might have a late one.

'I'll do it if you like,' Grace said, 'you might as well get home and have an early night.'

'Not at all, I'll go, I'm feeling much better actually. Must have been your healing hands.'

'What did I tell you?' Grace picked up her cigarettes and lighter. 'Amazing Grace!'

It was raining slightly and several of the smokers had umbrellas. Grace sidled under one of them to join Dion.

'Working on the pitch?'

Dion looked miserably across the sea of parked cars. 'Nah,' he said, 'I'm leaving it to Melvin and the cream of international creative talent. The King of the Rip-off.'

'You should get yourself a new partner,' Grace flicked the ash off the end of her cigarette.

Dion's eyes slid away for a moment, 'Yeah. I should.'

They both looked up at a shout from the door. It was Andrew and Bruce.

'Got to go kick some ass,' she said in gravelly New York tones, 'I'm an agent now.' And she went towards Andrew and Bruce throwing the end of her cigarette in a casual arc so that it came to rest on the roof of Myles Kitchen's Jaguar.

'Two things,' said Andrew when all three of them were seated in his office. 'First,' and he smiled hugely at Grace, 'your surprise party.'

'Sweet Jesus,' said Grace under her breath.

'But we'll leave that aside for the moment,' Andrew went on quickly, 'because the important thing is, nailing down this poster with your er … friend.'

'She's not a friend, she's a client.'

'Yes, well. That's as may be.'

'What does "that's as may be" mean?' Grace, who had been fidgeting with her lighter, looked directly at Andrew. 'That's as is, as I see it.'

Andrew was growing confused. He turned to his desk, which was littered with torn roughs for the pitch. Bruce appeared not to be listening. His head was bent, his arms hung down between his legs. Grace could see the little hollow at the nape of his neck just where the stubble of his hair began. Then he spoke.

'I thought it was all fixed, Grace.'

Grace took pity on him.

'Yes it is. As we agreed on the phone. Five thousand – one poster – one year buy out. OK?'

'Well …' Andrew picked up his Mont Blanc pen, which he always did when he wanted to remind people of his status. Grace got up and made to go for the door. Andrew dropped his pen as though it was red-hot and blustered, 'Absolutely splendid. We're all agreed then. Great. Good. Great.'

Grace smiled and then turned back to face him before sitting down again.

'So,' she said, reaching over to pick up Andrew's pen with a little raise of her eyebrows.

'Feel free. By all means,' said Andrew as though he intended giving her the pen as a gift. It gave her a certain amount of pleasure to watch the small tic pulsing on one side of his face as she bore down on the gold nib to scrawl the name of the product and the date.

'So Andrew, what's the schedule?'

'Ah,' said Andrew, picking up his diary and looking at its blank pages with a frown. 'I'll check with Angela, will I?'

Angela was the secretary shared by Andrew and Myles who was the only person in the building who knew where everyone should be at any given time. Myles and Andrew's lives were set, like those of recovering alcoholics, 'in the day'. Ask them at five in the evening what they were doing on the morrow and they became evasive. Grace used to think this was the result of a natural tendency towards mendacity but the truth was they didn't know. Angela knew and, when the time was right, Angela would tell them. No sign of her retiring, Grace thought sourly, even though she was well into her fifties. In an industry where no one was indispensable, Angela had the foresight to make sure she was.

She took no chances. All her notes were in shorthand of her own devising which would baffle the most astute code-breaker, and she had a filing system that would take an enigma specialist a lifetime to sort out. Apart from that, she kept a low profile in the agency and, while management took a more than usual interest in her health and discouraged her from foreign travel lest she plunge to her death in some disaster, she went about her business with the anonymous efficiency of an office cleaner.

Grace made her way back to her office, dodging pockets of rowing creatives and account handlers, lulled by the familiar taunts and retorts – the overblown rhetoric: 'Because it's got integrity – it's got passion …' deflated by the pragmatic: 'But it hasn't got a logo – OK? And I think the client might like to see their name somewhere. In nice big letters – right?'

'Any news?' she asked Mike, flopping down in her chair, pleased with herself.

'The best,' Mike told her. 'Pitch brief said absolutely, positively no radio or TV – just print.'

'Isn't God good?' Grace grinned at him, happy to see him back to his old self.

'So how's about I take you out for a posh meal to mark your going away?'

'My passing?'

'Absolutely.'

Grace thought for a moment. A quiet dinner with Mike would be nice but maybe she should stay home and ensure that Olga was all set for tomorrow.

'Oh what the hell,' she said, 'let's do it. Olga should be able to look after herself for a night.'

'I have to see this Olga. She's big on the "phwoar!" factor I hear.'

Grace winced. Somehow Mike being laddish always rang false – as though her father had commented on someone's bum. They agreed to meet in town in a hotel near a restaurant in Temple Bar they both liked.

'Well, well, well. How are things at the hub of the agency?' It was Andrew again. Grace sighed; Mike became very busy at his computer.

'Much the same as it was ten minutes ago, Andrew,' Grace said and picked up her cigarettes as a signal to him to get on with it.

'About this party,' Andrew said, a note of pleading in his voice.

'Oh for God's sake. Whatever you like Andrew. Whatever is "appropriate"? I bloody hate those things but don't mind me, you know?'

Andrew looked hurt. 'Grace it's for you. To show how much we appreciate your –'

'"Contribution"?' Mike suggested without looking up from his computer.

'Thank you, Mike. Exactly. Contribution.'

'Huge contribution,' Mike said, swivelling around to face Andrew. 'Huge.' Andrew backed out the door.

'What a total wanker,' Mike said getting to his feet and reaching for his jacket. 'Sandwich?'

'No, I'm getting my hair done.'

'Ah,' said Mike, 'I'm touched.'

The hairdresser's was crowded. She'd been lucky to get an appointment. The air was filled with the white noise drone of hairdryers and the acrid smell of colourants. The girl who usually did Grace's hair was on a day off – a piece of serendipity that allowed Grace to opt for the more outré young male stylist. Mark bathed her in smiles when she said the magic words: 'I want a complete change – I don't care what you do.'

He brought her some style books and started to flick through the pictures, all the time giving a running commentary.

'That might be nice. Is this too much? Oh this is lovely. Do you like this?'

Grace's attention wandered for a minute so that his voice seemed to recede and become lost in the Muzak of rhetorical questions that drifted round the salon: 'Planned any holidays? Going anywhere nice tonight? Is that water too hot? Shall I put a treatment on?'

'I'm sorry?' Grace came to with a start and looked down at the open page, which showed a model of about seventeen with cropped spiky hair, in a variety of reds and russets. 'Does this look like I don't give a fuck?' Grace asked.

Now it was the stylist's turn to say, 'I'm sorry?'

'I quite like that,' Grace said shyly. 'Do you think it's too – young?'

'Well it's pretty funky,' Mark said, and grasped a hank of her hair. Their twin reflections stared back in the mirror – Grace looking startled, the effect exaggerated by her eyebrows pulled up high on her forehead; Mark serious and judicious as though torn between the death sentence and life.

'Might be quite interesting actually.' Mark turned to call out the name of one of the colour specialists, 'Could you come here a sec Robbie?'

Robbie was a big butch girl with a shaved head, her face glinting with a variety of piercings. She wore faded dungarees, pockets stuffed with the instruments of her trade. When purchasing this garment, she had never enquired of a friend if her bum looked big.

'Whadja think?' asked Mark.

'Yeah,' said Robbie after a while, 'could be good that.'

'She wanted a change,' Mark explained.

Grace smiled ingratiatingly into the mirror. The two stylists smiled back, the smiles professional, not reaching their eyes. Grace badly wanted them to like her – as though that might determine the outcome of this impulse. As Robbie expertly combed, parted and slapped bits of plastic onto skeins of hair before plastering them with paste, Grace divided her time between looking at the other customers and returning to the picture in the book. The more she looked at the picture, the more nervous she became. She was going to come out of this looking like Phyllis Diller who, she reminded herself, was a figure of fun. Beside her sat a man in a pinstripe suit. The patter was different for men she noticed.

'Did you catch the Man U match? Wicked, right? Playing any golf? Schumacher's doing great isn't he?'

Apparently men didn't take holidays or go somewhere nice in the evening. The colour seemed to take forever. Her eyes started to water with the fumes. She leaned closer to the mirror and dabbed under her eyes where the mascara had run. This brought her attention to her eyebrows, which were simultaneously sparse and bushy. One of the hairs must have been two inches long.

'Do you think someone could pluck my eyebrows?' she asked a passing junior.

While she was at the washbasin having colour 'run through the ends', a tanned girl in a white coat came and attacked her eyebrows with a tweezers. 'Oh dear, we've let these go a bit,' she said to Grace as though it were an oversight for which they were both responsible. Grace, wincing at the removal of each hair, felt her eyes water again. Finally she was back before the mirror with Mark standing behind her clicking his scissors open and shut awaiting inspiration.

The man in the suit was still having his hair cut. The stylist snapped his scissors shut over thin air or, in his case, thin hair, and the pinstripe suit nodded approvingly.

Mark ran a comb through Grace's lank tresses. Even wet, the colours sang out. Grace swallowed. Mark snipped and cut for what seemed like hours. At some point during the cutting, Grace's mobile rang. Mark sighed and then stood back, scissors dangling accusingly. Grace took the call – immediately moving the instrument away from her ear as her father's bellow came down the line.

'There's a bloody foreigner here in your house. Says she knows you.'

'That's Olga. It's all right.'

'You never mentioned. The other evening when you were over – you never said.'

'I forgot Dad. And could you stop shouting? I can hear you perfectly well.'

Grace wondered what had induced her father to drop around. He rarely left his own home. He was looking for a paint roller apparently.

'What on earth made you think I'd have something like a paint roller?'

She smiled reassuringly at Mark, through the mirror. He made a little moue of impatience. Grace asked her father to put Olga on.

Cupping her hand over the mouthpiece, she whispered, 'I'm at the hairdressers. Which reminds me. Olga – do you think you could shave your armpits? For tomorrow?'

'What?' Olga's yell down the phone was almost as loud as her father's.

'You heard.'

'No.'

'No you didn't hear, or no you're not going to do,' Grace looked up at Mark who was now all ears, ' – what I asked?' Grace finished carefully.

'I like hair.'

'It'll grow back Olga.'

'No.'

'Shave your bloody armpits Olga. I'm your goddamn agent and that's an order.'

There was a long pause and then a sulky 'all right' from Olga followed by her father's voice, 'So I take it you don't have a paint roller then?'

'No,' shouted Grace, so that the whole salon turned to look at her. 'My father,' she said by way of explanation to Mark.

'Riiiight,' he said sliding a lock of her hair through his fingers and cutting along its edge, clean as a ruler. Grace stared into the mirror, no longer seeing herself, lulled by the rhythmic slice of the scissors and steady hum of blow-dryers. Sometimes three inches of hair would fall to the floor, sometimes just a fraction of a centimetre – an amount, Grace thought, hardly worth cutting at all. As her hair shrank, so her face seemed to grow until it became a great white moon in the mirror. Oh God. Oh God. Oh God. Oh God.

'This is going to be great,' Mark said, as though he had heard her. He ran his hands through her hair, which was almost dry by now, and teased it into spikes. Then he took a dryer and whooshed it this way and that so that each strand shone. He plunged his hands into a jar of wax and tweaked bits of it onto a strand here, a strand there. Then he stood back.

'Fabulous,' he said.

Grace looked in the mirror. Was it fabulous? Well it was different. And she did look younger. Did she look too young? Or rather did the hair look too young – and she too old? Older than her hair. No, she decided, she looked good – most importantly, the hair looked as if it might belong to her. As though she'd always been as vibrant, as careless as this.

'You'll need a much stronger lipstick,' Mark told her and, beside him, Robbie – a stranger to lipstick in her own life – nodded in agreement. Just as she'd finished paying, her phone rang again. It was Mike wanting to know what was keeping her. Grace immediately launched into a flood of explanation and apology until she stopped herself and said, 'Actually, I'm not going to bother going back Mike. I'll see you in the restaurant.'

'Oh. Right,' Mike fumbled the words in his surprise. Neither of them said anything for a moment or two but Grace didn't hang up. After a while she said, 'Are you there, Mike?'

'Yes.'

'Do most people have paint rollers do you think?'

She could almost hear Mike thinking.

'I suppose so,' he said at last.

'I don't,' said Grace but Mike didn't hear her because she'd already pressed 'end'.

When she got home, Olga was in the living-room clad in a vast towelling robe that had 'Ritz Hotel' embroidered in blue on the pocket. One of Lionel's travel souvenirs. Grace had forgotten all about it. Olga was flicking through TV channels and, without looking at Grace, allowed the robe to fall away and raised her arm to reveal one smooth, still pink armpit. 'Happy?' she shouted over the TV commentator who, in turn, was shouting over the roar of a football crowd. Then she turned round, took in Grace's hair and immediately turned back to the TV.

'Who's winning?' Grace enquired lightly.

Olga didn't answer. Grace went to the kitchen and got herself a glass of water. When she returned, Olga had turned the TV off and gave Grace's hair her full attention.

'It look good,' Olga allowed, reluctantly.

'You don't think it's too …'

'Too what?'

'Too too I suppose,' said Grace, throwing herself into the couch beside Olga. Olga smiled to herself.

'Your father. Very nice man.'

'Really?' Nice was not a word Grace would have ascribed to her father.

Olga smiled more broadly.

'Very nice. Very – virile.'

'What?'

Olga stretched, allowing her robe to fall open revealing, for a moment, her naked body. Grace looked at her searchingly and then said in a voice several octaves lower than her normal one, 'Oh no. You didn't. You couldn't …'

Olga assumed an expression of hurt.

'Don' worry. I do for free. Favour to you.'

'Oh Jesus Christ. Oh God.' Grace got up and started walking rapidly around the room. 'How could you?' she asked. Olga remained blank, then threw back her head and gave one of her shouts of laughter.

'Was choke. I was choking you.'

'Not choke. Joke. Joke, joke, JOKE,' Grace screamed and then, quietly, 'and it wasn't very funny.'

Olga shrugged; Grace grabbed a full ashtray from the table and threw its contents into the ashes of the fire.

'Anyway – I thought you said you didn't have any sense of humour.'

Olga reached for Grace's bag and helped herself to a cigarette. 'Maybe I get one.'

'I mean it's the most appalling – the most ridiculous thing …' Grace thought of her father for a moment and then she started to laugh almost hysterically. 'Oh dear God – what a thought. The mind boggles,' she said when she could get her breath. She collapsed back into the couch beside Olga.

'Hair very good,' Olga said.

'Shave very good too,' Grace said happily.

TWELVE

MIKE ARRIVED LATE at the restaurant. He entered with the busy intentness of the unpunctual and was half-way across the room before he stopped in his tracks.

'Jesus!'

Grace looked around to see what had caused this outburst. Then she remembered her hair.

'What do you think?'

'Very rock 'n' roll.'

'I kind of like it,' said Grace, running her fingers across the spiky surface of her hair so that it sprang up under her fingers in a satisfying way. Mike examined her more thoroughly.

'It is nice. Makes you look like you work in the "meedja".'

'I do work in the media – sort of.'

'Well there you are then. Wine?' Mike had opened the wine list and was flashing through its offerings with the slight frown of someone who had recently attended a wine appreciation course, which he had.

Grace wondered if she could get away with it. A glass wouldn't hurt.

'A glass wouldn't hurt.' She looked up, startled as Mike echoed her thought. He was grinning at her around the corner of the wine list. Grace thought for a second. Her over-riding feeling was one of fear. What frightened her was how much she wanted a drink. Not for any reason – she just wanted one. She grabbed a hunk of her hair and pulled at it quite hard.

'No,' she said finally. 'Need to keep my wits about me in my new role as agent to the redoubtable Olga. You have some though.'

Mike half-smiled.

'Please yourself,' he said and ordered an obscure Bordeaux wine, muttering something about a half-bottle never being enough and a bottle too much. Then they fell to studying the menu. They spent some time arriving at a choice that tempted them both so that they would have the opportunity to share. That was the pleasant thing about knowing someone well, Grace thought. You got to have the crab claws *and* the duck terrine. They talked with an agreeable cruelty about their colleagues at work and speculated about their various love-lives, their salaries – for the moment keeping a healthy distance from any personal confidences. They wondered how this one had got so far with so little talent, who was on the look-out for a new job and who would replace Andrew when he made concrete his dream of moving to (where else?) Tuscany to paint.

'Actually, he's not a bad painter,' said Mike defensively because he had, in a moment of weakness, bought one of Andrew's dreary seascapes. On the shores of Andrew's works it was always low tide.

'How much did you pay for that?' asked Grace, who knew the exact amount involved.

'Oh not much. It was almost a present really.' Mike marked the end of the conversation by pushing his terrine across the table so that Grace could help herself to a forkful. He sucked on one of her crab claws. 'Nice,' he said, 'bit garlicky. Hope you're not meeting Travis later.'

'I'm not meeting Travis period,' Grace said crossly. 'I was just being polite having lunch with him – that's all.' And then, because she was smarting at the snide tone she thought she detected in his voice, asked, 'And how's Annalise these days?'

'She's extremely well, thank you very much,' Mike said coldly, smearing the last of his terrine on a piece of ciabatta, 'she's just back from the Bahamas actually.'

Annalise travelled a great deal in a futile way, like a refugee, trudging through countries without ever really noticing them. She returned from hot countries as white and drawn as when she boarded the plane two weeks earlier. God knows how she afforded it.

'Tell us more about the Russian then,' said Mike realizing perhaps that the dinner was degenerating into a succession of sharp-edged exchanges. Grace told him snippets about Olga – anecdotes which she didn't need to embellish in order to render her more exotic. Mike laughed every time she paused for breath and then said the sooner Grace got rid of her the better. She told Mike the armpits story.

'Maybe that was what Bruce liked most about her,' Mike pointed out.

'Shit, I never thought of that.'

'How's the sleuthing going?'

Mike was looking at the pudding menu. He drank the last of the wine in his glass. He'd managed to finish the bottle after all.

'How do you mean?'

'Oh all that stuff about cooked books and stuff.'

Grace laughed.

'Oh that.' She took the menu and ran her eye over it. 'Are you having anything?'

'No. So?' Mike raised his eyebrows.

'So what?'

'So did you find out anything?'

Grace took a last look at the menu and then put it down on the table.

'Well,' she said, 'there were a few odd things. Remember the dairy spread thing? I told you about the extras.' Mike looked vague.

'Jesus you must remember. Anyway, apart from that, the charge-outs were weird.'

'Weird in what way?' Mike was trying to catch the attention of a waiter.

'I don't fancy coffee,' Grace told him. 'Will we just get the bill?'

Mike made a writing motion in the direction of the waiter who nodded. He turned back to Grace.

'Oh it doesn't matter,' Grace said, 'I'm not going to think about it till I've got this Olga thing out of the way.'

'And then what? Tell Myles?'

'I don't know.'

Grace sighed and put her cigarettes and lighter in her purse. She gestured at the bill that Mike was examining.

'Are you sure about this? We can go Dutch if you like.'

Mike threw a credit card on top of the bill.

'No, on me. I insist.' The waiter took the card away. Mike started to rifle through his wallet and, at the same time asked, 'Will you? Do something I mean?'

'Oh God, I suppose so. I mean if someone can invent three featured actors who didn't appear in a series of commercials and yet got paid – well, it can't be an isolated thing, now can it?'

The waiter returned with the credit card slip. Mike signed it and Grace stood up. Suddenly she wanted to be out of the place. The noise level had risen since they'd arrived and it was very hot. Mike remained seated and stretched out his hand.

'Grace?'

'What?'

'Let's stay a bit. There's something I wanted to …'

'We can talk in the taxi,' Grace said. 'Come in for a coffee at my place if you like.'

'OK.'

They went out onto the street where the air was curiously balmy. Dame Street stretched before them, rising towards Parliament Street, the lights of the cars creamy yellow in the magic that was magic hour – the dark sinking into the light – ink in water.

'That was nice,' she told Mike, 'too much food possibly, but nice.'

Mike didn't reply. Didn't need to. They walked along, occasionally side-stepping to avoid a group spilling out of a pub, responding to the overtures of strangers with good humour, smiling at the couple lost in a kiss.

'It's one of those nights,' Grace told him, 'one of those nights when you absolutely know you're not going to step in any vomit.' She smiled at him. 'So what was it you wanted to talk about?'

And that's when it happened. Grace had to rethread the spools of film in her brain. They were walking along in the warm almost darkness, chatting and now Mike was against the window of some hotel with a needle pressed against his neck and the young man holding the needle was saying, 'Just give me the money.' Mike looked suddenly haggard, his face cadaverous with fear. Grace wanted to scream – the street was crowded after all but although she opened her mouth, no sound emerged – just the sound of air being expelled. She tried to gather the force of a shout but now she couldn't seem to breathe in any direction – in or out. Mike had one arm raised and was flailing it uselessly, trying to find his wallet. He looked at Grace and then at her bag. She fumbled with the clasp and the very ordinariness of the gesture seemed to bring her breathing back to normal. Her hand closed around her wallet. She tried to speak. What she wanted to say was, 'I have money,' but what came out was, 'Have you ever considered working in commercials?'

The effect of this remark on both Mike and the would-be thief was identical.

'What?' They both exclaimed in unison. Grace tried to smile at the hypodermic holder and mustering all her charm said, 'You've a really interesting face.'

Mike had dropped his arm and was now slumped against the window. The thief lowered his needle. The three of them might be any one of the groups that had paused to chat along the street. Behind her, Grace could hear the clatter of high heels and a girl's shriek of mock outrage, 'Gedd off!'

Mike's attacker took a quick glance at himself in the window before saying, 'How do you mean – "inner-res-diing"?'

'Well,' said Grace, trying to avert her gaze from the pepper of pimples on the youth's face, 'you've got – a quality.'

She could see Mike's face – a mix of pain and rage. Ignoring him, Grace pulled out a card from her bag and handed it to the youth.

'Here's my card. I want you to call the number on it and we'll be able to tell you the date of the casting.'

'The casting?'

'For the commercial,' Grace explained. The boy looked at the card, turning it slowly in his hand.

'Of course,' Grace said in a firm, scolding voice, 'the drugs would be a problem. I wouldn't permit drugs of any kind.'

'I don't do drugs,' said the boy, who indicated the needle with distaste, 'I found dis in a skip.'

'Well please dispose of it safely,' Grace said primly before grasping Mike by the arm and walking purposefully back in the direction they had come leaving the boy standing at the window. When she thought it was safe, Grace looked back. The boy was still there. He smiled at her and raised his hand in a wave. Then he turned and walked away with quick, bouncy steps towards Christchurch.

'Oh my sweet Jesus,' Mike stopped and leant against the window of a bar where, inside, four girls screeched with laughter. He breathed shallowly for a moment.

'Grace, you are out of control. What possessed you? What possessed you to do something so – so daft?'

'I don't know. It just popped out.' And then she, in her turn, grew angry, 'And didn't it work? Didn't he buy it? Haven't we survived?'

'I don't know, Grace. I really don't know.' Mike peeled himself off the window. The girls at the table had just noticed them. 'Fuck off!' they mouthed through the window. Mike took a step back on the pavement. 'Enjoy our city you working-class English cunts!' he shouted. The girls gestured to him to come in.

'You're barking. Do you know that Grace? Barking!'

'Woof woof,' Grace said in a very small voice and then, as a taxi rounded the corner, raised her arm. They settled themselves into the back seat and Mike seemed to calm down.

'I'd like to see you putting that head-case in a commercial – even in a casting,' he said. Grace pulled her coat around her and smiled out over the mercifully silent taxi-man's shoulder.

'I'll be well gone by then,' she said tranquilly, 'he'll be your little discovery.'

'Bitch!'

And Mike started to laugh with relief until they were both screaming with laughter in the back.

'There's a fine if you're sick,' the taxi-man warned them, which, of course, made them laugh even harder.

'So,' said Grace when they'd quietened down, 'back to my place?'

'No.'

'I thought you wanted … ?'

'It was nothing. Nothing at all.' Mike leaned forward and gave the taxi-man his address and Grace's. They dropped Mike first. As they turned into his street, a taxi just ahead of them pulled in and Annalise got out. As always, Grace was startled by her ordinariness. Far from being a siren, Annalise was a drab, bony woman with a gaunt face, nondescript hair and a body innocent of curves. She didn't look like someone who had slept her way through the phone book.

'Isn't that Annalise?' Grace said when it became clear Mike was going to ignore the encounter. Mike didn't reply but rooted in his pocket for his wallet. Then he stopped.

'Tell you what Grace, you pay, I nearly got killed for this tonight.'

'Oh tosh!' said Grace, but there was a note of apology in her voice.

THIRTEEN

THE STUDIO WHERE the photo shoot was to take place was in a
laneway off Merrion Square. Along its length were small-time car
repair shops, fashion wholesalers, lock-ups and the occasional
mews apartment. The buildings seemed to list to one side, lolling
against each other for support. In some, the pebbledash facing had
come away from the brick so that it gaped like old wallpaper. A
half-hearted rain – more mist than rain really – hung in the air,
gathering in eddies over the skeletons of burnt-out cars. The laneway was unsurfaced and the gravel was pocked with slick, black
oily puddles. Olga and Grace abandoned their taxi at the top of
the lane to pick their way through the mud and oil spillages.

'It's just a bit further,' Grace said, not sure if this were true.
Normally she wouldn't attend stills shoots. Olga gathered her coat
(Grace's coat actually) more closely around her. 'Sorry,' said Grace
as they were circumventing a pile of tyres.

'Oh I am use,' Olga said with a sigh, 'I am use to place like this.'

Grace looked back at her crossly, about to say something, but
then they were outside the studio door which was freshly painted

and had a gold plaque: Jamie Jordan, Photographer. The door opened at the first ring and Olga and Grace walked in to a large space. Huge lights hung suspended from the ceiling and, around the edge of the studio, a forest of standing lamps of various sizes reared up out of the shadows.

'You're here! Great! Grace – good to see you and this must be Olga,' Jamie's voice billowed and roared around the studio and, as he came towards them, Grace fancied that the floor heaved and creaked. He was a huge man – well over six foot, which gave his girth an air of authority rather than corpulence. His shoulders were massive; his stomach thrust out from just below his neck almost filling the vast tent of black linen that was his jacket. Beneath his stomach, his trousers, anchored by a plaited belt, strained over his thighs and fell into neat, knife-edge pleats at his surprisingly dainty feet.

He took Olga's face in his hand, Olga as docile as a calf at market, and moved her head this way and that, humming all the while.

'Excellent, excellent,' he said at intervals.

Grace looked around to see who else was there. On a couch at the end of the studio she saw the two Irish clients, who sketched a wave at her. Bustling around in the mezzanine over the seating area she saw Pattie, the wardrobe woman, and Gerry and Anne – hair and make-up, respectively.

'Bring the stuff down here, Pattie,' Jamie yelled, 'I don't do stairs,' and confidingly to Olga, 'Last time I went up those stairs I managed to break two of the beams – snapped like matchwood.' Pattie came down with an armload of garments. Jamie lifted up the dresses one by one and discarded them:

'Too pretty-pretty, too boring, too shite, too blue, too total crap, too …'

Then he held up a red silk shift. It floated in his hand like a scarf. He paused for a moment then threw it at Olga who caught it adroitly.

'That's the one. Slip it on sweetheart.'

Olga dropped Grace's coat carelessly to the floor and, before she could take off more, Grace hissed at her, 'Upstairs.'

Olga shrugged and followed Grace up to the mezzanine where she took off her shirt and jeans and after a moment's thought her bra and panties. Grace smiled distantly at Pattie who was trying to look elsewhere. Olga slipped on the dress. Even with the smallest shift of air, the silk seemed to hover around her, like a mirage. Through its folds you could glimpse the curve of her breast, the line of her thigh. She stepped into the high-heeled shoes Pattie held out for her. 'Manolos', Pattie murmured to Grace and added, 'six hundred euro.'

'Bloody 'ell,' said Gerry as Olga turned slowly, examining herself in the mirror, 'you look pretty fucking amazing love.' Olga gave a tiny, almost bored smile. From below, Jamie shouted up at them:

'Minimum make-up – minimum fuck-around with hair – *comprende* Gerry? Anne?'

Grace made herself comfortable on a pile of backdrop curtains and wondered where Bruce was. Three-quarters of an hour later, he arrived accompanied by a steady stream of 'fucks' from which Grace extracted the information that Andrew had pulled him in on the pitch. By this time, Olga was made up and Gerry was doing the last minute tweaks to her hair. The sight of her silenced Bruce. Olga stood up.

'Totally, totally …' was all Bruce could manage.

'Are we nearly there yet?'

Jamie was standing at the bottom of the stairs. Olga glided down, a cigarette trailing in her hand. 'Don't burn the dress, hon,' said Jamie, but it was a plea rather than an instruction. Grace's mobile rang.

'Turn that bloody thing off,' Jamie said over his shoulder as he went over to the camera. Grace walked to the doorway to take the call. It was Lionel.

'I'm in the middle of something,' Grace hissed.

'Sorry,' said Lionel with uncharacteristic diffidence, 'this won't take a minute.'

'Well hurry up.' Grace looked over to where Jamie was placing Olga. Olga was laughing at something he'd said.

'It's just,' Lionel hesitated, 'look you haven't heard anything about the paper. About it going to the wall? Anything like that?'

'Going bust? Your paper?'

'I just wondered if you might have heard on the grapevine — through the media department or something.'

'No,' Grace said slowly, 'but I could ask if you like.'

'Thanks sweetheart.'

'I mean that would be awful — but you'd get some sort of pay-off, wouldn't you? If it's true that is.'

'Not if they're bankrupt.'

'Jesus. OK. Look I'll call you — as soon as I hear.'

'Thanks. Oh and thanks for helping Olga out. She said something about some ad she might be in?'

'Yeah. Got to go Lionel.'

Grace switched off her mobile and looked up the length of the room to where Olga was moving into different positions as Jamie encouraged with: 'Great Olga. Now kill the smile. Straight to me. Make fists of your hands. Lovely. More smoulder. Lovely. Drop your left shoulder — a bit more. Keep looking straight at me but turn your body a bit away. No the other way.'

Grace moved closer and Jamie gave her a quick smile.

Occasionally he moved aside so that Bruce could look through the camera. Olga stretched and shook out her arms. Jamie called for more stock, yelling at his assistant with the casual brutality with which photographers communicated with their assistants. 'You stupid cunt, what did I ask you for?' The assistant's expression didn't change. He wasn't too bothered. Soon he would be a photographer himself and have his own assistant. Grace glanced over at the two clients who were embarrassed at witnessing the humiliation of a fellow human being. They both smiled shakily at the assistant.

'Hold it!' Jamie took his eye from the lens and put his big, beefy hands on the general area of his hips. 'Pattie?'

Pattie came scuttling down from the eyrie of the mezzanine.

'What's that?' Jamie gestured at Olga who had abandoned her latest pose and was sitting on a director's chair in the corner, having a cigarette. Pattie looked at Jamie nonplussed.

'Sweat!' Jamie said in a modulated tone far more terrifying than one of his yells. Olga stretched and there were indeed dark stains forming under her arms. Pattie gasped. Olga looked over, conscious that she was being discussed. Then she looked at the dark stains with indifference.

'What you expect? Is bloody hot here. I'm a human being. I sweat. I have to pee …' and she got to her feet and started to amble towards the ladies' room.

'Not criticizing darling,' Jamie called after her, 'not a problem.' And to Pattie, 'Get them out or get me a replacement dress. Oh and whatever solution you arrive at, I want it yesterday.'

'Wouldn't be problem if Grace not make me shave arm,' Olga shouted from behind the closed door of the ladies' room. Grace looked at Jamie and shrugged elaborately.

'She's Russian,' she said finally.

Jamie's face and the faces of the clients immediately cleared and they all nodded sagely, as though Grace had explained an obscure philosophical conundrum that had been troubling them for years. The shoot went on for another couple of hours – some of it devoted to the now pristine red dress – then Jamie shot a roll or two with Olga in a black dress just in case the red was too 'sudden' for the overseas clients. And then it was over. Grace called a taxi for herself and Olga. In spite of the clients' entreaties, Olga had declined their invitation to dinner.

'I sick talk,' she said.

'Of course, of course. Naturally,' they murmured and their eyes followed Olga as she and Grace went to their waiting taxi.

They ordered in pizza and half-watched TV, too exhausted to do anything else. Grace became unreasonably annoyed during some American series based around a coven of sexually rapacious women.

'What's with this sheet thing? In every TV show, in every damned film, if the heroine is naked in bed, when she gets up, she wraps herself in the sheet and trails around the house in this – sheet! It's ridiculous. Have you ever, ever wrapped yourself in a sheet? Has anyone ever done that – ever?'

'You take thing too serious,' Olga said picking bits of anchovy off the remainder of the pizza, 'who give fock sheet – no sheet?'

'Yeah,' Grace agreed, then remembered Lionel's call. She leafed through her Filofax and keyed a number into her mobile.

'Something Lionel needed to know – I forgot,' she explained to Olga.

The call lasted five minutes and, when it was finished, Grace threw herself back in the couch.

'Shit,' she said.

Olga raised her eyebrows enquiringly.

'Lionel's paper seems to have gone bust.'

Grace explained while Olga nodded, her mouth drawn down. She had a finely honed appreciation of what being broke meant. Grace said there was always the house. If necessary she could sell it. It was far too big anyhow. Olga picked at a hangnail with great concentration.

'You think it's odd for me to bail out an ex-husband?'

Olga shrugged. 'You have papers for house?'

Grace laughed. 'I don't have the actual deeds here, that's not how it works – I don't know. They're with the solicitor or the bank. Lionel sorted all that. I hate bloody forms and all that bureaucratic stuff.'

'Deeds are important,' said Olga.

'I'll check them out tomorrow. OK? God!' Grace groped for her lighter. 'Anyway, I mightn't have to sell at all.'

'I think he get money on house before,' Olga said finally.

Grace felt her stomach falling away because she knew immediately, even through the fog of Olga's tenuous grasp of English, that what she said was true. Lionel had remortgaged the house. And Olga knew about it.

'Why didn't you tell me? I thought we were – friends.'

Olga tore a corner of crust from the pizza and started to rip it into small pieces. 'I didn't think it matter. I'm sorry.'

'He is such a total bastard,' Grace said after a bit.

'He don't think,' Olga said. 'I don't know him well but I know he don't think. We not together long. Once, twice.'

'I don't care what you did or how many times,' Grace said.

Olga began to tidy away the remains of their supper. She paused at the door, holding the pizza boxes inexpertly so that bits of crumb tumbled out of one corner.

'He lousy lover anyway. What you think?'

Grace wondered if she felt jealous and decided she didn't. Lousy lover. Now there was a thought. Was Lionel a lousy lover? For some reason a competition she'd seen on some late-night TV show popped into her mind. It was a line of men with every part of them hidden except for their penises. Their wives and lovers had to pick out their partner. Obviously most of them were pretty inattentive during lovemaking because the majority of them got it wrong. Grace could have picked Lionel's penis out immediately. But only because he had a tiny scar on the left side – a relic of the time when he was fourteen and got it caught in a zipper. With the passage of time, Lionel's version of the cause of the scar had been coloured somewhat. Now it was the result of a knife-wound in an alley in Marrakech or a ricocheting bullet in Sarajevo. When Olga came back Grace's curiosity got the better of her.

'That scar on his penis … ?'

'Yeah,' agreed Olga, 'lucky he had machete. Otherwise those Chechen bastards take off whole thing.'

Grace grinned and lay back in the couch.

'I think,' she said, 'one of us deserves a little drink.'

Olga raised her eyebrows.

'I'll stick to Saudi champagne. Apple juice and mineral water,' Grace explained when Olga looked puzzled.

Olga poured herself a shot of vodka and lifted her glass.

'To courage!' she said.

'And imagination,' Grace added.

Grace woke. The phone by her bedside was ringing. She looked at the clock and groaned. It was her father.

'Yes?' Grace said, shaking herself awake, 'Do you know what time it is?'

'Of course I know what time it is.' Her father's voice sounded strangely muffled. He mustn't have put his teeth in yet. A clatter at the end of the phone followed by his clearer tones suggested that he had now rectified the oversight.

'It's Saturday,' Grace pointed out.

'All the more reason to be up and about making the most of it,' shouted her father.

'Tell me why you're ringing,' Grace said as calmly as she could manage.

'I need you to take me to the hospital.'

Grace shot up in the bed.

'What's happened?'

'Your mother tried to kill me.'

'I did not,' her mother's voice interjected from the other phone and then in a child's voice, 'Please come Grace. He's bleeding. It won't stop.'

'Now are you satisfied you old bitch?' screeched her father.

'Grace? Grace?'

'Jesus Christ!' Grace yelled as she heard her name being called from the street outside.

'Look I'm on my way,' she said to her father, pulling on sweats and a T-shirt. She wrenched open the front door, 'Yes? What?' she screamed and then, 'Sorry. Sorry Red.'

Red stood on the doorstep and looked hurt.

'No need to get your knickers in a twist. I did say I'd be early. I've a nice little Beamer needs to be back before nine,' and he indicated a rakish black BMW parked at the gate.

'Thank God!' Grace said. 'Look, you have to drive me to my parents'. Something's happened.'

The streets were deserted, which was a good thing given the fact that they broke most of the traffic lights and all of the speed limits. During the course of the journey, which took only minutes, Red ran her through the merits and demerits of the car – 'Look at dat acceleration Grace. Excellent but she's a bit of a cunt in a corner. See dat?' – as they mounted the pavement and whacked against the side-mirror of a parked car.

When they drew up outside Grace's parents' house, she ran to the door fumbling with her key. Red followed more slowly, carefully pausing to put on the car alarm. Her father and mother were in the old surgery: Grace found them by following the trail of blood. Her mother was crying and making little fluttery gestures with her hands. Her father was sitting on the floor, one leg of his pyjamas rolled up. He'd applied a tourniquet to his calf.

'There you are,' he said querulously, 'about bloody time.'

'What happened?'

'Clipped an artery I'd say,' said Red who was standing behind her.

'Are you a doctor?' her father demanded.

'No,' admitted Red.

'Well then, I'd thank you to keep your opinions to yourself.' He raised one striped arm and stretched it out accusingly in the direction of Grace's mother. 'It was her. She placed the garden clippers exactly where I'd be guaranteed to step on them. And she had them sharpened only yesterday,' he added, resting his case.

'We need to get you to a hospital,' Grace said.

'What have I been saying? Dear God! Dear God almighty am I surrounded by idiots – by morons?'

Grace went to her father's side and Red ran over to take the other arm. They hoisted him to his feet and slowly made their way to the car, followed by Grace's mother who had donned an ancient fur coat over her nightie. At the door of the car, Grace paused and looked at the blood on her father's leg and at Red.

'Should I get something to put under him for the blood?'

'Leather seats, wipes right off,' said Red, easing her father into the front seat. Grace and her mother got into the back. They made the journey to the hospital with Red utilising all of his skills but rarely using all four wheels of the car. Grace's father seemed to have gone into a state of shock but her mother hummed to herself pausing only to mention to Red in her best cocktail party voice, 'I must say you are an excellent driver, Rhett.'

Accident and Emergency in the hospital was not too crowded. The last of the Friday night drunks were stumbling away nursing their hangovers and their wounds, and apart from an elderly man who had been attacked by his own dogs and a white-faced teenager with his mother, there were no other patients. The victim of the dog attack was arguing with his son or possibly his grandson. The old man was going over the incident and wondering which of the dogs, Lara, Scruffy or Shep, had been responsible for starting the trouble. The younger man, dragged from his bed so early on a Saturday, was in no mood for conversation.

'They need putting down. The lot of them.'

The old man's eyes filled with tears.

'Jesus Christ!' The young man went over to the coffee machine and put in a coin. Nothing happened. He banged it once or twice with his hand and then kicked it.

'Nothing works,' said the old man to no one in particular.

Red hovered beside Grace and her parents.

'Grace … ? I'll need to – you know – de car?'

'Oh God, yes. I'd forgotten. Go, go, go,' said Grace and then, 'Thanks Red. Thank you so much.'

'It was delightful meeting you, Rhett,' Grace's mother said, taking his hand. 'And your name. Such a coincidence. It was my favourite film you know.'

'Oh stop blathering,' Grace's father said, speaking for the first time since they had left the house, but he gave Red a brisk nod of thanks – a colonel approving the action of one of his men. The relative quietness of the department coupled with her father's 'Doctor' status meant that he was seen quite quickly. From behind the drawn curtains, Grace could hear him weathering the baby talk of the nurse.

'Just a little prick. There we are now. That wasn't so bad was it? The doctor'll be here in a minute.'

Then the rasping tones of her father, 'Not an Indian. I don't want an Indian doctor of any denomination. I've no time for Indians. Send me a blackie if you must.'

'We'll take what we get,' scolded the nurse.

After a while her mother went in to see him, but he sent her away.

'Get out. Get out. Haven't you done enough damage?' But when the doctor – Chinese as it turned out – suggested an overnight stay, Grace's father called out for her mother and the two of them held hands – her father stiff on the bed, her mother tensed in the chair – like victims of a flood waiting for the lifeboat.

Grace called a taxi and, after twenty minutes or so, it arrived. By then it was almost four o'clock.

'What happened to that big Russian woman – forget her name?' her father asked as they drove past the parked cars ringing the hospital.

'Oh shit,' Grace dialled the number of her home and after a while an out-of-breath Olga answered. Grace explained what had happened and that she was sorry she hadn't phoned.

'No problem. I was out. Josh take me to lunch.'

'What? Why did you have lunch with Josh?'

'He call and say lunch,' Olga yawned, 'we went pub in mountain. Oyster,' she added.

'I see,' said Grace more to her parents than to Olga.

The taxi dropped her off first and as she came in, she called Olga's name.

'Here!' shouted Olga from the kitchen. She was sitting at the table surrounded by a cluster of estate agent's brochures. Grace picked one up. It was a pub in West Cork. She looked at another and another. All pubs in various parts of the country.

'Josh get,' Olga said, immersed in a brochure.

'What … why?' Grace sat down.

'Is my dream,' Olga said simply.

'A pub in the country? That's your dream?'

Olga enveloped Grace in one of her smiles, 'Yes.'

Grace burst out laughing. Olga looked hurt. 'You think that strange?'

Grace stopped laughing and said, 'No, I don't think it's the least strange. In fact it's an ambition you share with about ninety per cent of the population. The other ten per cent already own a little pub in the country and are doing their damnedest to sell it without making too much of a loss.'

Idly she picked up a couple of the brochures. There was one in Kinsale. How pretty it looked in the sunlight with the sea beyond and its jaunty sign outside.

'And what on earth possessed Josh to get them for you? I didn't even know you'd spoken to him since the night he was here.'

'Oh I see him couple of time,' Olga said vaguely, gathering the brochures into a tidy heap. 'Oh and Travis ring two time.'

'Oh great,' said Grace flatly but after twenty minutes of Olga's badgering she eventually agreed to ring him back. He answered at the first ring.

'Waiting by the phone?' Grace said in a teasing tone she didn't recognize.

'No,' said Travis, 'you rang my mobile and I was holding it in my hand.'

'Oh,' Grace said feeling foolish.

'I was wondering if you'd like to grab a bite to eat,' he said easily, his voice receding at intervals as though he were doing something else at the same time.

'Something to eat? Tonight?' Grace asked, looking at Olga who was nodding her head furiously.

Grace put the phone to her chest for a moment and then lifted the receiver again.

'Fine, fine,' she said brightly. They agreed to meet in an Italian place they both knew.

It was a tiny restaurant with only six or seven tables and most were occupied. Travis hadn't arrived. The waiter looked at Grace indifferently and asked her had she booked. 'I don't think so,' said Grace and then was relieved when through the restaurant window, she saw Travis approach. She'd just started to say 'I'm with …' but the waiter had abandoned her and gone to the door where he enveloped Travis in a bear hug.

'Trav-ees, is too long. You want eat?'

When the waiter realized that Grace was with Travis, he bore down on her and kissed her soundly on either cheek and he placed them at a table in the corner.

'Well, you're popular,' she said when they'd settled themselves.

'Oh we all know each other round here,' Travis said, waving the proffered menus aside and ordering two melons with Parma and two linguini frutti de mare.

'OK with you?'

Grace shrugged, smiling.

'Do you want wine?' Travis wanted to know.

Grace shook her head. He ordered a beer for himself.

Dinner was a series of awkward pauses followed by animated bursts of conversation – Grace's driving lessons, her father's accident, Travis's encounter with knife-wielding teenybopper, a film they'd both seen. Once or twice, Grace thought she felt his hand graze her thigh but she might be imagining it. As the meal progressed, they grew more relaxed. At one point Travis indicated his beer.

'Shouldn't really be drinking this. I'm an addict.'

When Grace started at this, he said, 'Oh I don't do drugs now. On the straight and narrow. Except for this,' he added, taking a mouthful of beer.

'My daughter. My daughter's … eh … "in recovery" too,' Grace said, uncomfortable with the phrase. 'Emily. That's her name. My daughter's name.'

While Travis paid, Grace looked round at their fellow diners: a couple of tourists, eating without speaking; two young men, arguing about movies with more passion than insight; and a woman eating alone, younger than Grace. She had long, pale fingers between which she held a cigarette, using the same hand to turn the pages of her book. After another hug from the waiter for Travis and an enthusiastic handshake for Grace, they left. They paused outside on the street.

'Do you want to come back for … coffee?' Travis let the invitation hang between them like the punchline of a joke.

Grace plunged her hand into her bag and started rooting around in it. Her fingers closed around the objects it contained and played them out like beads – the cigarettes, the lighter, the matches, the lipstick, the compact, the wallet, the old bills.

'Well … ?' Travis said, leaning down so that he was level with her bent head. Grace looked up and laughed uneasily.

'No. Yes. I mean no. Yes. Yes.'

'I can see why the Abortion Referendum was such a close call.'

Grace laughed again, this time too loudly. She stopped and looked down.

'No, coffee sounds – good. Yes. Certainly. Hmmmm,' and she made a little humming sound and gave her bag a pat as though she'd found exactly what she'd wanted.

They both looked up as a taxi drew up alongside them and disgorged a group of giggling girls. A hen night Grace surmised hearing their English voices and watching, amused, as they alighted from the cab, their High Street finery taut against meaty thighs, their feet in cartoon shoes with huge platform soles and glittery straps.

'Whoooah,' one of them ventured at Travis in a laddish way.

'Have a nice night girls,' he grinned, holding the door of the taxi for Grace and giving the driver his address. Grace got in neatly, feeling suddenly old.

Travis's flat was on a busy road beside a bus stop – a red brick house with granite steps. Grace was on the third step when Travis indicated the basement. Two dead miniature conifers guarded the door, brown as the terracotta pots that held them. He fiddled about with keys while Grace tried to think of calming things like lakes and well-mown lawns. And ironing. Eventually they were inside. It was remarkably tidy, furnished in a way that suggested the contents had been the result of one Habitat transaction. There was matching shelving along each of the walls, some holding rows of books, some an eccentric array of *objets trouvés* – a big conch shell, a rusty tankard and a driftwood bowl. Travis sat down in one of the puce couches and let his arms hang down the back.

'So, do you still want coffee?'

Grace thought about this for a moment.

'Water. I'd prefer water.'

'Still or sparkling?' asked Travis. He was trying not to laugh.

Grace looked at him and then said, 'Where's the bathroom?'

'Behind you – first on the left.'

The bathroom was tidy too and smelt in equal parts of damp and cologne. Grace looked at herself in the mirror. Her reflection looked back at her, a shoplifter caught in the act.

'I want to go home,' she said to the face in the mirror.

Sometime later, Travis pushed the bathroom door open – it wasn't locked. He coughed once.

'Eh – what are you doing Grace?'

Grace was kneeling on all fours. Beneath her, on the floor, was a large mirror that had previously hung over the washbasin. It had occurred to her earlier that being on top while fucking mightn't be the best idea at her age. Grace was checking what she'd look like from below. She was worried that gravity might introduce a macabre element into what was meant to be well – sexy. But she couldn't say that so instead, she ignored Travis and turned back to the mirror. She didn't like the look of this at all. No one over twenty should ever go on top, she decided.

'I was – I was looking for my contact lens.'

'I see,' said Travis, levelly.

Grace got clumsily to her feet and started to fidget with her hair. She thought she might cry which wouldn't be the thing at all. What if he told people? Making a joke of this because it was a joke. It was completely ridiculous. She felt awkward and exposed. She hadn't the first notion of what to do next. She hadn't slept with anyone for ten years except for Lionel's brother and that was only out of spite. She sighed on a long, quivering downward note. Travis folded his arms.

'There's no need to make such a thing of it. We could just get a video if you like,' and he started to laugh.

'Don't you dare laugh at me,' Grace said bending down to heft up the mirror and, as she attempted to replace it in its original position, her jangled reflection glared out at them both.

'I was laughing at me actually,' Travis said.

'Really.'

'Yeah. I don't have a video machine. It was nicked a few months ago.'

He took one step closer and kissed her. And after a second of panic, Grace kissed him back. All of a sudden, everything seemed easy and all the awkward fumbling she had imagined passed in a dream. One minute she had all her clothes on – the next she was naked. They must have gotten from bathroom to bed somehow, but afterwards Grace had no recollection of that bit at all. She just remembered how good it felt – how good he felt. It was a bit like riding a bicycle she supposed. No, no. It wasn't at all like that. Of course there was the odd glitch, like when he said she reminded him of his mother, but that had something to do with the shape of her ear in the end so …

Grace lay back in the pillows and tried to drain her face of the smug expression she knew it bore. After a while, Travis got up and stretched.

'Want something to eat?'

Grace considered this for a moment and then decided she was quite ravenous with hunger.

'Yes. Yes I'm starving.'

He made scrambled eggs with Marmite soldiers.

'Perfect!' Grace said, taking forkfuls of it from her nest of pillows. Travis ate his own rapidly, standing up.

'Got to go,' he said when he'd finished.

'Go?'

'Work,' he said.

'But it's one in the morning.'

'I know,' he said, taking her plate, 'I'm late.'

'I'd forgotten you're a bouncer. Surely all the bouncing is well done by now.'

'Ah it's closing time where the real skill comes into play.'

Grace stretched under the covers and fingered the sheet, toying with the idea of draping it around her as a sort of experiment to see if all those movies and TV shows had been right.

'Stay if you like,' Travis shouted over the roar of the shower and Grace thought about it for a moment but got up and pulled on her clothes so that she was dressed when he came out, scrubbing at his hair with a towel.

'I'll go,' she said unnecessarily.

He stood for a second and then said, 'OK. Whatever. So ... ?'

Grace smiled at him.

'So.'

She had an absurd impulse to shake his hand but instead bobbed her head once or twice and mumbled something. Like goodbye. Walking up the street some minutes later, she couldn't be sure what she had said.

'That's the nice thing about older women,' she whispered to herself, 'they're so damned grateful,' and she let out a yelp of laughter occasioning a couple in a doorway to break from their embrace and look at her curiously.

FOURTEEN

ON MONDAY, Grace visited the building society and went through the motions of checking with them about the house, but she already knew. In a way she had always known. It's odd the things we can hide from ourselves. She had been as careful of herself as a person is around the bereaved: not wanting to think about anything that might disturb her, ignoring the obvious with a determination that was curiously lacking elsewhere in her life. How had Lionel managed to support two households on what was really quite a small salary? How on earth could he afford a house in the over-priced suburb where he occasionally lived with his new wife and family? She was too bemused by her own stupidity to feel angry about it. In fact, she even managed a chuckle or two, walking down the canal, with its comfortingly familiar flotsam and jetsam: the bones of a pram, picked bare by the movement of the lock and weather; the rusted keel of a car; the frolicky plastic bags; and, out of the dimness of water, the prow of a supermarket trolley, glinting against the light. It was quite painterly really. It reminded Grace of an exhibition she'd been to some weeks before. There was a supermarket trolley as one of the exhibits. It was titled 'Life' and a note beside it proclaimed soberly that it was 'Part of a Private Collection'. A private collection of 'Art', presumably – not a collection of supermarket trolleys. There was nothing remarkable about it although, Grace remembered, it was quite battered. Was that part of the art, she wondered? Was the battering something that had taken place between the artist and the work and intrinsic to the art itself – or was battering simply intrinsic to trolleys in general? Immersed in her own thoughts she was almost abreast of Emily before she was aware of her. They both looked wildly to either side for an escape route but there was no doorway to duck into, no side street.

'Emily!' Grace said, the name emerging on a note higher than she intended.

Emily stopped awkwardly and held her shopping bags in front of her for protection.

'Shopping?' Grace asked, followed rapidly with, 'What a stupid thing to say.'

'Was it?' She looked at Grace narrowly.

Emily had a way of making the simplest of exchanges carry more import than necessary so that offering her a cup of tea became fraught with subtext. With no shopping of her own to occupy her, Grace lifted up her handbag and started to turn it round and round in her hands. To an observer, Grace thought, they might have looked like two foreign agents about to exchange secret plans – or people involved in a drug deal.

She gave a nervous titter. Emily sat down on a nearby bench. After a moment, Grace joined her – two women, staring straight ahead, holding on to their belongings for dear life.

'So I hear you know Travis?' said Emily.

Grace felt her mouth drop open like a character in a sitcom. She must have remained like that for seconds because she was conscious of her mouth growing dry with a mixture of fear and shock. 'I?' was all she could manage.

'Oh I only know him slightly,' Emily said smiling, in control of the situation.

'How … ?' Grace said, destined it seemed to speak in monosyllables for the duration of the conversation.

'I can't tell you how,' Emily said.

Grace's head raced with various explanations for Emily's reply, each one more bizarre than the last. She tried to think clearly but her principal feeling was one of pure terror. Surely he'd never have said? He couldn't have. She took some deep breaths and tried to read Emily's reactions. Her ability to gauge other people's responses was one of the reasons she was good at her job. Grace always knew instinctively when a producer had come down as low as he or she could in a quote. She just knew. She looked at Emily carefully for some nuance in her expression but couldn't detect anything other than the usual truculence. And then Emily added:

'I know him through – I can't say.'

Light dawned.

'Oh, those bloody meetings – those NA things?' Grace said, laughing with relief.

'I didn't say that. That's so typical of you,' Emily fairly spat.

Grace felt strangely calm.

'It was your fault for bringing it up. And aren't those things meant to be anonymous? Isn't that what the "A" stands for?' Grace smiled to herself as the balance of power shifted in her favour. Then she immediately felt guilty and started speaking fussily and too fast.

'I met him years ago on a commercial. I don't know him at all,' and then, hastily, in case Travis had mentioned it, 'We had lunch to catch up. Nice boy,' she added, emphasizing the 'boy'.

'I hear he got you someone to teach you to drive.'

'Oh that? That's just a joke really. His cousin.'

'So are you going to keep it up?' Emily said, moving her plastic bags so their contents bumped around and resettled. Vegetables, Grace noticed. Lots of vegetables.

'No, no. Just lunch to see how he was getting on.'

'I meant the driving lessons.' Emily looked into Grace's eyes until Grace dropped hers and fell to rooting about in her bag.

'Cigarette?' she said, holding up a packet with a bright smile.

'I don't smoke,' said Emily, getting up.

'Why don't you call round?' Grace said, rising to her feet as well. 'It's not good that – that we …' Grace sat down again on the bench and then said, 'What did I ever do to you?'

Emily took two rapid steps towards her so that Grace sat back in fright. Emily's face was puckered, as though her mouth was full of food – as though she'd stuffed her mouth with something rancid, something vile – but then her face relaxed and she smiled coolly.

'Nothing, Mum. Absolutely fucking nothing.' And she walked away, the bags with their knobbly contents slapping against her long, thin thighs.

Grace remained on the bench for some time, hardly conscious of the cars crossing the bridge, the blare of horns, and the judder of lorries braking at the traffic lights. She didn't even hear her mobile, which must have been ringing for a long while. She picked it up, 'Yes?'

It was Olga to say Red was at the house and had she forgotten. Olga had put him in the kitchen and added darkly that she was 'keeping eye on him'. Grace got hurriedly to her feet and decided it would be quicker to walk than try to get a taxi. She set off at an almost run, ignoring the two calls that came through on her phone. A battered Toyota she didn't recognize was parked at the gate and, when she went in, the house appeared empty. She went down to the kitchen. Olga and Red were sitting on either side of the table, watching each other. Olga got to her feet – the movement causing her towelling robe to fall open – and glowered at Red, but Red seemed unconcerned and merely turned to Grace to say, 'Bit of a problem wit de motor, Grace, she's cuttin' out.'

Olga had tied her belt more tightly and, intrigued perhaps that Red was the only man she'd met so far that didn't find the sight of her naked breast compelling, sat down again.

'Could be carburettor,' she said, narrowing her eyes.

'Could be,' Red said, weighing this up. 'Do you know something about cars?'

'I only know cheap,' Olga shrugged.

'Dey don't come any cheaper dan dis love,' Red told her.

'I think she means "Jeep",' Grace said.

'Right,' Red said, rather impressed, 'want to take a look?'

Olga shrugged again and got up.

'Do you want to put some clothes on first?' Red suggested.

'No,' Olga said and, after a moment, he followed her out to the car. Grace went upstairs. She could see them both from her bedroom window, the upper parts of their bodies bent over the car engine. Red was enunciating the names of various car parts in slow, careful tones while Olga muttered something in her own language – their equivalent names in Russian, Grace supposed. After some time she heard the putter putter of the engine. She looked out again. Olga was fiddling with the engine; Red was behind the wheel. The engine roared into life. Olga straightened up and put her hands on her hips, a broad smile on her face.

'Sound woman,' Red said, revving the engine.

During the lesson, Red apologized for the car, which had been 'loaned' rather than 'borrowed' – emphasizing the subtle difference.

'So what do you think of Olga?' Grace asked, curiosity getting the better of her. Red gave this some thought.

'Knows her way round an engine,' he said and then, enigmatically, 'and not a bad-lookin' woman at all for her age.'

'What age do you think she is?'

'Older dan she looks,' said Red, refusing to be drawn. He then explained to Grace that Olga was not a Ruskie – in the usual sense of the word.

'She'd acshally be more of your Chechnyan, Grace.'

'Chechen,' Grace pointed out, 'and I suppose you think they're all gangsters.'

'Noratall,' Red told her easily, 'dey're just business people. And,' he added, as though this made the subject beyond argument, 'her da was a bally dancer.'

'A ballet dancer? Really?'

'Dere you are Grace. You don't ask de right questions, do ya? More clutch! More clutch! Lovely.'

When the lesson was over, Red left her home with the instruction that she be sure to thank Olga – that she was 'a star – arigh'?'

Having relayed the message, which seemed to please Olga enormously, Grace told her what she had found out at the building society. Olga spread out her hands in an 'I told you so' gesture. She also told her about meeting Emily.

'Everyone hate mother,' Olga told her comfortingly, 'is normal.'

'Do you hate your mother?' Grace asked. Olga drew herself up.

'I love my mother, love my mother.' She shrugged, 'But then my mother dead.'

They had some lunch and Grace picked up her messages, trying to ignore Olga who was reading aloud from a magazine. 'He had a big cock, the big – the biggest I have ever seen.' Olga enunciated slowly and carefully. She was trying to improve her English by reading from a copy of *Penthouse* she had found in the couch.

'Why don't you read from the newspaper,' Grace suggested.

'I want make conversation, not speak boring politic,' Olga told her.

The first message was from Mike. He wanted to know why she'd taken a day off without telling anyone. That everyone hated her especially him. Oh, except for Bruce who'd seen Olga's shots and they were totally amazing.

Next was Lionel, barely comprehensible between the groans. He'd done in his back, when in a Norman Rockwell moment he had tried to hoist a twin on either shoulder. The twins had escaped with minor injuries. Could he come back? He was ill. He was a broken man.

'Good!' said Grace keying in his number.

'Grace darling, thanks for calling back.'

'I've just been to the building society you bastard.'

There was silence at the other end of the phone, then a groan, 'Grace, I'm in agony here.'

'I'm feeling pretty sore myself,' Grace reminded him just as Olga interjected with 'Trust! Trust!' Grace glared over at her but noting that she was still deep in *Penthouse*, held her hand over the mouthpiece to say, 'Thrust. I'd say it's probably "thrust", Olga.'

'Are you talking to someone?' Lionel demanded.

'I was going to sell the house you pig and give you half. How stupid is that?'

'It's very kind,' Lionel said after a bit, 'you always were kind. I only did it for Emily.'

'What?'

'She needed to pay for that place she went to – when she was you know – sick and so …'

'Why couldn't you do it on VHI?'

'Well I sort of let that slip – I mean you're never sick Grace and …'

'Anyway that was only a few thousand. You could have just borrowed it from the bank.'

'I know, I know,' Lionel was speaking in a sing-song pleading voice which Grace found even more irritating than anything he was saying, 'but then I thought – why not you know buy a house? And then there was furniture. And you still had a house because I was paying the mortgage after all so it wasn't as if you were on the side of the road.' His voice dribbled to a halt. Grace did not answer and Lionel pleaded.

'So could I come over? Just for a couple of days. Till my back's better. I've no job Grace. I'm at the end of my rope to tell you the truth.'

'I'll think about it.'

She filled Olga in and told her how pleased Bruce was with her pictures and was just about to go upstairs but her mobile rang again.

'I'm still thinking about it,' she barked into the phone.

It was Andrew. Could Grace do one teensy thing – enormous favour – could she go to London to attend a casting because everyone in creative was up to their tits?

'I don't think I can go to London,' Grace started to say but suddenly Olga was on her feet and was nodding furiously.

'London. Yes. Yes,' she said. Grace placed her hand over the phone.

'I don't want to go to London.'

'I need go,' Olga said. 'Please, I go with you. Please.'

Grace returned to Andrew.

'Actually I probably could do it. If it's really necessary,' she said, making a variety of gargoyle faces in Olga's direction.

'I will remember this Grace,' Andrew said, in his very serious voice.

'I'm glad to hear it.' Grace threw the mobile in the general direction of her bag. Olga was smiling at her in a way she probably imagined was winning.

'So why do you want to go to London?'

'I need to – the man I used to work for owe me money.'

'And which man was this?'

'He had model agency. Models for catalogue. He owe me ten – maybe twenty thousand.'

Grace sat back in her chair and was just about to speak when the phone rang again.

'Oh for Christ's sake what?' Grace said into the phone.

It was Andrew again, a man unused to the crust of a voice on a telephone, a man whose life was oiled by Angela, who nursed him like a tender, tropical plant. Often Grace heard the 'Mrs Danvers' voice of Angela through the closed door of Andrew's office: 'You sound tired, you should take better care of yourself. Your health is more important than anything else. Have you tried stewed lovage with barley?'

Her variety of cures was gleaned from a slender knowledge of the alternative medical profession and strange potions handed down from her grandmother.

Grace sighed and tried to sound both contrite and efficient.

'I'm sorry. I thought you were my husband.'

Andrew melted just a bit but retained a hurt dignity.

'I see. The day after tomorrow would be good. Incidentally, the posters are going up tonight. Oh and bus-sides. Had to call in all the favours but we made it. The clients are very pleased.'

'Great. I'll tell Olga.'

And, once again Grace threw her mobile on top of her bag, this time remembering to turn it off. Then she turned back to Olga.

'Ten or twenty thousand pounds? That's a lot of money.'

'I was young. I trust him.'

'And he'll give you the money – just like that?'

'Oh yes.' Olga smiled. 'This time he pay.'

'I don't know why but at the moment, everything you say sounds like a bad TV thriller.'

Grace made to brush her hair away from her eyes in a gesture that had been a habit for years, but now there was no smooth flap of hair for her to brush – just a soft bristle of sideburn. She looked at her muted reflection in the windowpane – the clumps of red and russet sticking out of her head with an electric savagery. Underneath the hair, her face was pale and drawn, the softness around her jaw emphasized by the droplets of rain that slid down the glass.

'It's raining,' Grace said, more to herself than to Olga.

Olga looked at her with concern.

'You like tea? I make tea?'

Grace sat down on the kitchen chair – the one with the loose slat at the back so that she could turn it round and round in its socket – an activity she found comforting. It was the primitive action itself that soothed her, the rhythmic twirl of wood, like an African woman coaxing sap out of cane. Olga placed a mug of tea in front of her and then sat down opposite.

'Stop that. The chair?'

'Oh, I'm sorry,' said Grace who'd hardly been aware she was doing anything.

'I fix,' Olga told her, 'I fix chair.'

'I rather like it. I'm sorry if it annoyed you.'

Grace sipped some of her tea. It was very strong and very sweet. She didn't take sugar normally but it tasted good all the same.

'I don't know where I am,' she said.

'You are at a time of change in your life. Like me. We both change.'

Olga reached across as though she might take her hand but instead she gave Grace a matey punch in the shoulder. Then she too had a sip of her tea.

'So much sugar,' she said contentedly, 'I like sugar.'

Olga took two cigarettes from Grace's pack and passed one to Grace.

'You worry Travis not call?'

Actually, Grace was worried that he *would* call. She didn't know what to say to him. She told Olga what Emily had said, how terrified she'd been because her daughter knew him. Terrified of what? Olga asked. Grace didn't know. She was embarrassed, she supposed. So was she ashamed she'd slept with someone her daughter knew or was she just ashamed she'd had an encounter that probably wouldn't be repeated? Was she ashamed that what she remembered of Travis's flat was the smell of mould in the bathroom and the tawdriness of the off-the-peg furnishings – that there was so little to show for thirty-eight years? Was her real fear that Mike would find out, or Lionel, and that they'd laugh at her? Or was she frightened of that moment – that moment when she'd lain in the nest of pillows and felt such a longing for it to go on – to become something? No. Unlikely. What was it she felt watching his lean body, the curved convex of his buttocks, and the long line of his spine? It was homesickness. She was homesick. Homesick for that time long ago when she could have wandered around his flat, perfectly at home with her perfect body, not even thinking about it.

'I hate being old,' she told Olga.

Olga nodded. 'Is shit – is shit all right.'

And for the first time Grace noticed what Red might have seen – something that none of the others had seen – not even Jamie whose lens-sharp eyes could spot the tiniest imperfection at fifty feet.

'What age are you Olga?'

Olga didn't answer but got up brusquely and, with uncharacteristic fervour, washed their tea mugs.

FIFTEEN

LATER THAT AFTERNOON, Travis did phone. He spoke to her in a casual, easy way as though she were one of a list of acquaintances he needed to call. The only reference he made to Saturday night was to say, 'So you got home all right?'

'Demonstrably,' Grace said, an edge to her voice. Travis's voice grew cooler and more distant. A boundary had been crossed. Furious, Grace realized he thought she was being petulant because he hadn't called.

'I met Emily,' she said tightly.

'Ah,' said Travis and then he laughed softly, bringing the call back to its light tone.

'Why didn't you tell me you knew her?'

There was a crunching sound from the end of the phone.

'Are you eating an apple?'

'Carrot.' It sounded more like 'darrow' because his mouth was full. He swallowed. 'I couldn't tell you Grace because I know her in a particular way that precludes my discussing her.'

'You're remarkably articulate for a fucking bouncer,' Grace

said, disgusted with herself. 'But you could tell her that you knew me you bastard.'

'Well I don't know you in "a particular way", well – not in that "particular way",' and he laughed again. 'Emily and I are members of a group of people whose whole basis is 'anonymity'. Now I would never even discuss this with you but clearly Emily, without meaning to, has.'

'Oh shut up about your fucking AA or NA or whatever the hell it is. You're like bloody Masons with your rules and your rituals – you're pathetic.'

'Look I tell you what Grace. I'm going to hang up now.'

And he did.

Grace cried two loud angry sobs, more shouts than sobs really, and then she grabbed the thing that was nearest to hand – it happened to be a rather nice decanter – and hurled it at the mantelpiece. The decanter shattered and, in its journey, also dispatched two candlesticks, a tumbler of water and three ceramic tiles.

'Good,' said Olga approvingly who, attracted by the noise, had just come into the room.

'I'll get a dustpan and brush,' said Grace, all passion spent.

'Oh no. You must leave,' Olga told her, 'you must leave like this at least twelve hours. It work better like that,' she explained and, laughing to herself, went out closing the door behind her.

Grace sat for a while surveying the destruction and then remembered her father.

'Oh God.'

She called a taxi and shouted up the stairs to Olga that she had to check on her parents.

'Is OK. I go out for dinner,' Olga yelled back, and then came to the top of the stairs wearing a cream dress Grace had forgotten she owned. Olga did a twirl.

'Who are you going out with?' Grace asked, pulling on her coat as she heard the taxi pull up.

'Josh,' Olga said with an annoyed little sigh as though she'd already mentioned this fact several times.

Grace went out the door feeling strangely light-headed, as if she'd skipped a meal.

Her father was in the garden. Cursing. ('Bastard thing!') He was wearing large green wellingtons, the side of one cut to accommodate the bandage on his leg. He was bent down and she saw the sheen of his scalp through his hair.

'Hi Pops.'

Her father was wrenching at something in the ground.

'Bloody, bloody, bloody thing.'

As the whole clump came free he reared back, and almost fell over. He staggered and then stood straight holding the clump triumphantly in his hands. Worms were trying to wriggle back into the dark earth clinging to the root. Her father dropped his prize.

'So what brings you here Grace?'

He lifted a spade and plunged it into the earth. There was a sound of mush and the quick staccato of grit. The garden seemed muted as dusk merged its myriad shades into a single dark greenness. The digging soothed Grace. She sat down on the garden seat, mosaicked with bird droppings, and didn't say anything at all for a while, just listened to her father digging.

'Am I a bad mother?'

Her father rounded on her.

'You haven't even asked me a word, not a word about my leg and now you're here pestering me with stupid questions.' He glowered at her and then thrust out his chin, 'Am I a bad father?'

'How the hell would I know – and how is your leg?'

'It's fine thank you for asking,' her father said, running the words together.

Grace picked at one of the curls of bird dropping on the seat. 'Nobody made such a fuss then. For instance, I don't think you ruined my life.' And although she hadn't meant to at all, Grace started to cry. Her father kept on digging. After a while, he spoke.

'I'm awfully fond of hellebores; they don't appear to mind the shade.'

He slid the spade into a dark green clutch of leaves. 'You're not meant to divide some of them but I can never remember which ones.'

He looked at the cutting for a moment as though the answer might come to him and then turned to Grace impatiently:

'Well come on can't you? Water! Water!'

Grace poured a stream of water into the hole her father had dug. They both waited while the lake of water subsided, sinking into the earth without trace save for the dark glisten of the hole. Her father placed the cutting and shovelled in earth around its sides finishing with a final 'heeling in' with his wellie.

'Sink or swim!' he told the plant and then he stretched. Grace could hear the bones of his vertebrae crack, each one an individual note. He sank to his knees, his breath wheezing. Grace moved to help him.

'I'm fine,' he said angrily and remained on his hands and knees for a moment before levering himself up with the aid of the trellis.

'Was I a disappointment to you?' asked Grace

'Jesus Christ could you give me peace for five minutes Grace?'

'Sorry.'

Out of the corner of her eye, Grace glimpsed her mother. She was holding a garden fork like a lance and she was running. Her father noticed at almost the same time. 'Oh God,' he said, but there was a note of admiration in his voice. Then he moved Grace between himself and her mother's headlong charge.

'She won't hurt you,' he said reassuringly.

Her mother arrived, puffing.

'You forgot your fork!' she said, plunging it into the toe of her father's wellington boot. He looked down in consternation and lifted his foot completely out of the wellington (it was his good leg). The boot remained where it was, speared to the ground.

'Hah!' He said, managing to stay upright by leaning on Grace's shoulder, 'Missed!'

Grace's mother sat down on the garden seat.

'I'm so sorry,' she said.

'Beth? Beth?'

Beth was Grace's mother's name but her father rarely used it. Now he said it with such tenderness, and sat down beside his wife.

'She's not well,' he said to Grace, 'not well at all.'

Grace's mother curved herself into a ball at the end of the garden seat.

'Leave me alone,' she said.

Grace's father stood up, leaned in, lifted his wife and carried her like a tired child towards the house. He limped a bit – one leg clad in its ripped wellington, the other in a thick, grey woollen sock. Grace considered pulling the fork out of the pinioned wellington but decided to leave it where it was. Maybe Olga was right – that you should leave things, that it worked better. She followed them into the house.

She stood in the doorway of her parents' bedroom while her father took her mother's clothes off with difficulty, as though each garment surprised him by its very existence. He was like a man sorting through a skip. He wrestled and pulled, tearing at each piece of clothing. Her mother didn't want to be undressed.

'Let's go dancing Jack,' she said, 'let's go dancing.'

Eventually her mother, clad in a modest, pale blue nightie, was pinned to the bed like a butterfly. 'Hospital corners,' her father said proudly. Her mother lay with her pointy face yellow against the white sheet.

'You cannot imagine how beautiful she was,' said her father. He stroked her thinning hair that wisped around the pillow.

'She was "something else",' he said, awed by the unfamiliarity of the phrase itself which he must have heard somewhere.

'Something else,' echoed her mother.

'Sit with her a minute, will you pet?'

Grace sat on the satin stool beside the dressing table. She ran her hand across its raised pattern. She remembered it so well – that feel – and yet she couldn't remember sitting here much at all. The smell of powder, face powder, filled her nostrils. The smell of her mother bending over to kiss her when she was young, when they were both young. Her father returned with his ancient doctor's bag. He removed a hypodermic and pulled back the tucked-in sheet.

'Roll over. There's a good girl.'

For a moment, her mother's lean, wrinkled haunch was revealed. Her father squirted a tiny jet from the needle, slapped for a vein and plunged the needle into the papery flesh. Then he tucked her in again, tight as a drum. He looked at Grace.

'I need to sleep too,' he said.

He stood up and once again, Grace could hear his bones crack. In an individual way, each bone flexing and realigning. The oddest thing.

'Well, she should be out for twelve hours or so,' he paused, 'unless I've killed her.'

And her father laughed. Then he stopped laughing.

'You are a good mother my own sweet Grace.'

SIXTEEN

GRACE AND HER FATHER were sitting in her parents' kitchen. It was a room unchanged for forty years and demonstrated the worst excesses of the fashions of that era. There was a great deal of Formica and thick, chipped glazed pottery. Grace's father was having his supper: sardines which he ate out of the tin and a piece of sliced pan.

'Are you sure you wouldn't like some?' he said, the genial host.

'Absolutely positive,' Grace said.

'An excellent dish,' her father said, indicating the tin of sardines with the pride of a man about to embark on the carving of a pheasant.

'I don't doubt it.'

'Extremely good for the bones,' her father explained. He looked up at the clock that hung in a corner of the kitchen.

'Emily should be back soon.'

Grace made to get up.

'Stay a while,' her father said, mashing a sardine onto a piece of bread and popping it into his mouth hungrily, 'stay and talk to her.'

'How did she come to be here in the first place?'

No answer. He just chewed with the concentration of someone counting each mastication. He probably was.

'She came here – well she broke in here initially – when she was still, still …' he nodded to himself, unwilling to put a name to Emily's condition.

'I found her in the surgery and she was quite angry – quite aggressive. I said she was welcome to anything she could find – mostly laxatives, I told her. Nothing interesting.'

'Oh God, I'm sorry,' Grace said.

'Then she'd come sometimes – for money. I gave her some once or twice.'

'Oh God.'

'I'd no experience to speak of in the field. Tried to get her to see someone but it was no use. People find their own time I suppose. And she did, didn't she? Fair dues to her, I say.'

'What are you doing here?' Neither of them had heard Emily come in.

'She's my daughter my dear. This is her home – was her home.'

He indicated the empty tin on the table, 'There's another of those in the cupboard if you fancy it and,' he looked up at the ceiling, 'eggs I think, bacon.'

'I've eaten, it's OK,' said Emily.

'Well that's all right then,' said Grace's father cheerily. Then, rather theatrically, he stretched and said, 'Well I'm off,' and he went out of the kitchen, closing the door behind him.

'So how are you?' said Grace.

'Twice in one week!' Emily said. 'Next thing you know we'll be having cosy girly lunches.'

Grace tried to breathe deeply and evenly, to keep calm.

'I just wanted to know how things were since you got out of that place.'

'I've been out a year and a half.'

'Dear God, it's not as if I put you in there Emily. What did I do? What the fuck did I do?'

Emily sat down and gave a hard bark of laughter.

'Don't you remember? Don't you even remember?'

Grace didn't know. She didn't know what she remembered. The whole episode was like a headlong dash to some far-off destination where all the focus was on the arriving, and the details of the journey itself were just a series of flashbacks, the chinks of memory afforded a drunk in a blackout. Not that Grace was drinking then. She was just busy. Busy proving to the agency – and to Andrew who had just been made creative director – that she was brilliant. Brilliantly busy, busily brilliant.

Visits to this treatment centre – this place that Emily had decided to go – were another chore to be squashed into her already overcrowded days. What did she remember? She remembered the first time she'd gone there, for Emily's 'assessment'.

'What does that mean?' Grace wanted to know. 'Is it like an interview? To see if you'll "fit in"?'

And Emily had said, 'Oh don't fucking bother then. I'll do it myself.'

And Grace had said, 'Said the little red hen. Remember? When you were young there was a story I read you and one of the lines in it was, "I'll do it myself, said the little red hen".'

'You're amazing. The things you remember. The stupid things you remember.'

They had gone there on a February morning. There was a heavy fog and the fuzzy lights of the oncoming cars seemed to shimmer. The taxi-man muttered darkly to himself.

'I normally work nights – this is crazy this is. Crazy!'

He honked at the car ahead of him that was prudently travelling at twenty miles an hour.

'Oh I'm sure it will clear,' Grace said and as they drew nearer their destination. The fog dispersed, leaving only a few tendrils of mist and a certain opacity to the landscape. It would be twilight all day, Grace thought – always nearly dawn or just dusk. She gave an audible sigh of relief, realizing that up to a week ago she had been scheduled to shoot a commercial today that was all exteriors. It had been cancelled at the last minute.

'Thank you God,' she said.

'What?' said Emily.

'Oh just … we were meant to be shooting today. Imagine what it would have been like – and they'd no money for weather insurance. So,' and Grace grinned at Emily, 'thank you God!'

Emily stared at her mother, her expression impossible to read. So what else is new? Grace thought to herself.

'Is that the place for alkies?' the taxi-man asked, mentioning the name of the centre.

'We're visiting a friend,' Grace told him.

'Yeah, right,' said the taxi-man and both he and Emily started to laugh as though they were old friends.

The house – the centre – was of grey stone with steps leading up to it. It had the abandoned air of a property too long on the market. There were a few cars parked in front. The steps were pockmarked granite and the stone gaped at each rise as though each step had been stretched to breaking point.

Grace and Emily waited in the cramped hallway. Or rather Grace waited; Emily stood on the steps, chain-smoking cigarettes. Her knuckles were blue with cold and illness. The girl in reception took phone calls, answering in a cool, no-nonsense voice. Occasionally, she seemed to take calls from friends, greeting them with a delighted 'How are you?' but maybe they weren't friends because the conversations were pointedly solicitous. Were they 'still hanging in there?' Were they 'getting to their meetings?' Then the person at the other end would make some query which either elicited a cheery, 'They're really good,' or a sad diminuendo of, 'Not great I'm afraid.'

During one of the rare moments the receptionist wasn't on the phone, Grace asked her if it would be much longer – that she had to be somewhere. The receptionist spread her hands and shrugged.

After almost an hour, Grace was told they could go in. She went out to get Emily who was now sitting on the bonnet of someone's car, playing with her hair. She looked up at Grace's call, reluctantly climbed down and clumped across the gravel in her big shoes, which, Grace noticed, could do with mending. Actually everything Emily wore could do with mending and cleaning – or burning. Grace felt a stab of anger. What would these people think of her? This woman in her pale suit with her freshly coiffed hair, her un-scuffed shoes and her Cinderella daughter wrapped in a man's coat that had once been black but was now greenish and smelt of mould. The receptionist indicated a room directly behind her. Grace made to knock and then just opened the door. It was a hot, untidy room filled with books and boxes. It smelt of gas fumes, country hotel cooking smells and cigarette smoke.

The woman behind the desk didn't look up but continued writing. Grace hovered beside a chair. Emily leant against the door.

'Sit, sit,' said the woman, looking up finally.

Grace sat in one of the two chairs and after a moment, Emily threw herself into the other. The woman started to ask Emily questions. Some diffidence – or maybe it was just fear – made Grace close her mind to what was going on around her and after the initial question about what type of drugs, slipped into a day-dream. Now and again she would come back to herself.

'Has your addiction ever led to your arrest? Are you presently awaiting the outcome of court proceedings?'

The woman's biro scratched purposeful ticks as Emily answered in monosyllables, occasionally glancing at Grace as though she were an intruder.

'We will be able to take Emily right away,' the woman said to Grace. 'Did you bring her case?'

Grace nodded. The woman started to sort through files on her desk talking all the while.

'No phone calls for one week, no visitors for two weeks.'

Grace felt a great flood of relief but hid this with a timid, 'Isn't that a bit draconian?'

The woman ignored her and continued, 'However we will expect you to attend "family days" which are every Tuesday.'

'Every Tuesday. I see. And that will be what – an hour?'

The woman smiled in a wintry way.

'Oh I'd put aside the full day. We expect you here at nine-thirty and we finish up around four-thirty.'

'But I …'

'I don't want her here,' Emily interjected with the longest speech she'd made all day.

'You don't have a choice,' the woman said but, in spite of the words, Grace felt that the woman cared more about Emily than she did about her. It struck Grace that the woman didn't like her – didn't approve of her.

'I'll be here,' Grace said, 'I'll just have to make arrangements.'

'Good,' said the woman, 'Now,' she said to Emily, 'let's get you settled in. Where's your case?'

'It's in the hall,' Grace said.

The woman went out of the office and returned with the suitcase. It was an old one of Lionel's and the peeling luggage tags, frayed reminders of his journeys, seemed tacky and out of place. The woman opened the case and started examining the contents.

'Now look …' Grace started to say but Emily quelled her protest with a fierce glance. The woman sifted efficiently through the case, lifting out Emily's sad collection of jumpers and jeans, her grey underwear. She lifted out a pack of Tampax and checked each one. She opened every bottle and box in Emily's wash-bag. She squeezed a minute worm of toothpaste onto her hand and smelt it. She removed two books, a Walkman and a bottle of perfume and placed them in a large brown envelope.

'What are these?' she asked Emily holding up a card of tablets.

'I get headaches.'

The tablets joined the rest of the things in the envelope. The woman looked at Grace as though surprised to see her still there.

'You can go home now,' she said.

Grace felt such a surge of relief and release that it was difficult not to shout out loud. She thought she ought to hug Emily, to make some gesture, but one look at Emily's bony, unforgiving figure told her that this was out of the question so instead she patted her arm with one hand while, with the other, she stuffed some notes into her pocket.

Emily and the woman disappeared through a door and Grace asked the receptionist to call her a taxi. The receptionist indicated a small brown box on her desk. On it someone had written in biro, 'Calls 30 c'.

'Oh,' said Grace after a moment and rifled round in her bag until she came up with some coins.

'Shouldn't be long,' said the receptionist and then she smiled at Grace.

'It will be fine, really. Everything will start getting better now. I promise you.'

Normally any small kindness in times of stress reduced Grace to tears but on this occasion she didn't feel anything. Except hunger. She felt starving. Maybe it was the smells of cooking that issued from somewhere underneath reception although they were hardly appetizing – the sour institutional smell of cabbage and the thick, woolly smell of boiling potatoes.

'I'll wait outside,' Grace said.

'Have a smoke,' the receptionist suggested.

'I don't,' Grace said because she didn't then.

Grace left the reception and walked backwards like an inexperienced courtier leaving the royal presence. Once on the steps, she clattered down and made for the shrubs that skirted the drive. She wandered aimlessly through the dank green, the speckled, shiny leaves giving off a smell of graveyards. Somewhere deeper in the shrubbery, something had died and a smell of putrefaction seeped out from the undergrowth. The taxi came within minutes.

'Visiting someone?' he asked Grace after a while.

'No,' said Grace for reasons she couldn't fathom, 'I'm a doctor.'

What a long time ago it all seemed. In her parents' home, all was quiet. Her father must be asleep and her mother certainly was. Emily was curled up in an armchair, turned away from Grace.

'What did I do wrong? It was your idea to go there,' Grace looked out the window. Emily let the question hang for a long beat.

'It was all about you,' and, in a horrible parody of Grace's voice, '"Actually I think I'm alcoholic myself".'

Grace didn't have time to respond because Emily raced on, her voice rising, 'And you never came when you were meant to come – you'd just wander in when it suited you and make my time there shit if you really want to know.'

'I came when – when I could. I wanted to see you. It wasn't prison after all.'

'And then "family days" you were – you were either making notes about your fucking job or else you were just talking shite because you hadn't been listening to what you were meant to be doing as a "concerned person".' Again the cruel echo of Grace's voice, '"Must phone casting agent. Check wardrobe. Get costing on radio campaign." Fuck me!' Emily finished, 'You were a god-damned liability.'

Grace felt herself getting angry. The unfairness of it – the injustice. Trekking out to that awful place week after week. Making excuses at work, the lies about medical treatment for a day each week. Mind you, everyone was very nice to her about that, assumed she had cancer. But it was true, her mind had been elsewhere. She'd tried to inure herself against it all – this strange parallel world where everyone shouted at each other and used a special language that she couldn't learn, didn't want to learn.

She remembered the first time she'd gone to visit Emily – visit her, as opposed to attend those Witches of Salem productions known as 'family days'. It was a Sunday and it was raining – relentless, driving rain that beat down on the roof of the taxi and wet Grace through during the few seconds between the car and the house. She'd followed directions down to the dining room.

The room was full of people and covered in a pall of cigarette smoke. Children ran between the tables, screaming and laughing as though they'd just been let out of school. When her vision cleared, she could make out some of the groups of people – every sort of person you could imagine all trapped together in this room filled with smoke and the smell of tea. It was like a disaster movie – disparate characters all drawn together and dependent upon each other simply because they happened to be in the same earthquake-riven street or burning building.

Grace spotted Emily sitting in a corner with a middle-aged man and a much younger man with a shaved head. Grace walked over with a bright smile. Emily looked up and indicated the empty fourth chair. Grace sat down and then didn't know what to do with the two carrier bags she was holding. Eventually she put them on the floor beside her.

'Pat, JJ,' Emily said, by way of introducing the two men. They both nodded unsmilingly at Grace. The older man looked like a coal-miner. His face was deeply fissured and black within its creases. His fingers were stained with nicotine and two of his fingernails were scrunched up and deformed as though someone had caught them in a vice. The younger man had a small puckered scar over his eye, which gave him a quizzical, urbane air. Or would have done if he hadn't got the letters H-A-T-E tattooed on the fingers of one hand. His other hand's only decoration was a series of old cuts and was unleavened with a complementary tattoo of L-O-V-E.

Grace didn't know what to say and the other three didn't appear to feel the need to say anything. After a while, Pat said to Emily, 'Are you on tea?'

Grace wondered was this some patois. Tea? Some drug? But then Emily got to her feet.

'Yeah, sorry, got to go. I'm on tea. Doing the set-up. OK?'
Grace got up.

'Of course, I'm sorry. I was delayed. There was a meeting.'

'Don't worry about it,' said Emily calmly. Then she picked up
the two carrier bags and peered inside.

'What's this?' she asked, pointing to a flat package.

'Smoked salmon,' Grace admitted.

Neither Emily nor the two men reacted for a moment and
then all three of them burst out laughing. Grace hovered for a
moment, fiddling with her bag then she leant towards Emily and
kissed her on the cheek – or rather a place in the air quite close to
her cheek.

'Nice to have met you,' she said to the two men, and then she left.

And what else had happened during that six weeks? Oh yes,
there was the weekend she'd missed visiting because she was in
London. So she'd gone up one Monday evening, just on the off
chance. There was a man sitting on reception – one of the counsellors. He agreed to let Grace see Emily for five minutes. He
directed Grace to the laundry. It was after seven and the centre
seemed empty although Grace could hear voices in the distance.
The laundry was located next to the kitchen. Emily was ironing
sheets.

'Hello,' Grace said softly.

Emily looked up startled.

'How did you get in?'

'They let me come in – just for a minute.'

She went over to Emily and hugged her. Emily was unusually
compliant. When Grace stood back, Emily was crying.

'Oh Emily, oh darling,' Grace put her hand out and smoothed
back Emily's hair which, she noticed, was lank and in need of
washing.

'I'm so tired,' Emily said.

'You don't have to stay,' Grace said, 'I'll take you home right now,' although she was filled with dread at the thought of it.

Emily wiped away her tears with two hands, like a child.

'No it's OK. It's good here. I'm OK.

'Here, let me.'

Grace took the iron from her and started to smooth the sheet, which Emily had almost completed. Emily sat down on the floor. Grace began to enjoy the action of the iron, its rhythm. Then, from the doorway, they heard a voice.

'What are you doing Emily?'

Emily jumped to her feet guiltily; Grace put down the iron. It was one of the counsellors.

'They said I could come down – just for a minute.'

The counsellor lifted up the sheet Grace had been ironing, scrunched it up and threw it on the floor.

'Are you completely mad? You stupid, stupid ...' Grace began but Emily stopped her with a scream of, 'Mum!'

Grace looked at Emily and the man. The strange thing was they seemed like a couple – a family almost – and she, well she seemed like an intruder doing the ironing. The other thing she remembered clearly from Emily's time in that place was one of the family days when, once again, Grace had lost track of the proceedings. She couldn't cope with the contrast between her normal life and what passed for normality in that place. She'd have a quiet breakfast at home, make a couple of phone calls to work, laugh or get cross about the latest crisis but it was all so gentle – the undulating pattern of work and its workings.

And then she was expected to join the cast of some mad theatre workshop where everyone screamed and burst into tears and raged at each other. It was like being out for a walk in a quiet, orderly park and suddenly finding you've wandered into a wildlife preserve. The only thing you knew with any certainty was you'd better be careful out there. No one seemed to have any time for Grace's modulated responses – her anxiety to be fair, her capacity to repeat endlessly the phrase, 'on the other hand …'

This particular morning she'd drifted away somewhere only to be brought to herself by the sound of a hysterical child crying. The child was describing what it was like living with her alcoholic father and the child was screaming while tears slid down her father's cheeks and everyone else in the room had a stillness about them. Grace got to her feet in a sort of dream and started to walk towards one of the counsellors. A voice she hardly recognized was shouting, 'Shut up! Shut up! Shut up!' and then from somewhere she heard Emily say, 'No you shut up,' and the counsellor saying, 'That's very good Grace,' and that was when Grace told him to go fuck himself and she left.

She left and she didn't go back. She didn't go back and two weeks later Emily left too. She phoned Grace and said she was out and that she'd moved into a flat with someone she'd been with in the Centre.

Outside, it had started to rain. Emily looked as if she'd fallen asleep but Grace could see her eyes – dark, watchful. Grace picked at the tassel on a cushion. It was greasy and frayed. It was the same cushion she remembered from childhood. She slapped her hand lightly against it. A small cloud of dust rose, making her sneeze.

'I just didn't want you to get hurt,' she said to Emily.

'I was hurt,' shouted Emily.

'What hurt you? Who hurt you?' Grace felt a coldness enter her whole body as it occurred to her that maybe she had been blind. Maybe something awful had happened and she ... she ... she hadn't noticed. Hadn't cared enough to notice.

'What – what happened?' she said, her voice low but full of force.

Emily sighed and shook her head.

'I don't know,' she said in a colourless voice, 'nothing special. I just. I don't know what really,' and then realized what Grace had been imagining and she laughed dryly.

'Nothing like that,' Emily said. She untwined herself and sat round to face Grace with her hands crossed over each other like a figure in an old photograph.

'Why does there have to be a reason? Why does everything have to be about an incident – an especially horrible thing that happens to someone? Nothing happened. Nothing at all.'

Grace felt suddenly so tired she could barely speak.

'Well I'm sorry then. I'm sorry for nothing.'

She sat there, her eyes sticky with sleep and then she smiled over at Emily, 'You're such a sad soul.'

And, after a while, Emily smiled back at her.

SEVENTEEN

'**J**ESUS CHRIST!' Grace said so explosively that the taxi-man slammed on his brakes, imagining some hazard that he had missed. She was on her way to work, driving past the familiar terraces of houses, the canal bridge, and the long black sheen of the canal when suddenly, as they rounded the corner, Olga loomed into view. She seemed to be striding towards them, all sixteen feet of her, the red dress shimmering around her, her eyes at once threatening and inviting.

'Sorry, it's just, she's a friend of mine – the woman in the poster?'

The taxi-man squinted out through the windscreen and gave a low whistle. Then he turned round to look at Grace with a renewed interest.

'Great looking bird – woman,' he said.

'She's Russian,' Grace said.

'She's a fine big woman, isn't she?'

'She looks bigger on the poster. Taller.'

'But she'd still be on the tall side, right?'

The taxi-man slowed down in order to examine the poster further. Behind him a bus honked, its brakes pumping.

'Where's the fuckin' fire?' the taxi-man yelled out the window, gathering speed.

'Bloody buses,' he muttered and then rolled up the window hastily as the bus began to pass them, its exhaust spewing jets of black, acrid smoke. 'Shaggin' things are filth. Will you look at that?'

The bus drew alongside, the driver's mouth working furiously, cataloguing a series of silent threats and expletives. Behind him, on the side of the bus, the figure of Olga appeared again – this time half-smiling, as though she knew a secret.

'Jesus, she's everywhere! "The Lady in Red" – wha'?' laughed the taxi-man, Grace's presence in the back having afforded him a brief encounter with fame. Grace imagined him later in the pub adding curlicues to the anecdote.

'I had that woman in the posters – the one in the red dress in the back of the cab the other day. She's a big woman but not as big as on the posters like.'

Grace smiled and punched in a single digit on her phone. It was answered on the tenth ring.

'Olga? You're all over the city! Take a taxi into the Green and have a look. There must be five sites between the house and there – oh and look out for buses.' Grace paused, 'I see. Well there's twenty euro on the window-sill in the kitchen.'

'Was that her?' asked the taxi-man, who had pulled up outside the agency.

'The real McCoy,' Grace told him, handing him a note and waving away the change.

It was early and Mike wasn't in yet. The agency was quiet, catching its breath after the frenetic activity of the recent pitch and readying itself for the next. Myles was on a drive for new business, which meant the agency was pitching on an almost daily basis and, even though the creative department was empty, there was still a whiff of adrenaline in the air. The ghosts of the troops waited in the trenches for the next onslaught. Of course, advertising wasn't a matter of life and death; like football, it was far more important than that.

But today Myles would bite his tongue when he saw people doing the crossword or reading the paper. He and Andrew would loosen the leash and allow all their puppies to run the full extent of a metaphorical park whose attractions included a late start in the morning and a long lunch – a reward for putting their all into the last endeavour. Just for today.

However, because this gesture annoyed Myles more than he could say, he vented his ire on anyone who hadn't been involved in the pitch, like Grace and Mike. He'd be checking on them pretty soon, trying to sniff out evidence of a lack of proper industry – a morbid interest in the net, for example.

Grace turned on her computer and started sifting through previous casting lists. She always made a note of anyone interesting for future projects. But, as her lists were all in separate files, the task was taking longer than it should. Mike usually kept a master list. She went over to his computer, turned it on and started scrolling through the files.

'What are you doing?' Mike's voice was very quiet and Grace found that when she turned round, she did so feeling guilty.

'Nothing,' she said, 'I was just checking something.' She gave a short laugh, 'I wasn't reading your mail for God's sake.'

Mike stood beside his chair, a patient expression on his face.

'Oh. Sorry.' Grace got up and was about to sit in her own place but then felt the need for a cigarette.

She went out and met Bruce who was just coming in. He was grinning broadly, an expression so unusual for him that it looked a little frightening.

'So what do you think of her, Grace? Did you see any of the posters on your way in? You must have done.'

'She looks very – very big,' Grace said, lighting her cigarette, her hand cupped over the match against the slight wind. How satisfying was any new skill, she thought, however inconsequential.

'She looks fantastic, Grace. You're a total genius.' Bruce gripped her elbow briefly and Grace smiled at him.

'I phoned her and told her to go out and have a look.'

'She'll be blown away!'

'Olga? I don't think so.'

Bruce turned this around in his head for a while before admitting, 'You're probably right. She's something else, isn't she?'

Grace was startled to hear that phrase used again so soon and in exactly the same way, Bruce's young voice giving the words a slight ironic twist while the older tones of her father the night before had plucked the phrase from some little-used cupboard at the back of his mind – a place where he kept things he admired but didn't fully understand. Grace nodded slowly to herself.

'Yeah. She's something else all right. I'm glad it worked out Bruce.'

Grace tossed her cigarette into the gutter that ran down towards a shore-hole, which was already stuffed with butts, and went back to her office. Mike was hunched over his computer, pecking two-fingered at the keyboard.

'What are you doing?'

'Checking on radio deadlines.'

'Great,' she said, mystified by the coolness of his tone.

'Sorry about the other night – stupid. I don't know what possessed me really. Panic I suppose.'

'What? Right. No, fine. Don't worry about it. Oh, and Myles wants to see you.'

'What does he want?'

'No idea.' Mike leaned towards his computer staring at the screen with great concentration.

Grace picked up her coffee mug.

Mike glanced over his shoulder.

'I'd go now if I were you. It sounded urgent.'

Grace banged her mug back on the desk and made her way over to Myles's office. Angela sat on guard outside. She looked up and when she saw Grace she picked up the phone and said, 'She's here.'

'Is there anything wrong Angela?'

Angela shook her head and reached into a drawer from which she retrieved a small phial of Rescue Remedy.

'No,' she said, unscrewing the cap, 'I'm fine. Couldn't be better.' Then she leaned forward and whispered, 'Do you want some?' She indicated the herbal remedy.

'Bit early for me,' Grace said, chuckling at her own joke. She was still smiling when she opened the door into Myles's office.

Myles was standing with his back to her, looking out the window.

'This is very difficult,' he said without turning round.

'Difficult?'

'Very difficult.'

Grace moved closer to the window to see if the difficulty lay out in the street. Myles conducted a running battle with parking meter attendants. His strategy veered from angry encounters in the street followed by phone calls to his local councillor to conciliatory measures such as the provision of tea for the meter attendants on cold days. She peered down but there was no sign of a brown uniform anywhere.

Myles sighed and returned to his desk, easing himself into a large leather chair. He indicated a chair opposite – a smaller, much lower version of his own – and placed his hands side by side on the leather-bound blotter pad. He picked up his pen, looked at it for a moment and then put it down again. Grace cleared her throat encouragingly. Finally Myles spoke.

'Obviously everyone's private life is,' he paused meaningfully, 'private. And I would never – nor should I – or anyone …' he looked at her severely for a second, leaving the words hang. 'However, given the circumstances of putting a colleague's life in danger,' he leaned forward, 'and I don't think I exaggerate here.'

Grace blinked once, trying to make sense of Myles's half-formed sentences, and then tried to catch up with what he was saying now.

'If you have a problem – well, I sympathize of course but when it starts to interfere with relationships – like Gerry Taylor for example.'

'Gerry Taylor? You think I'm having a relationship with Gerry Taylor?'

Now it was Myles's turn to look mystified.

'Did I say that?'

'To be perfectly honest Myles, I don't know what you're saying. I am at sea. Lost.'

'We're all very concerned Grace.'

'Concerned about what for God's sake?' But Grace's voice wasn't quite as strong as she intended it to be. Obviously Olga's story about the mixed medication on the night of the dinner with Gerry Taylor hadn't worked. 'I was on medication.'

'Well you'd think you'd have learnt your lesson the night with Gerry Taylor.'

So he wasn't talking about Gerry Taylor. Grace's mind started to race and then came to an abrupt halt at Myles's next words.

'Mike in particular is concerned.'

'Mike?'

'And apparently it's been going on for some time, culminating in that appalling night he spent with you last week.'

'What appalling night?'

'You embarrassed him in a restaurant – he had to practically carry you to a taxi and then you nearly got him killed by some drug addict. Well, seriously injured anyway.'

'I wasn't drunk that night. I didn't have anything to drink.'

'Don't make things worse Grace. Look,' Myles reached out his hand as though he might take Grace's, which was clutching the edge of the desk, but she whipped it away, 'look I think you're going through some kind of crisis. You've given up your job.'

Grace tried to speak but all that came out was a splutter before Myles went smoothly on.

'You're obviously depressed – I mean look at what you've done to your hair.'

'My hair? My hair!' Grace's hand furrowed across her head, feeling the reassuring coarseness of the strands through her fingers. 'I like my hair.'

'Well there you are,' Myles said kindly.

'Give me your phone,' Grace said, her voice achieving some low but carrying timbre that brought a nervous Angela to the door.

'It's all right Angela,' Myles said.

Grace dialled directories and asked to be put through to the restaurant she and Mike had eaten at. The owner answered the phone. Grace knew him quite well. It was a restaurant she visited often. She pressed the speaker on the phone so that Myles could hear both ends of the conversation. She asked the owner if he remembered her being in the previous week.

'Yourself and Mike? Of course.'

'Was I drunk?'

The restaurateur laughed.

'Of course you weren't.'

'Was I drinking?'

'No. You don't drink.'

'Did anyone carry me out?'

'Is this some kind of bet?'

'You could say that.'

Grace killed the speaker and hung up.

Myles frowned and then after a moment mumbled, 'Mike said.'

'Mike says a lot of things. And anyway it's not any of your god-damned business what I do. What were you going to do, fire me?'

Grace was shaking with anger. One hand was gripping her knee so hard it hurt. She picked up a pencil from the desk and snapped it in half. Annoyed by the puniness of this gesture, she reached for something heavier. There was a metal statuette on the corner of the desk commemorating some award or other but Myles, sensing what she was about to do, said:

'Grace, I'm the victim here.' And, of course, when he said that, all Grace could do was laugh. Myles joined in uneasily, at the same time making conciliatory gestures with his hands.

When Grace got back to her office, Mike wasn't at his desk. Grace grabbed her cigarettes, lit one where she stood and walked towards the back door, drawing deeply. A couple of people looked up as she passed but no one said anything. Out in the air, she finished the cigarette, ground it underfoot and went back to her office, almost colliding with Mike who was returning from making a cup of coffee.

'You complete fuck. What are you at?'

Mike sat down at his computer, placing his coffee beside him. 'I don't know what you're talking about.'

Grace made a little explosive noise.

'Oh really?' she said and was about to continue when her phone rang. It was Andrew. She listened in silence as he rambled on using words like 'misunderstanding' and 'natural mistake' and 'over-reaction'.

'Oh fuck off Andrew,' Grace said and slammed down the phone. Almost immediately it rang again.

'Grace – can we talk about this?'

'I can't waste time in idle chit-chat Andrew. The pubs opened ten minutes ago.'

'Don't be like that Grace.'

Grace looked over at Mike. He was still staring intently at his screen as though he'd heard nothing. She put down the phone and went next door to Andrew's office. He got to his feet and made to walk towards her, but Grace forestalled him with:

'So what's there to talk about?'

'I just wanted to assure you,' Andrew clasped his hands in front of him as though he were addressing a meeting, 'to reassure you that I for one never believed for one second any … anything,' he finished lamely.

'I'm touched.' Grace was beginning to enjoy occupying the high moral ground until she suddenly realized that what she wanted more than anything else at this moment was a drink. So strong was the compulsion that she didn't hear Andrew and he had to repeat what he had said.

'Will you still go to London?' he asked. 'I really can't leave now. The minute we've finished one pitch we're straight into another. You can stay over if you like.'

'I planned to stay over,' Grace told him. 'Oh, and would you mind awfully if I took Olga?'

Andrew thought about it for a moment.

'Fine,' he said, 'that will be fine. Call it a going-away present.'

'I thought I'd just call it "Sorry Grace" if it's all the same to you.'

Andrew adopted a wounded look swiftly replaced by one of relief as Angela came in, the several chains and bangles she wore tinkling as she walked. She was carrying Andrew's diary, some letters to be signed and a glass containing an orange liquid that was probably soluble vitamin C. Both Myles and Andrew were more vitamin fortified than a truckload of cereals.

Grace went back to her office. Mike was on the phone talking to someone – or pretending to. His well-bred, musical tones rose and fell, responding to some imaginary interrogation at the other end. 'Right … right. OK … right … right.'

Grace began to feel sorry for him, trapped in his own subterfuge.

'Right … OK … right … right.'

She walked over, took the phone from him and replaced it in its cradle.

'Right. OK,' she said using the same hollow tone he had been using on the phone.

Mike looked up – all bewildered annoyance.

'Grace, I was in the middle of,' and then he lost interest and simply sat slumped in his chair, staring at the floor.

'I just want to know why you did it. How could you say something like that? Was it a joke? Were you getting back for the other night?'

Mike continued to stare moodily at the floor.

'It wasn't about the other night,' he said finally, 'but I suppose it was like that. It was, it was an impulse. It just seemed to be a good idea.'

'I thought we were friends!'

'We are friends Grace. It's just – you wouldn't leave that money thing alone.'

'What money thing?'

'Oh – that someone was skimming,' Mike laughed without humour, 'misappropriating funds.'

'Oh that,' Grace could hardly remember her half-hearted attempts at detective work, 'that was just … I don't know. Anyway,' and she laughed, 'so far my investigations have revealed that the only one who could be operating that particular scam is me.'

Mike shifted in his chair but still didn't look at her.

'Then what were you looking for on my computer?'

'Jesus Mike, give me a break. I was looking for people we'd pencilled at castings. I know you put all the names in one document – mine are all over the place.'

'Oh,' Mike said, so low she almost didn't hear him.

'Jesus,' Grace said, equally softly, 'only I could have done it – or you.'

Mike stayed where he was, picking at a thread at the hem of his jeans. He opened a drawer in his desk and felt around inside. He took out a book of matches from the restaurant he and Grace had eaten in a few nights before. He showed her the box and gave a short laugh, then he lit a match, watched the flame for a moment and held it to the thread at the hem of his jeans. The flame caught and flared for a second before fizzling out, leaving a shiny black ball the size of a pinhead where it had been. Pleased at his handiwork he replaced the book matches tidily in his drawer.

'I just wanted to make sure that whatever you said, no one would believe you,' and he turned back to his computer.

'But how did you think you'd get away with it? All I had to do was ring the restaurant.'

'I thought I'd get away with it because – well, I knew you'd started drinking again. You had wine that night in your house after the shoot and I know you didn't drink for years because you've a problem and I just thought … O, God knows what I thought.'

'Outside!' Grace said with sudden decision, grabbing her coat and not looking to see if Mike was following her.

'Where's your car?'

Mike pointed at the metallic silver BMW parked nose in to the kerb across the road.

'Keys?' Grace stretched out her hand, not looking at him.

Mike hesitated.

'What do you want the keys for?'

Grace didn't answer, just halted in the middle of the street, her hand held out impatiently.

Mike reached into his pocket and handed her a set of keys.

She looked at them shakily, and then pressed the button on the automatic locking device hoping it was the right one. Bingo. She wrenched open the door on the driver's side. Mike rested his hands on the car roof.

'You can't drive, Grace.'

'Yes I can. Get in.'

Mike paused, then went round and got in the passenger side.

'It's not an automatic,' he said.

'Good. I can't drive automatics.'

Grace had already turned on the ignition. Mike massaged his knees and as Grace slammed the car into reverse and shot out into the middle of the road, screamed: 'Grace!'

Grace tried to tune out every sound except that of the car engine and Red's voice which, if she concentrated, she could hear somewhere in the porch of her ear – as though she had kept all his instructions, neatly stacked in anticipation of just such an emergency. She moved rapidly through the gears, weaving around a double-parked van and spinning the steering wheel violently to avoid a cycle courier zipping out of a side street. She sped towards a set of traffic lights, pressing the accelerator almost to the floor as she cleared the junction just as the amber light turned to red. Mike was shouting a variety of things, one moment angry, the next pleading, but Grace couldn't hear him. She threaded the steering wheel swiftly through her fingers and turned into a laneway lined with parked cars and delivery vans, the car's tyres squealing in protest. She increased speed muttering under her breath, 'Please God, please God.' There was room for only one car. She made it to the end of the laneway without encountering anything coming in the other direction. She turned left and decreased her speed to thirty miles an hour. The moment she did this, she began to lose her nerve. Her hands were suddenly covered in sweat and she couldn't keep a grip on the wheel. She slowed and, shaking, managed to manoeuvre the car into a loading bay. She turned off the engine. They both sat, staring out through the windscreen. After a while Grace said,

'Do you think you could drive it back the rest of the way? I'm all driven out.'

Mike got out and walked around to the driver's side. Grace slid across.

'I'll probably have lost my space now,' he said.

She grinned at him.

'No you won't. I'm feeling lucky today.'

He shook his head and then said, 'So you can drive.'

She rolled her shoulders, which were knotted with fear and tension.

'Yeah. I can. Just not very well yet.'

Grace's luck was holding out because their space was still unoccupied. Mike parked the car in the same spot and they walked to a nearby park to talk.

The first time, it had been a mistake, he said – a genuine mistake. It was shortly after he arrived and he assumed that all the artists in a commercial received the same repeat fees. The fact of the matter was that one of the actors had negotiated treble the amount of the rest of the cast. He allocated the top fee to everyone. It had been so easy that next time he did the same thing, only this time he kept the extra for himself. There were so many ways to beat the system. Double billing for hotel rooms, bills for limos that were never used, airline tickets. So long as he kept his head and kept the amounts small, it was foolproof.

'But why? Why take the risk?'

'Because I'm broke.'

Annalise, he explained, was an expensive woman. When Grace, as carefully as she could, pointed out that Annalise was an expense that should be shared out amongst a whole army of men, Mike said it wasn't as simple as that.

'Yes it is, leave her. Leave her and get on with your life.'

'I love her.'

'Do you?'

Mike sighed. 'No.'

Grace turned her body so that she was looking directly at him. 'So?'

It turned out that Annalise owned everything. The house, the car. If Mike walked away it would be with a couple of suitcases. No, he corrected himself, a couple of bin bags – even the suitcases were hers.

'Were you ever happy?'

Through the gate of the park, a group of tiny children from the local French school filed neatly in, the girls in their navy dresses with white collars, the boys in sailor suits – all wearing little straw hats. They were joined together by a long ribbon that each child held with its left hand, each tiny fist holding on tight. Then the teacher clapped her hands once and the children dropped the ribbon and cascaded across the park like beads from a broken necklace, their squeals cutting through the air, their hats cartwheeling down the slopes of the hill, their faces alight with freedom.

'Yes,' Mike said, 'yes we were.'

They'd been childhood sweethearts he told her, giving the phrase a cynical twist. And then, when he was eighteen and Annalise seventeen, she'd fallen pregnant. There seemed to be nothing for it but to have an abortion. And after all, they had their whole lives. They got married four years later and started trying for the family they had postponed. Grace nodded.

'But you couldn't.'

'No. We tried everything. I've wanked into more plastic cups! It was her – not me. Anyway, what does it matter who it was?'

'But you encouraged her to have an abortion,' Grace didn't look at Mike, 'that's what she can't forgive.'

'Not true. I tried to stop her. I begged her. Begged her not to.' Mike flexed his fingers, which were wrapped around the slats of the bench on which they sat.

'That's what she can't forgive,' he said.

Somewhere in the trees, a bird sang. It was a repetitive, irritating sound consisting of two notes – as if the bird was sound checking for an outdoor concert. ('One two, one two, one, one.')

'Not all birdsong is sweet,' Grace said.

'Will I go to prison?'

Grace could feel the first of the sun on her face. She closed her eyes and said, 'Why would you go to prison?'

'You're not going to tell?'

Grace rocked backwards slowly on her hands as the children wove a pattern of navy and white on the hill. The wind caught their screams just as the abandoned ribbon floated up to weave a capricious pattern against the pale blue sky. A woman in a suit clawed it back again, flailing at it as though it had offended her.

'No. I'm not going to tell.' She watched the children, now restrung on the necklace of their bondage. 'Why should I? Fuck them!'

They walked back along the tree-lined pathway, their shoulders occasionally touching.

'I will leave her,' Mike blurted, just as they reached the agency.

Grace squeezed his arm and gave his cheek the briefest kiss. His skin was soft and warm like a boy's.

EIGHTEEN

'WE STAY IN BIG HOTEL?' Olga wanted to know.

'It's not a hotel. It's a club.'

'Oh,' Olga went up the stairs with the heavy-stepped menace of a teenager.

'It's very smart. You'll like it,' Grace called up after her. Olga paused on the top step.

'We go to restaurant?'

'If you like.'

Grace sat down feeling strangely light-hearted, as though she were going on a holiday. It was a holiday in a way. The casting would only take up a couple of hours of the afternoon and after that they could shop, have a nice dinner. She went upstairs to finish packing. Their plane was early in the morning and, in the taxi to the airport, they passed several giant Olgas. Grace could see the taxi-man looking at Olga in his rear-view mirror.

'Is … ?'

'Yes it is,' Grace cut across him.

'Very nice!'

Olga yawned. They travelled business class. Grace was anxious that Andrew's apology be as heartfelt as possible. While she waved away the breakfast, Olga fell upon it, eating every morsel of her fry as though they were on their way to a country rent with famine. They arrived in the club at just before eleven and stood in the tiny reception area while the girl behind the desk completed a leisurely conversation with a friend. Grace signed the register. While Olga was less than pleased that the club did not provide a porter, there was really no need. Olga was as strong as two porters. She lifted both Grace's case and her own like bags of sugar and set off up the narrow, winding staircase at a brisk trot. When Grace advised her to slow down – that there were still four more flights to go – she gathered speed. Their rooms were adjacent. Olga looked around, unimpressed by the small pile of leather-bound books, the velvet pillow and the pristine white bedcovers.

She examined the bathroom, tossing the bottles of shampoo and shower gel into her handbag, and fingered the towels as if she intended buying them – which of course was the last thing on her mind. Having checked that Grace's room was exactly the same as her own – apart from the selection of books and the colour of the cushions – she threw herself down on the bed. From this vantage point, she could see the mini-bar in the corner. She jumped up and wrenched fiercely at the door of the fridge. Grace hastily produced the second key attached to the door-key. Olga's face lit up when the door opened.

'Champagne?' she asked.

Grace would have liked a glass of champagne. She would have liked several.

'No,' Grace said, 'I don't want a drink. But you have some.'

Olga looked at Grace and, ripping the foil from the bottle, opened it with a soft, expert 'plunk'. She poured a glass for herself and then grabbed a tin of nuts, which she ate by tossing them into the air and catching them adroitly. Well, most of them.

'I like this place,' she said, taking a sip from her glass and looking around nodding approval, 'very home.'

'Very home if you've got a mini-bar and a maid,' Grace said. She had given up correcting Olga's English. It exhausted both of them. Olga had found a box of chocolates in the fridge and was ripping them open. She took a bite of the chocolate. Its liquid centre squirted out but she caught it neatly in her hand.

'You'll spoil your dinner,' Grace said. 'By the way, is there anywhere you'd particularly like to go?'

Olga thought for a moment, chewing slowly.

'I like to go ...' she mentioned a restaurant frequented by celebrities and impossible to get into unless you'd booked several months in advance.

'How did you hear about it?' Grace was curious.

'Magazine,' Olga said languidly. 'I like to go there.'

Grace laughed, and went next door to her own room where she phoned Andrew to tell him they'd arrived and promised to phone him later that evening to say how the casting had gone. She washed her teeth in the yellow half-light of the bathroom and went back to Olga's room. She gave her fifty pounds sterling and told her she'd be back at four.

'Then we go shopping?' Olga asked.

'Yeah. We'll go mad on your fifty pounds,' Grace said.

Olga reached into her bag, delicately removed a credit card and passed it to Grace. Grace looked at it.

'This is Lionel's!'

'He won't miss.'

'Eh, that's not the point Olga.'

'I do for you.'

'What?' Grace sat down on Olga's bed and looked at the card again.

'Mr L. Sherwin' it said with Lionel's indecipherable signature – a single curving line with a squiggle in the middle.

'I mean, Olga – what use is this? It says "Mr". They're not fools. And what about the signature?'

'Signature easy and in shop, no one look. All they see is "commission". I work in shop. I know.'

'Is there anything you haven't done?'

Olga thought for a moment. 'No.'

Grace inspected the card. It was just one of the many credit cards Lionel held and it reminded her of the ease of his life compared to hers. The frugal way she used her cards – her anxiety to pay on time to avoid a penalty. It reminded her of the years of struggle. All those years when she believed he had given her the family home, so she didn't complain. She remembered that pulse of gratitude that overcame every slight, every hurt. She told Olga she'd think about it.

The casting studio was located just a few streets away from the Club but Grace, who had no sense of direction, was late anyway. The casting agent was blonde, aged about thirty and wore a very short leather skirt and a lacy black jumper through which you could see portions of a fuchsia bra. She had the bright, singsong voice of an air hostess and many of the attitudes as well. For instance she kept enquiring after Grace's wellbeing in a variety of meaningless phrases: 'Coffee? Water? Nice flight? Not delayed were you? Traffic bad? All right?'

('Actually I witnessed a murder on the way up the stairs, I need to call the police.')

'Are you sure you won't have anything? Coffee? Mineral water?'

Grace sat down in one of the three leather chairs, which were the last word in fashion a decade before. They were less ubiquitous now, because they were extremely uncomfortable. Once seated, Grace's knees were in line with her nose and she had to crane her neck to see anything at all. She looked at the list the agent (Sharon – or possibly Sherin) had given her. There were twenty-six names. Normally, there were creatives with Grace and she just facilitated the casting but quite often Andrew let her do it on her own. She had a flair for it.

The door opened and the first girl appeared. Grace switched her mind to automatic and allowed instinct and experience to take over. She spent several minutes with each interviewee but in fact she knew within the first five seconds who was right. She didn't know how she knew, she just knew. It was a certainty that had nothing to do with a mental process. Indeed, if she'd allowed herself to think, she was lost. She would have started dithering, questioning herself.

The two and a half hours passed not unpleasantly. Grace, real-izing she was a client for once, and entitled to make demands, asked for an ashtray and smoked several cigarettes. Eventually, it was over. Grace had short-listed five names and waited for the time-coded tapes so she could bring them back to Andrew.

'Could you put a pencil on these?' she asked the casting agent, indicating the names she had asterisked. Sharon (Sherin?) nodded approvingly.

'Oh yes, she's very good. Oh she's lovely, isn't she? Oh yes. Lovely, lovely.' Grace got the impression that if she'd decided to cast one of the leather chairs, the casting agent would have endorsed her choice enthusiastically.

A little tired and dry-mouthed from too many cigarettes, Grace made her way back to the club. It was just on four. She went up the winding stairs and knocked on Olga's door.

A haughty, 'Who?' through the panelling.

'Who do you think?' Grace said crossly.

The door opened. Olga was wearing a La Perla slip which Grace had kept in a drawer for years waiting for an occasion that never seemed to present itself. Olga had no concept of personal property. This, Grace suspected, had less to do with her socialist roots and more with the fact that she saw life as something to be colonized and, to be fair, she was equally generous with anything she herself owned. 'Take,' she said carelessly if Grace happened to admire something like a bracelet or a pair of earrings.

On the floor lay a number of miniature bottles and the empty half-bottle of champagne had now been joined by two empty half-bottles of wine. Grace wasn't too concerned. Olga seemed to have an infinite capacity for drink and, other than a tendency to laugh more loudly, alcohol had little or no effect on her. Olga gave truth to this by reaching soberly for her dress accompanied by the enquiry:

'We go shop now?'

Olga turned round to be zipped, holding her hair up from her neck. She sat on the bed patting beside her for Grace to sit down too. Olga reached out for the notepad and pencil beside the phone and handed both to Grace along with Lionel's credit card. Grace hesitated but, without looking at the card, ran the pencil across the pad. Olga compared what Grace had done with the signature on the card.

'Is perfect!' she said, delighted. She jumped to her feet.

'We go. You don't need practice.'

Grace opened her mouth to tell Olga that she could not possibly do this, but the sound of her mobile intervened. It was Lionel.

'Sweets,' he shouted over the traffic noises Grace could hear in the background, 'do we have any insurance policies, savings policies – anything like that?'

Grace held the phone a little way from her ear and stared for a moment at the pale green wall opposite the bed. Then she pressed the end button.

'Let's go,' she said to Olga.

They went to a designer shop off Bond Street because, Olga explained, the staff got bigger commissions there and would be less likely to check too thoroughly. They would already be feeling anxious about the sale. All that was required was to enhance that anxiety. They would be a double act. Grace, the extravagant one – eager to make the purchase – Olga would be more cautious.

'Sort of "Good cop, bad cop",' Grace said.

Olga looked at her sharply.

'It's a TV thing.'

There were three other customers in the shop and Grace became slightly alarmed. Olga shook her head infinitesimally.

'Is OK. Don't worry,' she whispered.

There were two salesgirls wearing expensive, severely cut designer clothes – replicas of which hung around the walls. Grace ran her hand tentatively along the rail, feeling the soft materials drift between her fingers. On a shelf that ran above the clothes rail were arranged three styles of shoe, so delicate they seemed to be part of the shop's design rather than something you could buy.

'Need any help?'

Grace jumped.

'We just look,' Olga's voice had taken on a new timbre. It was milky, low and steeped in money.

The salesgirl moved back a step or two where she hovered like a predator. Grace looked at Olga. Little remained of the Olga who had arrived on her doorstep with her torn tights and lazy sexuality. Olga's capacity to take everything in her stride, to be surprised at nothing, did indeed lend her that illusive quality of wealth – of someone used to being pampered. It helped that she was wearing a very beautiful cashmere coat which Grace, in a moment of madness, had purchased the previous year.

Olga took an armload of dresses and pushed Grace into the dressing room. Grace checked the size of the first dress, which was two down on the one she normally wore. She slipped it over her head. It fitted perfectly but, while its cut made her figure look both slim and curved, there was a blandness about it that was all too familiar. She went out, and stood before the long mirror. The salesgirls made soft cooing noises. Olga shook her head. The two salesgirls looked at Olga resentfully. Grace put on the next dress. It made her look like a gnome. A very well-dressed gnome, but a gnome nevertheless. She didn't bother going out. She tried on the next. It seemed a little tight as she pulled it up over her hips but, when she put her arms through the sleeves, it fitted perfectly, if a little snugly. She did up the zip. The shoulders were cut so they just cleared the top of her arms; the neckline was cut straight across so that her neck looked longer, more fragile. It moulded itself around her waist and hips and fell down to just below the knees. Even without shoes, she looked inches taller. She called for Olga who tore open the curtain and then regarded her unsmilingly.

Olga let the curtain fall and disappeared to return with a pair of the shoes Grace had seen earlier. Grace put them on and walked out. She looked at her reflection in the mirror. Her hair stood up in its surprised little spikes, her eyes looked large and frightened and the dress – well the dress was perfect. She found herself smiling, her eyes drawn down to the hem, just below her knees; her legs looked longer and slimmer and the delicate lines of the shoes; their heels so thin they seemed to have been drawn with a pen.

'I don't like.'

Grace and the salesgirls turned to Olga, united in their disbelief.

'What?' All three of them exploded at once. Olga examined her nails blandly.

'Is too – black.'

'It is black. Black is the colour it is. That's like saying it's too dress.'

'That too,' Olga said.

'It's absolutely made for her,' one of the salesgirls said a little combatively to Olga and then smoothly to Grace, 'It's absolutely perfect.'

'I'll take it – and the shoes,' said Grace.

Olga sighed, bored.

'I think you should wait. Try other shop then,' and she smiled distantly at the salesgirls, 'if you don't find better, come back.'

Even though Grace clearly remembered their plan, she still found her eyes welling up with tears at the very idea of leaving the shop without the dress.

'I'm definitely taking it,' she said, removing Lionel's card from her bag, so immersed in the commerce that she'd forgotten its provenance.

Olga moved towards her but the salesgirl was quicker. She grabbed the card and swiped it through.

'Just have to wait for clearance,' she said, holding the card in her hand but keeping her eyes on Olga. The shop grew silent. Grace could hear her heart beating and then, after what seemed a lifetime, the 'ticker ticker' sound of the machine as the white slip emerged. Grace grabbed it and signed it with a flourish; the sales-girl smiled at her brilliantly and returned the card.

'Have it your own way then,' shrugged Olga as Grace went to take off the dress. Later, with both purchases cushioned in mounds of tissue and placed reverently in bags, Olga and Grace left: Olga looking sulky, Grace triumphant. They didn't speak until they'd turned the corner.

'Yes!' yelled Grace, flinging her arms around Olga.

'I tell you is easy,' Olga said, 'now is my turn.'

This time, Grace was the cautious advisor. She had agreed to get her friend's purchases on her card because her friend had been mugged earlier, but she made it clear that she regretted the generous impulse so that the salesgirls were even more anxious to speed through the transaction. Everyone looked at her with nervous anticipation because Grace had the whip hand. Grace had the card.

'I really don't think it suits you, Olga,' she said firmly, holding the card away from the eager hand of the assistant. Like stealing candy from a baby.

NINETEEN

OLGA AND GRACE were sitting in the bar of the club. Grace's new shoes hurt just a bit but she didn't care. They ordered champagne for Olga, mineral water for Grace. Then, in the mirror over the bar, through the flanks of bottles, Grace glimpsed a girl exactly like Emily – who might have been Emily. She turned around. The girl wasn't in the least like Emily, except perhaps for her thinness and the smallness of her face with its taut little chin and emphatic cheek bones. The girl was drunk. She swayed and then sat down very suddenly in a low velvet chair. The man she was with looked at her with contempt. He was drunk too.

'I thought that girl – she reminded me of Emily,' Grace said as their drinks arrived.

Olga appeared not to have heard. Grace had already pointed out a famous writer and a very famous director but Olga had been unimpressed.

'She's not even like her,' Grace said.

Olga took a sip of her champagne.

'Some peoples find it hard to know who they are, what they want,' she said. 'You're very alike.'

'Alike? We couldn't be more different.'

'Whatever you say.'

'What makes you say we're alike?'

'Nothing at all,' Olga said. She seemed on the verge of laughter.

'Anyway,' Grace said, deciding to let the matter drop, 'it's pretty pathetic to be still groping around when you're my age.'

Olga nodded slowly. Grace couldn't be sure whether this was in agreement with what she had just said or simply a comment on life itself.

'Grace! How absolutely wonderful to see you!'

Grace turned around. Bearing down upon them, threading his way through the now crowded bar, was Geoffrey Simmons, his plump face wreathed in smiles, his Boss suit skating smartly over the imperfections of his figure. He took Grace's hand, squeezed it and then kissed her on both cheeks.

He worked in politics. He was a spin doctor really and Grace had only met him about three times, but after the first time (it was at a dinner party) he'd always remembered her and seemed to feel such genuine affection for her that Grace suspected he might have mistaken her for someone else. Or perhaps that was his job – to remember people and make them feel special.

'You look terrific. Terrific!' he said standing back to get a better look. Grace found an expression uncomfortably close to a simper come over her face. 'And who is this?' He'd turned to Olga who was examining him idly in between sips of her champagne.

'This is Olga,' Grace hesitated and then hurled a handful of consonants up in the air in the hope that they would fall on the bar in a rough approximation of Olga's surname.

'Wonderful!' said Geoffrey, taking Olga's hand and kissing it. Olga glared at him. Geoffrey was even more charmed. 'I'm stuck over there,' he said to Grace, indicating a table of sour-faced men in suits and also, to Grace's horror, Gerry Taylor.

'Pharmaceutical company,' he went on, looking over at his companions with a certain amount of distaste. 'Trying to persuade them to locate in Ireland. Well, have to find something to put in all those empty software factories,' and he laughed hugely as though he'd told a joke. Grace found herself laughing with him. He was like that. You felt drawn to him in spite of yourself. She supposed that was why he was such a success.

'What I'd really like to do is take the two of you out for dinner,' he said, 'but …' and he spread his hands regretfully. 'No chance of that I'm afraid.'

At that moment, Gerry Taylor looked across at them, squinted at Grace then rose to his feet and made his way across to the bar.

'Well, well, well,' said Gerry, 'twice in one week.'

'You know each other?' Geoffrey asked.

'Oh, yes, Grace and I are old friends,' said Gerry, but he was looking at Olga.

Then he turned back to Grace.

'Last time I saw you, you were a little the worse for wear,' and he shook his finger mock-scoldingly at Grace who badly wanted to hit him.

'We had dinner a couple of days ago,' he explained to Geoffrey, 'Grace was a little …' He stopped and gave a guffaw of laughter. 'Must have been something you ate Grace.'

Grace looked at him witheringly, but he went on.

'Don't you remember?'

'Remember what?'

'Must have been something she ate.'

'I don't know what you're talking about.'

Gerry rested a hand companionably on Grace's shoulder and,

when he'd indicated to the barman to bring another round, continued.

'It was at a drinks party in Grace's house – a hundred years ago. Wine and cheese,' Gerry curled the phrase to place it back where it belonged – back when he and Grace were at college.

Grace couldn't remember having a party. Then she did. It was for her eighteenth birthday – about forty college friends all standing around uneasily drinking mulled wine and eating cheddar cheese on sticks while Grace's parents roamed the room, as though they had wandered into the wrong house.

'It was hilarious,' Gerry went on. 'This friend of Grace's, what was her name Grace, Olive? Olivia?' He gave her a playful punch, 'Give me a bit of help here Grace.'

'I can't remember.'

'Anyway, she got absolutely sozzled – completely hammered – and two of the fellows there have her by the elbows and are helping her out along the path. She's throwing up and she's so far gone her toes are dragging along the ground with them on either corner and then Grace's father appears on the doorstep. And do you know what he said? "Poor girl. It must have been something she ate."' Gerry gave a shout of laughter so that several people in the vicinity turned round.

'Good one,' said Geoffrey.

'Dad said that? How sweet. How sweet of him,' and Grace felt a little prickle in her nose preparatory to tears but stopped herself. How could she have forgotten something like that? That her father, so bluff, so abrupt, could be capable of such delicacy – of such kindness.

'I thought we go to dinner,' said Olga, jolting Grace back to the present.

'So where are you going?' Geoffrey wanted to know.

'We're trying to decide where to go,' Grace said, recrossing her legs for no other reason than that she loved the feel of the material of her dress against her skin. Olga mentioned the restaurant she'd talked about earlier. Grace looked at Geoffrey wryly.

'Why didn't you say so?' said Geoffrey, whipping a mobile out of his pocket and pressing a single digit.

'Who's that?' he said in a peremptory voice and then, 'Charles? Of course it is, of course it is. Look, Charles, I've two special friends I'd like you to accommodate tonight. That's right. Sherwin, Grace Sherwin. Eight o'clock?' He looked questioningly at Grace who nodded. 'Thanks Charles.' Geoffrey popped his phone back in his pocket and beamed at them both. 'Now how easy was that?' he said comfortably.

'I'm impressed,' Gerry Taylor nodded with approval at Geoffrey, 'you must give me that number.'

'Absolutely,' agreed Geoffrey and looked at Grace with amusement, inviting her to join in the lie. 'Just as soon as I can get my hands on a pen.'

As they waited to be shown to their table in the restaurant, Grace inspected the diners. She noticed two TV soap stars, a famous American actor, an impossibly successful theatre impresario, two members of the latest boy band and a politician she'd seen interviewed earlier on TV while she was getting dressed. She conveyed all this information to Olga in an undertone.

'Yes I know him,' she said of the American actor, her voice impatient. A waiter showed them to their table. Olga leaned forward, 'So he's a doctor, this man?'

'What man?' Grace had meanly forgotten all about Geoffrey Simmons – author of their good fortune.

'The man in the club.'

'Yes – I suppose he is,' Grace said, picking up a menu, 'he's a spin doctor – you know.'

'Spin doctor? I like doctors. And the other one was there the night in the restaurant?'

'Yes,' Grace admitted.

'I prefer the doctor,' Olga said and then got to her feet. 'I need go to ladies' room.'

Grace watched in amusement as Olga made her way through the tables. Every eye, including that of the American actor, followed her slow progress across the floor – the hair swinging, it seemed, in slow motion; the recently purchased dress revealing her creamy back; the perfectly sculpted bones of her shoulders.

While she was gone, Grace managed a few covert glances in the direction of the American movie star. He was eating 'bangers and mash' – a speciality of this chic restaurant. Irony carried too far, in Grace's opinion. The American seemed to agree with her. He looked at his recently delivered plate as though it contained the head of a close friend. He appeared smaller than in his movies and older. Grace smiled at the cliché. She stole another look from behind her menu. Yet there was something about him – something irreducible. Grace had known many actors and the fragility of their egos, how easily rocked they were, how readily they tumbled from the confidence of a success to the terror of finding the next job. But there must come a moment, she thought, when an actor crosses over to a place where his confidence is unassailable. She looked over again and, mortified, discovered he was looking directly at her. She dropped her eyes.

Olga returned and took the menu. She looked boldly across the room at the American. 'I'll have anything except those,' she said pointing at his plate. They had grilled vegetables and sea bream. While they ate, Grace probed gently about Olga's business in London. They were leaving at noon the next day. There wasn't much time.

'I go see him after here.'

'So late?'

'He doesn't get home till late. He work.'

'Would you like me to come with you?'

'He doesn't like strangers,' Olga said but she gave Grace a grateful smile all the same.

'Is he …' Grace felt a little foolish actually saying the words but she blundered on, 'is he a sort of gangster?'

Olga laughed shortly.

'He's business man.'

'I see.'

'He publishes catalogue. He owns club. Maybe he sells some drug. Small time. He's nobody.'

'Are you afraid of him?'

Olga gave a short derisive laugh.

'Are you crazy? He afraid of me,' and she took a last mouthful of fish, shaking her head slowly that Grace should have imagined anything of the sort.

'He was bad part of my life. Now I have good part. I meet nice people like Josh.'

'I don't think I like you seeing so much of Josh,' Grace said, looking at the weave of the tablecloth with great attention.

Grace felt so close to Olga at this moment that she wanted to wipe the slate clean, to get all the nameless fears set to rest at once. And maybe the excitement of the day had been replaced by guilt (she had resolved to phone Lionel later and tell him about his credit card).

'You're too …' Grace couldn't think of a word.

'Too what?' Olga said quietly, 'too old, too foreign, too used?'

'He's very young. In himself.'

Olga lit a cigarette and blew a jet of smoke straight at Grace.

'One minute you tell me he was born middle-aged – then you tell me he's a naïf. The fact is you know nothing about him. You don't think about him at all. You rarely speak of him. And you try not to think of Emily just in case, just for a second you see that she is exactly like you. She *is* you. And Josh – he might as well be someone you meet every day on a bus. What is it they say? "You know him to say hello to"?'

Grace was so shocked by what Olga had said that it took her a while to grasp the other peculiar thing about this speech. Olga's English was rapid, fluent and virtually without accent.

'What happened to "I donta spika da English"?' Grace hissed. 'Lying your way into my house.'

'It's habit,' Olga said, reverting to her previous hesitant, guttural intonation. 'I get more work that way and,' she scrunched out her half-smoked cigarette, 'I get to hear more.'

'Oh right. Good.' Grace didn't know what to say. What she wanted more than anything was to run to the door Olga had opened and slam it shut. She wanted to get back to where she was before. She didn't want detail. She didn't want to stop and look and pick over things. She wanted to let things be. To go on, somehow.

'He's just a nice boy. He's funny. He makes me laugh.'

Grace looked up in surprise.

'Does he? I'd never think of him like that. He always seems so serious.'

'That's because you don't think about him much.'

Grace bent down to her bag on the floor. She picked it up but, once it was in her lap, she couldn't remember what she'd wanted from it. She slid the zip to and fro. She felt – not sad – so much as left behind. It was as though she'd arrived breathless at the departure gate of some airport only to discover that the plane had taken off. It's pointless to feel angry. All you can do is shrug philosophically and wait for another flight. Sitting there in the restaurant, it was as though she were in that airport marking time, getting through it as best she could.

'Excuse me?'

Grace looked up, startled.

The actor was standing at their table. Grace shook herself back into the present and smiled uneasily at the American. She felt a surge of warmth and familiarity as though it were her oldest friend standing there because, with a career that spanned twenty years, he had become a friend; all the characters he played merged into one pleasing person (he never played villains) – a person you could rely on, someone who could be counted on for a certain dry wit and, of course, someone who would discover in the last frame just how much he loved you.

'We were wondering if you ladies would care to join us for a drink,' he said, looking at Olga rather than Grace.

Olga got to her feet.

'I don't think so,' she said.

The actor was shocked. This was a whole new experience for him. He smiled that famous, crooked smile that melted the hearts of women from Bangkok to Banagher.

'Excuse me?' he said.

But Olga was already striding towards the door. Grace wasn't sure what to do. Finally she said in a small voice, 'I love your work.'

The actor looked at her properly for the first time. He arranged his face into his public one – the press conference face designed to woo fans to his next movie. He was preparing himself for a gracious, much rehearsed 'thank you', when the idiocy of what she had said struck Grace and she burst out laughing.

'I'm sorry,' she gasped and followed Olga, leaving the actor standing as though waiting for a note from his director.

Out on the street, Olga suggested they take two taxis and she would go straight to her meeting. She smiled reassuringly at Grace.

'Is no problem,' she said, making the broken accent another secret they shared.

Back in her bedroom, Grace looked at herself in the long mirror beside the door. Her reflection left her feeling oddly let down. It was just a dress after all. Nothing special. She checked her mobile. There were messages from Lionel and Travis. She decided to leave Lionel and pressed redial for Travis. When he answered, he sounded as if she'd caught him during a hill-climbing expedition. She could hear muffled voices in the background, traffic, but overriding everything was the howl of wind.

'Grace?'

'Where are you?'

'Work. It's blowing a gale here.'

Travis told her to hold on and moments later his voice came back, this time speaking normally. He must have gone indoors.

'So how are you?' he said.

'I'm fine,' she said. She looked across at the mini-bar but lit a cigarette instead.

'Look Grace,' Travis paused.

'Let's forget about it,' Grace said, 'I over-reacted.'

There was silence for a moment on the other end of the phone and then Travis's voice again.

'Grace, I called because … I'm seeing a bit of Emily and,' he paused again, 'I just wanted to tell you, that's all.'

Grace took a long drag on her cigarette, burning her throat. She coughed.

'Are you all right?'

'I'm fine,' she said, her throat raw. She took a breath.

'If you ever tell Emily about us I'll kill you,' she said and then, realizing that this sounded softer somehow than she intended, 'I mean that. I mean that I will kill you.'

Travis's voice came back, speaking evenly.

'What do you think I am?'

'I think you're one of those people who fuck up the world because they think telling the truth is a good quality when actually it's a shite quality.'

'Don't worry. It never happened.'

'No,' Grace agreed, 'no it didn't.'

She could hear Travis shouting to someone else that he was on the phone for Christ's sake, then he came back, 'So … ?'

Grace wanted to hang up but instead she said, 'This must have been some whirlwind romance. She was just a friend less than a week ago.'

'Well there you go. That's life.'

'Is it now. Is it? Anyway, you're too old for her.'

She could hear Travis's dry chuckle.

'I don't think too much about age really.'

'Can I trust you?' Grace's voice seemed to hang in the air, like a recorded speech with just a bit of echo on it.

'Yes you can. If you let yourself.'

Grace held the phone for a second and then said, 'Goodbye Travis.'

She felt too tired suddenly to do anything. She unzipped her dress and threw it on the back of the chair and crawled under the thick, white duvet. Outside she could hear the first of the several rubbish trucks that operated through the night in this area rattling down the street. Somewhere far below, a girl screamed.

Someone knocking on her door woke her. She looked at her watch – it was three-thirty.

Grace felt a little sick, the faint nausea you feel when woken suddenly from sleep. Olga stood at the door. One of her eyes was pink and half-closed. There was blood on her mouth.

'Oh Jesus. Oh Jesus.'

'It looks worse than it is.'

'What happened?'

'Nothing.'

'Oh Olga. Do you need a doctor?'

'No. I need a drink.'

Olga walked over to the mini-bar and then stumbled.

'Bastard kick me in the rib.'

Grace went to the mini-bar and got out two small bottles of vodka. Her hands trailed over the remaining bottles. The brandy, the gin, the whiskey. She wanted one of them so badly that it hurt.

'Do you mind if I drink?' Olga said, suddenly solicitous.

'God no,' Grace laughed, 'I hate it when people don't – because of me. I hate that.' This was only half true at the moment and, as Olga poured both small bottles, one-handed, into a glass, the urge to reach out and take the drink from her was almost irresistible.

Instead she went into the bathroom, got a towel and wet it. She got ice from the freezer and wrapped it in the towel.

'Here.'

Olga placed the towel gingerly against her eye.

'You should see the other guy.' And she laughed throatily ending on a moan as she grasped her ribs.

'I take it you didn't get your money.'

Olga lowered the towel for a second and glared at Grace out of her good eye.

'Of course I get the money.' She nodded to herself. 'Pig won't hit anyone else for a while.'

'What happened?'

But Olga was on her feet, still holding the towel. The ice was beginning to melt and dripped on the floor.

'I go to bed. It's been a long night.'

'Are you sure there's nothing … ?'

'I'm OK. No worries.'

The next morning, Olga's eye had turned a variety of colours but, thanks to the ice, was only slightly swollen. Her lips looked as if she'd had an unsatisfactory encounter with collagen. Their plane was at noon.

'About the money,' Grace began.

'Why do you go on and on about the money?' Olga snapped.

'I just …'

'Let me worry about money.'

Olga was sitting at the mirror in Grace's room applying concealer to her eye and mouth.

'Did you get the full twenty thousand?'

'Yes.'

'That's a lot to just have in your handbag. I mean one look at that amount of money and then you and it's going to be "now where did I leave those rubber gloves?" ' Grace laughed shakily. Olga gave an exasperated sigh. Then she smiled.

'I'm not going to take it in. You are.'

'Me?'

Grace felt a tremor of fear. She felt she would be even worse at dealing with Customs than Olga. She glanced at her face in the mirror. Already it was seamed with guilt and terror. In fact, all her life, the expression that most often fell across her face was one of guilt. What did she think she'd done? She remembered that, when she was in college, she'd had a friend given to shoplifting. She used to bring Grace along as a decoy – Grace's demeanour always attracting the attention of any staff or security, while her friend was free to pilfer to her heart's content.

'What if they search me? What will I say?'

'Take it or not, it's all the same to me.' Olga seemed to have lost interest in the whole business.

Somewhere at the back of Grace's head, a small voice said, 'Just say "No".' But unfortunately the voice belonged to Nancy Reagan with her scraggy neck in her pink Chanel suit, smiling that desperate, toothy smile while behind her, Ronald hovered, glazed with love and forgetfulness. And Nancy Reagan had been talking about drugs after all, not money. This was money – money that was Olga's by right, Grace reminded herself.

She took a couple of breaths and muttered, 'It's not as if it's drugs.'

'Exactly,' Olga said shortly and went back to rebuilding her face.

When they were packed, Grace made a last trip to the bathroom. When she returned, she asked Olga for the money.

'It's already in your case,' Olga said, hefting both cases easily, in spite of her bruised ribs.

Grace asked for the bill at reception. Olga's mini-bar incursions accounted for a substantial part of it. Grace smiled at the thought of Andrew's face when he would be required to sign off on her expenses. Then she laughed – he'd probably think it was Grace who'd laid waste to the bar. She suddenly felt very light-hearted. How pleasant it was to be guilt-free about that at least; to be able to face into this journey without a hangover. She looked over at Olga who, eyes covered in dark glasses and lips outlined in vermilion, looked remarkably fresh, as though the previous evening had included nothing more than a spritzer or two.

TWENTY

'STOP SMILING. You look like idiot,' Olga hissed.

Grace straightened up from the luggage carousel but already Olga was marching towards the exit, teetering slightly on the very high heels she was wearing. Grace placed her suitcase on the trolley. Her hands felt slightly slippery as she started to push it. She told herself she was being ridiculous. On an impulse she leant down, doing her best to appear casual, and unzipped her case. On top was a plastic-wrapped packet containing, not money, but something white. Grace felt the walls begin to swim in front of her eyes. She shut the zip quickly to conceal the package – the sort of package that she had seen in so many films, so many TV series. A package she'd seen often on the news, piled high and flanked by triumphant police.

Grace could hardy breathe. She looked towards the Blue Channel. It seemed so far away. She'd also seen programmes about smuggling. The surveillance footage so accurately captured all the little tics and nervous habits of the smuggler: the feigned insouciance which only served to highlight the sheen of sweat on an upper lip; the attempts at light-hearted banter with a Customs official; the compulsive yawning – thinking it masked their intent when, of course, any Customs official knows that yawning is the result of extreme tension.

As she neared the gap into Customs, Grace found herself simultaneously sweating profusely, yawning and saying merrily to the bored Customs officer, 'Lovely flight – I don't know why I get so nervous.'

Her overnight case seemed to pulse like a beating heart. Grace was now hyperventilating and the only thing preventing her from falling over with fright was the trolley itself. She'd gone beyond fear and had reached a state of fatalism.

'Could you open that bag please?'

'So this is it?' she said to herself.

She decided she'd admit everything at once and not go through the humiliation of a search. The man in Customs had a face pitted with acne scars. His hair was spiked and bleached at the tips. Grace thought he should have a serious haircut – one more in keeping with his job. It was like a policeman with a pierced tongue. But she comforted herself with the realisation that he looked about Josh's age. She could cry a bit. Maybe she'd remind him of his mother and he'd take pity on her.

Her world had contracted to a tiny pinhole of terror. She didn't even think about Olga – of Olga's betrayal – it was just her, the suitcase and nothingness.

'Could you move along please?' The voice was quite sharp and she realised the Customs man must have had to repeat the phrase. 'Ma'am?'

Grace looked around. Behind her, an Iranian man was lifting several carrier bags from his trolley and placing them on the bench. The Customs man was looking at her with the bright, 'Can I help you?' expression he had perfected during his training. He was gesturing at her with his eyes, waving her through. He started to sift through the contents of the Iranian's luggage. Grace gave a sound somewhere between a sigh and a sob.

She pushed her trolley along the white-walled exit area and emerged into Arrivals allowing all the tension to drain from her body, feeling the beginnings of elation – rapidly replaced by rage. Just ahead of her she saw Olga.

'Olga!' she screamed and suddenly the sea of people behind the red barrier at Arrivals surged forward.

For a moment, she didn't know what was happening – where she was even. There was a flash of white light as though somewhere in the distance, there had been an explosion. There was a lot of shouting. At the edges of her eyes, she was conscious of black shadows rolling in like clouds and she knew she was going to faint.

'Grace? Grace?' Andrew was leaning over her. She couldn't lift her hand. Was she paralysed? But then she realized her palm was stuck to the tiles with a piece of chewing gum. There was a cigarette butt beside her nose. She tried to sit up.

'Don't move her. She might have broken something.' It was Myles Kitchen.

'Andrew? Myles?'

Grace began to slip away again. She heard Olga's voice.

'I tell her to eat but she no eat.'

Olga was kneeling beside her.

'Are you OK?' she whispered.

The white lights started to flash again. Grace pushed herself up on one elbow.

'You cunt,' she said. There were photographers pressing in from every side. Olga looked at her, surprised.

'I am big hit!' she told Grace.

Grace looked around for Andrew, who was behind her.

'Grace this is phenomenal – it's amazing. It was on the news last night. People are stealing the posters. On every phone-in show, Olga was the main subject – it's just extraordinary. The clients are thrilled.' He stopped for a moment and arranged his face into an expression of sympathy, 'But the important thing is – how are you?'

'I'll be fine,' Grace grabbed Olga by the wrist. 'I just need to go to the bathroom.'

Somehow she and Olga made it across the hall to the nearest ladies' room. A woman applying lipstick at the mirror took one look at Grace and decided to abandon her task.

'You, you,' Grace couldn't continue. A ball of something like phlegm was stuck in her throat. She was shaking. Unable to speak, she reached down to her case and wrenched the zip open.

'What's that, you cow?'

Olga scratched the side of her mouth with one long nail.

'It's flour.'

'It's what?'

Olga reached down and picked up the shrink-wrapped package. She turned it over. It said 'Durum Flour'. There was a tiny Italian flag on the top and a sheaf of wheat. Grace leaned against the tiled walls.

'What did you think it was?'

'I don't know.' Grace burst into tears. Olga went into one of the cubicles and returned with a wad of lavatory paper.

'Here.'

'Thanks.' Grace blew her nose thoroughly and mopped her face. Olga lit two cigarettes. Grace took one of them gratefully.

'We only get away with four, five puffs,' Olga said, eyeing the smoke alarm. There was a timid knock at the door.

'Er Grace?' It was Andrew.

'Yes?' Olga shouted.

'Just wondering er …'

'Go away.'

'Right, right.'

Olga pushed her dark glasses on top of her head and looked at herself in the mirror.

'Shit.' She turned back to Grace.

'Did you think it was drug? Did you think I put drug in your bag?'

Grace looked down at her cigarette then risked another puff before running it under the tap.

'I just, I opened the bag to see where the money was and I saw –' she indicated the packet of flour, 'that. I mean what was I supposed to think?'

'That it was a packet of flour,' Olga said evenly.

'You should have said.'

'I forgot. So shoot me.'

'Why flour?'

'I get bored the day you go to the casting. I go for walk in Soho – find nice Italian shop and I think I'll buy some and make proper pizza. I make good pizza – I used to …'

'Don't tell me. You used to work in a pizzeria.'

Olga smiled slowly and blew a column of smoke in the air.

'And where's the money?'

Both women jumped as the smoke alarm sounded. Olga tossed her cigarette butt into one of the lavatories.

'I tell you about the money when we get home,' she said and replaced her glasses.

Andrew was waiting outside the ladies' room together with several photographers.

'A few more shots?' he suggested. 'Glasses off maybe?'

'No, no,' Grace interjected. 'Glasses on. Air of mystery.'

Andrew nodded approvingly.

'Excellent work Grace,' said Myles coming over from where he had been talking to two of the reporters, 'now, we need to talk about Olga's future. I thought we'd go across to the airport hotel and thrash the whole thing out.'

While he was saying this he carefully presented a pleasing profile and adopted the lofty smile of a statesman, just in case anyone was still taking photographs.

'We tired. We go home,' Olga said, matter-of-factly. 'We talk tomorrow. Maybe,' she added.

'Grace?' Myles's voice had the desperate note of someone left in charge of an unpredictable and possibly dangerous delinquent.

'Oh, I think it can wait till tomorrow,' Grace said and then, in spite of Andrew's offer of a lift, she and Olga went out to the taxi-rank leaving Andrew and Myles standing in Arrivals. Over their heads, there was a banner, which read, 'Welcome Home Daddy'.

'Focking vulture,' Olga said when they were settled in the cab.

'Where to?' said the taxi-man, bored and then, 'Jesus!' He turned round in his seat to face Olga. 'It's you, isn't it?' he said.

'Yes it's me,' said Olga coldly.

'Wasn't sure with the dark glasses but I knew, I just knew.'

They drove home to the soothing mantra of the taxi-man's repeated exclamations of, 'I don't believe it. I do not believe it!'

Once in the house, Grace could do no more than stumble up the stairs, leaving the bags in the hall. She lay down on the bed fully clothed and within seconds was asleep. It was dark when she awoke – aroused from sleep by the headlights of cars that strobed across the ceiling.

'Olga?'

There was no reply.

She got up, took off her clothes and went into the shower. She stood under the jet for what seemed an age, allowing the water to play across the back of her neck. She shampooed her hair. Clad in sweats and a jumper, she went barefoot downstairs. She turned on the light in the hall. Through the open door of the living room she saw that Olga was asleep on the couch. She closed the door softly and went down to the kitchen and rummaged around in the freezer. All she could find was a pizza, which struck her as extraordinarily funny. She sat down, gasping with laughter.

Olga came in, tousled, wiping her good eye.

'What's so funny?'

Grace held up the pizza box.

'Dinner. Dinner's funny.'

Olga nodded distantly, still half-asleep.

TWENTY-ONE

'SO TELL ME about the money.'

They'd ended up eating an omelette rather than the pizza and were drinking coffee.

Olga ran her finger round the top of her mug.

'I didn't get the money.'

'I thought …'

Olga gnawed at the inside of her cheek.

'I went to the house and tell him he owe me. That the money is mine. He laughed at me. I got angry. I slapped him. So he hit me a few times. He say if I annoy him again the only job I'll get is with a freak show. Then he poured me a drink and said best thing we forget it. He get one of his men to drive me back to the hotel.'

'Can't you do something? Sue him?'

Olga laughed with genuine mirth.

'Good idea. I'll do that.' She took a sip of coffee, careful to drink from the unswollen side of her mouth. She put the mug down.

'You're such a naïf, Grace.'

Grace looked down at the table.

'I didn't let some bastard take me for twenty thousand pounds and then laugh in my face,' she said.

Olga looked at her and smiled slowly.

'Oh really?'

Grace took a cigarette but didn't light it.

'Well it's the last time anyone will take either of us,' she said and after a pause, struck a match and lit her cigarette.

'How much more money you think I get for this thing – this poster thing?'

Grace thought for a minute. It was oddly liberating to find herself doing the exact opposite of what she had done for years, which was ensure the agency paid as little as possible.

'Oh a lot – a lot of money. We have them, as they say, "by the short and curlies".'

'What is this "curlies"?'

'Balls Olga. We've got them by the balls.'

Olga nodded to herself, on familiar terrain at last.

The phone rang. Grace picked it up. It was Lionel.

'Hi Lionel,' Grace's tone was more cordial than usual, conscious that she owed him three thousand sterling's worth of sympathy and kindness.

'It's official. The paper's closing,' his voice caught for a moment, 'I'm fucked.'

'But they can't do that. There has to be some pay-off – some lump sum – you've been with them for a hundred years.'

'I'm not staff.'

Grace felt guilty and stupid. The trip to London was like a horrible drunken spree where you half-remember stuff you want to forget.

Gerry Taylor's contemptuous little smile when he'd met her in the bar, the dress – that really rather ordinary dress. She felt her face grow hot now at the memory of her imagining that she had drugs in her bag. It was like one of the stupid, wildly off-centre ideas she used to get when she was drinking years ago. When her life was a fog and she always seemed to get things mixed up. Once she'd seen a mother struggling with a child and she'd intervened. She'd thought the child was being kidnapped. What was wrong with her?

She started to cry. She could hear Lionel.

'Oh sweets. There's nothing to cry about. We'll be all right. Something will turn up.'

Grace's sobs grew louder.

'I spent a whole lot of money on your card in London. I forged your signature. I'm sorry. I don't know what's wrong with me. I think I'm going mad. Like Mum.'

'On my card? My credit card?' Lionel's careful tones hung in the air.

'I'm sorry.' Grace looked up to see Olga, who had followed her up from the kitchen and was sitting on the bottom step of the stairs, glowering at her.

'Give me,' Olga said, standing up and taking the phone from Grace.

'Hey bastard,' she said into the phone, 'you fock with house so she have nothing and you give her zero for kids plus you don't deserve job 'cos you are shit reporter.'

She dropped the phone and walked with a casual rolling gait down towards the kitchen.

'Lionel?' All Grace could hear was breathing at the other end. 'Lionel?'

'I'm not a shit reporter.'

'I know, I know,' said Grace.

'Don't worry about the card. Fuck it. I mean, it's only money,' he said, regaining some of his former swagger, 'and tell that bitch cow that I'm sorry I got her out of Russia. Oh, and tell her as pole dancers go, she should stick to car maintenance.'

'I'll phone later, OK?' Grace hung up just as Olga emerged from the kitchen carrying a glass and eating a chocolate biscuit.

'He tell you he get me out of Russia?'

'Yes.'

'Well is true. I owe him.'

'How … ?'

'Oh he get me on team of interpreters. Pretty good when he thinks I speak just a bit German and bad English.'

'And you were a pole dancer?'

Olga dropped a piece of biscuit on the carpet which she tidily picked up and popped in her mouth.

'Yeah. He tell you that? He say I was shit?'

Grace nodded. 'And Red tells me your father was a ballet dancer – so much for inherited talent.'

'It's not quite the same as ballet, you know, the pole dance,' said Olga.

TWENTY-TWO

GRACE WOKE FEELING RESTED. Too rested. She looked at the
clock. It was almost half past nine. She jumped out of bed just as
the phone rang.

'It's half past nine Grace, where are you?' came Myles's querulous voice.

'Oh, for God's sake,' said Grace and hung up. Almost
immediately, it rang again.

'I'm coming for fuck's sake,' Grace shouted.

'Don't come on my account,' said her father frostily.

'Oh, sorry Dad. I thought you were the office. They're hound-
ing me.'

'That's the Civil Service for you,' said her father.

'I don't work in the Civil Service.'

'I know – you resigned, still, you can't overlook the attractions
of security and a decent pension.'

Grace ground her teeth uselessly. 'So Dad, was there anything
special?'

'No, nothing special.'

'How's Mum?'

'Well,' admitted her father, 'dangerously well. She's having a clear-out at the moment.'

'Oh.'

'She's got everything out on the street. She's astonishingly robust.' As always, a note of reluctant admiration had entered her father's voice. 'Fortunately she couldn't get the couch through the living-room door so I've somewhere to read the paper,' he gave a merry laugh. 'I'd kill her if I could get away with it.'

'Dad!'

'But she seems to thrive on poison, and a blunt instrument is out of the question. She can run faster than a ferret.'

'What about … ?' Grace was going to say 'a nursing home?' but she stopped herself, knowing it was useless. They'd die from their wounds, locked in a struggle on the battlefield, her parents – two old soldiers.

'Would you like me to come round and help you haul everything in again?'

'No, we rarely use saucepans and I never liked the chairs anyway.'

'Where is she now?'

'Asleep.'

'Right,' Grace said, her mother's drugged face hovering briefly before her, 'just as well I suppose.'

'Goodbye, Grace. And, 'don't let the bastards grind you down'. Bloody bureaucrats. The uncivil service.'

'Right. I'll remember that Pops.'

Grace went down to the kitchen. Olga was already there. Her eye looked slightly better.

'Why didn't you call me?'

'I thought you needed the rest.'

'If anyone else rings I'm going to rip that damned thing out of the wall.' Olga was making toast.

'What's that?' Grace asked, looking at something pink on a half-eaten slice.

'Em,' Olga said.

'Em? Oh ham. I'm not sure you should be eating that. I can't remember when I last bought ham. It's weeks old.'

'I have iron stomach,' Olga told her, patting her midriff with satisfaction.

'So today you have money meeting with agency?'

'Yeah,' Grace spread some butter on toast, 'I'm quite looking forward to it.'

'What you think Josh come too?'

'Josh?' Grace chewed slowly. It hadn't occurred to her to include Josh but now it seemed like a very good idea, if only to show Andrew and Myles that they were serious. 'Maybe he isn't free.'

'Yes he is. I phone. He's coming round.'

Grace was a little put out but then felt a certain relief. She told Olga about the call from her father, how he refused to absorb what exactly it was she did for a living. Or rather, had done for a living. Olga tore a strip of fat off her ham and then lowered it into her mouth like a strand of spaghetti.

'What does Emily do? Her job.'

'She …' Grace tried to remember Emily mentioning her job but she couldn't think of one occasion when the subject had come up. Presumably she had a job. She couldn't be out just walking the streets till eight or nine at night. She couldn't be devoting whole days to those meetings of hers. Grace looked at Olga.

'I don't know, I have absolutely no idea.'

Olga made a face. 'You are a family without curiosity.'

'Which in itself is a curiosity,' Grace said.

'No. Is sad.' Olga picked up the buttery knife and threw it carelessly into the sink. 'I go dress,' she said and closed the kitchen door behind her.

Josh arrived some twenty minutes later looking different. Grace couldn't quite put her finger on it. He was wearing a suit as he always did during the week. He looked as well cared for as usual. Even as his mother, she couldn't find it in her to call him handsome – his face was too slack, his mouth too small and too damp, his eyes a nondescript browny yellow. Hazel. Hazel was probably written on his passport. But apart from these drawbacks he had, as they say, made the best of himself: his hair was tidy, his nails manicured and buffed to an expensive sheen, his shoes were highly polished, his suit well-cut.

'So how's the world of high finance?' At least she knew what he did for a living.

Olga came down minutes later. She had reverted to her own wardrobe and was wearing a very short cotton skirt, which looked home-made, and a denim jacket. She was bare-legged and on her feet were high-heeled, strappy sandals studded with beads, some of which were missing. Josh looked at her as if she were wearing couture. They drove in Josh's car at a rather slower pace than the last time; as he drove, Josh ran them through the game plan. They'd just listen to the offer, then they'd go outside to discuss it.

'That always unnerves them,' he explained. Grace gave him an idea of costs for everything from single posters to TV campaigns while Josh nodded, occasionally flashing smiles to Olga who was sitting in the back.

'The thing is, they need us more than we need them,' Josh told them.

'That's a matter of opinion,' said Grace, who was counting on her ten per cent to get her through the remainder of the year. Josh looked at her sharply.

'Whatever you do Grace, don't let them know you're that hungry.' He concentrated on his driving and then said, 'I'm sorry about the house. I didn't know. I'd have stopped him – stupid old fool.'

'Don't talk about your father like that,' Grace said surprising herself.

Once they'd parked at the agency, all three of them seemed unwilling to leave the safety of the car. Grace rooted in her bag for cigarettes. Josh, she could see, was about to demur but changed his mind when Olga said, 'Oh, great. Give me.' Grace lit both their cigarettes and, taking pity on Josh, opened her window.

'We can't afford to blow this,' Josh said, suddenly looking very young.

'I trust you,' Olga slid her arms down over his shoulders and, for a moment, rested her head on his.

Grace picked up her bag and reached for the door-handle. Once in reception, she placed Olga and Josh on one of the matching electric blue couches. The cream ones had lasted even less than the normal three-week rotation time. Then she went into her office.

'Anything happening?' she asked Mike who was already working on his computer.

'No – just tidying a few things up,' he said.

'Very wise,' said Grace.

'So, your new discovery is an overnight sensation,' he said, swinging back on his chair.

'Yes,' Grace said, 'and,' she leaned forward conspiratorially, 'I intend making them pay through the nose for her.'

'A new career! You don't hang about do you?' Mike looked at her, as though everything that was happening was as a consequence of his advice.

'So – into battle,' Grace said, picking up a sheaf of files.

'What are those?' Mike asked. Grace looked at the pile of manila folders in her arm.

'God knows, just something to frighten the shite out of them.'

'Well, up the revolution.' Mike lifted his arm lazily into the air and made a half-hearted fist. Grace blew him a kiss.

TWENTY-THREE

'**Y**OU'RE BEING RIDICULOUS. No way are we going to pay that amount.'

Andrew threw down his pen and looked over at Myles for support. Myles was deep in his notes, a slight frown on his face. Olga was spread-eagled in one of the boardroom chairs, tearing a cardboard coaster into very small pieces. She looked like the stranger in a bus station your parents advised you not to talk to. Josh sat comfortably, occasionally flashing his cuffs so that his shirt sat just so over his wrists. In front of him there was an expensive leather folder, which earlier he had removed from an equally expensive leather briefcase. His hands were relaxed and clasped in front of him. Grace felt something quite unfamiliar. It was pride, she realized.

'I think we should start saying six hundred thousand as opposed to nearly a million. Purely in the interests of accuracy,' he said.

'It's out of the question.'

Grace could see that Myles was getting angry, something he normally never allowed himself to do. He was letting it get personal. Josh took a sip from his cup.

'This is wretched coffee,' he said, 'is there any tea?'

Andrew gave an explosive sigh. Josh opened his folder.

'Now,' he said pacifically, 'let's see where we have a bit of consonance – a measure of agreement.'

'We have none. There is no area where we agree,' Myles said and then looked up sharply as Olga untwined herself from the seat and went to the door.

'Ladies' room,' she said removing a cigarette from the package she was holding. Moments later they could see her through the window, walking up and down the street, smoking.

'Look at her, for Christ's sake. We're not talking Christy Turlington here.'

'Well get Christy Turlington then,' Josh said, and closed his folder.

Outside the window, Grace could see Olga ambling over to a car that had pulled in beside her. She was leaning on the roof of the car, her cotton skirt barely covering her buttocks. She was laughing at something the driver had said. The awful thought occurred to Grace that Olga was about to walk over to the passenger side and climb in. But Olga merely laughed again, slapped the roof of the car and the car drove off. She took a last drag of her cigarette and threw it into the gutter. Andrew was staring meaningfully at Myles.

'I think we're all getting a little sidetracked here,' he said using an upward inflection as though he expected Myles to contradict him. 'What we need to do is to arrive at a compromise.'

'A compromise by definition is an agreement arrived at where both parties make concessions and achieve a solution acceptable to both.' Josh's smile embraced the whole table. 'The problem is, you don't seem inclined to make any adjustments. You just want us to concede – to give in and,' he paused to take a sip of the tea which

Andrew had poured for him, 'much better,' he said and then, 'where was I? Oh yes, compromise.'

'We are not paying this woman half a million pounds for a couple of posters and that is final.'

'Well we were talking euros but if you want to work in old pounds, the equivalent is actually four hundred, seventy-two thousand, five hundred thirty-eight pounds and forty pence. Roughly. For six hundred thousand euros.' Josh smiled again. Grace was beginning to enjoy herself.

'Let's be honest with each other at least.' Josh leaned forward, his body language unconsciously echoing that of Myles so that both men wore expressions of easy candour, their hands loosely clasped on the table, their smiles as open, frank and artificial as a boy band's publicity still. 'It would be a mistake to base these negotiations on,' Josh smiled winningly, 'what is essentially a lie.'

'Lie? What lie?' asked Myles.

'That we are talking about some Mickey Mouse deal worth a hundred grand.'

Myles's smile didn't falter but the knuckles of his clasped hands whitened. He directed his gaze at the blank TV monitor above Josh's head.

'One hundred thousand euros and that's our final offer.' He slammed down his pen.

Josh laughed with such genuine amusement that even Myles and Andrew joined in. But then Josh stopped laughing and his face went blank as though his mind was already on his next meeting.

'I'm sorry,' he said getting to his feet, 'normally I've no sense of humour about money but that offer is so laughable that, well …' Josh placed his folder tidily in his briefcase and walked out of the boardroom. Grace paused in the doorway and turned back to Andrew.

'Well one good thing came out of this meeting,' she said and both Andrew and Myles looked at her eagerly. 'It's the first time in a fortnight you haven't mentioned my going-away party.'

Back in the car Olga said, 'That not go so good.'

'On the contrary,' Josh told her, 'it couldn't have gone better. A tenner says they'll be back this afternoon. They'll offer two, we'll come down to five, we'll compromise with four.' And he turned round and kissed Olga full on the lips for quite a long time.

Grace examined the railings on the other side of the road. Josh was quite an old twenty-four she conceded, and Olga was sort of ageless. Grace began to hum an old Abba song. As Josh backed out onto the roadway, he and Olga joined in until their voices filled the car.

'Money, money, money,' they sang, over and over again because none of them could remember the next line.

And Josh was right. At four o'clock the phone rang.

'I'll put you on to Josh,' Grace said, making a face at him and pointing at the phone.

Unable to listen, Grace went down to the kitchen where Olga was pouring drinks. Five minutes later, Josh came down. He had a serious, inscrutable expression. He didn't say anything. He just raised his right hand and slowly lifted up his index finger, then the second finger, the third and, when he lifted up the fourth, Grace gave a great whoop of triumph and Olga's face opened into a big, lazy smile.

'Were they furious?' Grace wanted to know.

'Not at all. What have they got to be furious about? It's not their money after all.' Josh sat down and dropped his arms behind the back of the chair, looking utterly relaxed. 'They just needed time to work that out.'

Grace felt a great weight lift off her to be replaced, almost immediately, by a feeling of fear. Everything seemed to be happening so fast. Too fast.

'Is anything wrong Grace? Mum?' Josh asked.

'Oh no, everything's fine. Couldn't be better really. I saw Emily the other night.' Grace went on in a rush. 'She seems a little happier. Enjoying her job I think.'

Josh thought for a second. 'Yes she does like it. It's what she should have been doing all along.'

'Oh, I totally agree,' Grace said, trying to ignore Olga's cynical smile.

'Being outdoors all day,' Josh continued.

'She's always liked animals,' Grace said, suddenly seeing a vivid image of Emily sitting on a horse.

Josh laughed.

'Well I don't think the animal life is what attracted her to it. I imagine she kills quite a lot of them.'

Grace's face cleared.

'She's a gardener!'

'Well of course she is,' Josh said, 'what are you on about?'

'I'm just – I'm not making any sense,' Grace said, 'excitement I suppose. Too much adrenaline. And how does she get to – eh – work ? To eh …'

Josh looked at Olga who was looking down into her empty glass, anywhere but at Grace.

'To the Botanic Gardens?' Josh said.

Grace made a little explosive noise. 'Where else?'

Josh turned to Olga. 'Grace lives in a dream you know. I don't think she had the remotest idea what Em did.'

'Of course she know,' Olga was replenishing her glass and then she gave Grace the smallest smile of complicity.

'You'd think I knew nothing about my children. You'd think I was a bad mother.'

'I don't know Grace, were you?' asked Josh. 'You were forgetful. A forgetful mother.'

'I was not.'

'I thought we celebrate – not fight,' Olga raised her glass to them both.

'We're not fighting,' Grace sat down and smiled tightly. Then she got up and went into the living room. After a bit the other two followed. Josh seemed more cheerful. He lifted his glass and clinked it, rather loudly against Olga's. 'Three cheers. To Olga.'

'And my agent, and my financial adviser,' finished Olga.

All three sat companionably for a moment. Josh tasted his drink and made a brief moue of distaste, 'Jesus! I hate vodka,' but he drank it anyway.

'I remember you leaving us in the cinema once.'

'Enough already,' Olga threw her eyes up to heaven.

Josh stared dreamily into his glass and then out the window and beyond so that Grace felt afraid. Afraid of what he might see there.

'Yes. In the cinema. One minute you were there, the next minute you were gone.'

'I don't remember that.'

'Well there you are. That's what you did.'

'No.' Grace put down her glass, 'And what did you do?'

Josh picked up a cushion and held it for a minute. Then he threw it at Grace – quite gently, as though they were having a game.

'What do you think I did? I was five for fuck's sake. Emily was barely four. We waited.'

'You waited for me?' Grace couldn't help feel a surge of gratitude – of love.

'Yes we waited. But you never came, Grace. You never came.'

'How?' Grace didn't know how to continue.

'Someone from the newspaper came – from Dad's newspaper.' Josh smiled, 'He bought us chips.'

'I'm so sorry.' Grace tried to remember the incident. Surely she would remember something so dreadful. Like something a mad person might do. Had she been mad then?

Josh picked up another cushion. He passed it from hand to hand. Olga took the cushion from him.

'Leave her alone, is no big deal. So she left you in a movie theatre. You should be so lucky to be in a movie theatre.'

Josh sat down on the floor between the TV and the bookshelves. 'It was a big deal,' he said, almost to himself.

Olga hunkered down beside him, her face gentle, soft. 'So, what was the name of the movie?' she asked

'You know, I can't remember,' said Josh.

'Well then,' said Olga, 'it was no big deal. Otherwise you'd remember.'

'It was *Sabrina Fair* – a re-run,' Grace said, almost to herself – she picked up the cushion Olga had thrown on the couch. 'It was the cushion that reminded me. I brought cushions for them to sit on because they were so small then.'

'I hope the man from newspaper bring them back – the cushions,' Olga said, her voice flat and practical.

'No, no he didn't,' and Grace began to laugh.

After a while, Josh did too.

'Let's go out. Let's go out – go mad,' Olga said.

Josh was suddenly all business. He keyed in a number on his cell phone and said, 'Louisa? Hi. It's – oh,' he grinned at the two women, 'well spotted! So have you got anything for tonight? Nine-ish? For three. What?' Then he smiled just at Olga, 'Oh, definitely Louisa – very heavy smoking.'

The restaurant was a big, buzzing place – the tables too close together so that the waiters had to sashay between them, their trays held high, their long white aprons brushing against the backs of diners as they twirled and spun and deftly delivered plates of pasta, the restaurant's speciality. Their table was barely big enough for three and was covered in cutlery, glasses, bread baskets, butter pats, little dishes containing flavoured oils and olives, and tall salt and pepper pots that trembled and threatened to fall every time a waiter passed. It was a restaurant where everyone seemed to know each other and the waiters' task was made even more difficult as customers swung back on their chairs to engage people on other tables in conversation. It had the feeling of a crowded railway station where you are swept along by a tide of people, managing to climb aboard, adrenaline pumping, just as the doors of the train slam closed.

Grace wasn't sure she liked it. But she could see that Olga loved it. Per-haps she'd spent a great deal of time in crowded stations, catching trains at the last minute. A number of people had fallen silent at their entrance, pointing out Olga to a neighbour or fellow diner although these were people used to celebrity. Olga seemed oblivious – Josh covertly pleased.

He opened the wine list with a flourish, studied it intently, making little faces, ranging from grudging approval to a pursed-mouth annoyance. All of a sudden, he took on the expression of an uncertain little boy – ready to sulk.

'Will you be having wine Grace?'

Grace readied herself to exert extreme forbearance but then, strangely, she found she didn't need to. She didn't want any wine.

'No,' she said, 'no thanks.'

Josh's face softened with relief. He ordered a bottle from the top end of the list. Grace smiled, anticipating his disappointment because Olga would drink it as she drank all alcohol, thirstily and with complete indifference. Grace and Josh had pasta while Olga had steak.

'Why pay all that money for something I make when there is no money?' she said.

They talked in spurts, having to shout, to repeat things. It was a restaurant where conversation was limited to sporadic questions and short answers, at least in the front part where they were. The back was quieter, more intimate. They were having coffee when Josh said: 'God – look who it is! Emily! Emily?' shouted Josh, standing up and waving his napkin.

Grace and Olga turned round to where he was looking. Emily was coming out of the back of the restaurant. She was with Travis. His hand was at her back, easing her through the throng of tables. Emily was laughing at something he had said.

'Em?' Josh shouted again. Emily looked over. She squinted against the glare, the tumult of people and then, recognizing Josh, waved and said something to Travis. Then she saw Olga and Grace and bobbed her head in greeting. She seemed about to continue on their path to the door but Travis redirected her until they were both at the table.

'Well, small world,' Grace and Travis said, almost in unison. 'You remember Olga, Emily,' Grace said, 'oh and eh Travis,' she made her voice hesitate, 'this is Olga – and,' she laughed 'Olga this is Travis – we worked together yonks ago.' Grace suddenly felt overwhelmed with gratitude that they were in this noisy, high-pitched restaurant so that her inane introductions seemed gay and social rather than taut with awkwardness.

She could hear Travis asking Olga if she were the woman on the posters and Josh laughing and asking if they'd like to join them – an empty invitation as the table clearly couldn't accommodate them. Grace smiled up at Emily. She'd had her hair done and it formed little commas around her face. She had on lipstick and her eyes were smoky and lustrous. She was wearing a thin summer dress speckled with a pattern of varying shades of blue and mauve. Grace's napkin fell to the floor. She bent to pick it up and, in doing so, saw Emily's shoes – delicate blue shoes with tiny heels. Her legs were pale and recently shaved. There was a tiny bead of dried blood where she had cut herself. Grace felt such a stab of love and fear for her – as though the razor had gashed her own skin. She sat up and anchored her napkin more firmly on her knee.

'No,' Travis was saying, 'we'd better be getting along. Great meeting you,' he said to Olga, 'and nice to see you again Grace.'

'Ditto!' she said lightly and then to Emily, 'You look lovely Emily. Really.'

Emily hesitated and then she leaned forward and brushed Grace's cheek with her lips, just for a second, and then she and Travis left, his hand hovering at the small of her back but not touching it.

TWENTY-FOUR

THE LAST THING Grace expected to see on the step was a policeman. A policeman and a man – the words of some pub song rattled through her head – two policemen and a man, down by the river saw-li-ah.

'Mrs Sherwin?'

'What?'

'You are Mrs Sherwin.'

'Yes?' Grace agreed, her voice thin with a frantic edge to it.

The uniformed guard looked down the road – his colleague smiled at Grace.

'Do you think we could come in?'

'Why?'

Grace looked at them, simultaneously seeing, out of the corner of her eye, a soft-top Golf GTI slowing down. Driving it was Red. Grace's mouth dropped open. She just couldn't help it. She found herself motioning frantically with her head like a character in a bad play. By now Red had noticed her visitors and was drawing away. The detective and the guard looked after him, suspiciously. Grace raised her arm and started to wave gaily.

'Just a neighbour,' she said.

'Nice car,' said the garda, resentfully.

'Oh, I don't think it's his,' Grace told him with a mad little laugh.

'His dad's then,' said the garda, cheered by this news.

'So?' The detective was moving impatiently from one foot to the other. 'Can we come in?'

The fact was that Grace was not unused to the presence of police on her doorstep. On two occasions she'd been visited by police to tell her that they had Emily in custody. On those occasions she'd found herself on the defensive; as though it were she who'd passed out in a park or stolen the lipstick.

One time she'd cried. She'd said: 'It's not my fault.' The garda then hadn't replied. He'd just looked away as though bored. Perhaps he was just bored with the mundanity of the charges involved.

She looked at the faces of the two men to see if she could read anything in them. It wasn't her parents anyway. She'd been talking to her father only minutes before the ring at the door.

The men were growing impatient.

'Can we come in?' one of them asked again.

'By all means. Certainly.' Grace threw open the door and started to wave her arm around in a hostessy way. She led the way into the living room, agitatedly plumping cushions as she went and indicated that they should sit. Neither man seemed inclined to sit.

'Do you have an Olga Koza … ?' The guard gave up after the first syllable, 'A Russian woman staying here?'

'Olga?'

'Yes.'

'Yes?'

'And she is resident with you?'

'Resident with me?' Grace's voice seemed incapable of behaving without an interrogative curve at the end.

'And she has been in this country how long?'

'About a week and a half,' Grace said, relieved to be able to utter a sentence that ended with a full stop rather than a question mark.

The man, the detective, was doing all the talking while the guard's eyes cased the living-room like an estate agent. This notion was cemented by his next words.

'You've a spot of damp over the window there. You'd want to have that seen to.'

Grace and the detective looked over to the window, and the detective frowned, whether at the idea of the presence of damp or because the guard had spoken out of turn Grace didn't know, but she took unreasonable consolation from the fact that the guard had made such an idle – such a friendly – remark. This feeling of relief was swiftly dissipated by the detective's next question.

'And this woman's status in this country?'

Grace wasn't sure what he meant. Social status? She hesitated.

'She's my friend,' she said finally.

The two men looked at her. Then all three of them looked at the ceiling, Grace nervously, the two men with curiosity as Olga's voice rang out.

'Grace, I can't find my focking stockings. Did you see?'

'Is that the woman in question?'

Grace's thought processes emerged from the fog around which they had been blundering. Papers. They were looking for Olga's papers.

'Woman?' Her conversation had moved back to question marks again.

'May we go up?' asked the detective over his shoulder.

Grace shrugged, frantically trying to remember the telephone number of a solicitor friend of Lionel's who had been nice to her once at a party.

The two men climbed the stairs. Grace followed.

The door of Olga's room was open and she was going through the drawers like a housebreaker.

'Focking things!' she shouted and then turned round in surprise at her visitors.

'These men are from the police,' Grace said. Olga put her hands on her hips and grinned.

'I didn't think they worked for the buses,' she said.

This nonplussed Grace and the men, but then the guard laughed, took off his hat and twirled it in his hands.

'We just need to see your passport,' the detective said.

'It's in my bag,' said Olga, retrieving her bag from under the bed.

Grace waited, for a moment as curious as the police to see what would emerge.

But the guard had started to laugh and was pointing at Olga.

'It's you, isn't it?'

Olga smiled lazily.

'I knew it was you the minute I came into the room. The minute!'

The detective was frowning again, anxious perhaps not to convey the impression that he was gratified by this encounter with near celebrity.

Olga reached into her bag and took out a passport. The detective took it.

'I'm British citizen,' she said casually.

'Your name is Olga Jones?' the detective said in disbelief.

'My name is Olga Kozarzewski Jones. I am divorce from my husband Mr Ewan Jones. I have paper.' She walked over to her suitcase and opened a zip at the side. She gave some papers Grace couldn't see to the detective.

'I return to my maiden name,' Olga said in a bored voice.

The detective flicked through the passport.

'You're older than you look,' he said, getting his own back.

'Sorry to have disturbed you,' he said to Grace as she showed the men out, 'we had … information.'

'I see,' said Grace. 'Can you tell me where this "information" came from?'

'I'm afraid not.'

'Did it come around lunchtime yesterday? From Myles Kitchen?'

The two men, reluctant to look Grace in the eye, busied themselves checking each side of the street. When they judged that suburbia was sufficiently safe to allow him to speak, the detective replied, 'I'm afraid I can't say.'

'Don't worry about it,' Grace said and closed the door.

She took the stairs two at a time. Olga was still opening and closing drawers, cursing about her stockings as though nothing had happened.

'Bastards!'

'Oh they just do their job,' Olga said and then, triumphantly, 'There they are! Great!' She retrieved a pair of stockings from under a pile of magazines.

'I didn't mean them – I meant the agency. The bastards must have done it so they'd have you over a barrel and be able to call the shots.'

'Then why they agree yesterday afternoon?'

'They didn't sign anything did they – did they?' Grace sat down on the bed and took a cigarette from the pack beside Olga's bed. 'Hah!' she said, 'but we got them, we got them,' then a thought occurred to her.

'You never told me you were married.'

Olga was tidying or rather moving the things on the floor with her foot into one pile in the corner.

'You never ask.'

'To an Englishman?'

Olga took a cigarette.

'Pig.'

Grace nodded sympathetically.

'Did he – hit you?' Until London, the idea of anyone hitting Olga seemed ridiculous but now less unlikely.

Olga shook her head, blowing smoke through her nose in two impatient plumes.

'No. Nice man. He farm pig. I marry for passport. Stay with him one month. Leave him – and his pigs.'

They both jumped at the sound of Grace's mobile ringing in the other room. It was Red.

'Jesus Grace. Dat was close. What did dey want?'

'Someone reported Olga to Immigration.'

'Who'd do dat?'

'We know who. It's OK.'

'Bastards!' said Red.

'Isn't it one of your main concerns that Immigration do a good job?'

He ignored that.

'Anyway Grace, I had to leave de Golf back sharpish. Pity. Would have been a nice day for it.'

'You wouldn't have a car of your own handy?'

'I can get one.'

'Of your own Red.'

She could hear a steady tattoo through the phone as Red drummed his fingers against his newly-shaved skull.

'Oh never mind. I'll get a taxi.'

Grace had told her father she'd drop over. He'd said that her mother was having one of her good days.

'I could get de brudder's van.'

'Are you sure?'

'Don't put on dat smarmy voice you use wit your clients for me Grace.'

He'd hung up before she could think of a reply.

Red deposited Grace outside her parents' home then disappeared down the road, the van catching fitfully as he changed gear, the exhaust trailing diesel fumes. Grace used her key and once inside shouted, 'Pops?'

'He's in the garden,' came a voice from the kitchen.

Emily was drinking coffee at the kitchen table. Grace's mother, looking remarkably alert, was making scones.

'Hello?' said her mother, her head to one side.

'It's Grace,' she said hastily, circumventing any confusion in her mother's mind. Sometimes she thought Grace was her long-dead sister, occasionally that she was canvassing.

'I know,' said her mother crossly, cutting out shapes in the scone dough with a cup. She placed them side-by-side on a baking tray, popped them in the oven and then looked around with a satisfied air.

'Well that's that!' she said. Then her expression changed. Her eyes darted around the room, frightened, like a child lost in a crowded supermarket. Grace didn't know what to do but fortunately Emily got up and took her grandmother's arm.

'Would you like a little lie down?'

Grace's mother glared at Emily and spoke crossly.

'I've scones in.'

'We'll watch them,' Grace said.

'Watch what?' her mother was looking at Grace with her head to one side as though the answer to this question might be amusing. A slight smile played around her lips.

But Emily was leading her gently out the door and Grace could hear Emily's voice.

'The scones you silly old thing.'

From inside Grace's bag, her mobile sounded. 'Yes,' she said tensely into the phone.

'Grace?'

'Lionel!' Grace spoke carefully, 'How are you?'

'I'm OK sweets.'

'Any news on the paper?'

From the oven, the smell of baking drifted around the room.

'Gone, kaput. All done bar the shouting.'

'And how are you holding up?'

Lionel had put his hand over the mouthpiece but she could still hear his voice. 'Shut up you little bastards – bugger off!' Then an indecipherable series of female shouts and complaints and Lionel's voice again. 'Grace, for God's sake let me come back. This is – it's over between …' Then there was a yowl of pain and Lionel's voice saying, 'I'm bleeding. Jesus Christ I'm bleeding!'

Emily had returned. Grace looked over at her and made a face.

'I'm at the parents', Lionel,' she paused, 'OK then. Use your key.'

'You're a star Gr …' and then the line went dead.

'I think your father has tired of playing "Happy Families",' Grace said to Emily.

'Never was his game.'

Grace went over to the kettle and pushed the switch. She opened a cupboard.

'Not that one,' Emily said, 'the far one.'

'Oh.'

Grace went to the other cupboard and found the tea caddy. The kettle boiled, a brief tumult in the quiet of the kitchen. She brought her tea over to the table and sat down opposite to Emily.

'So how are things going with Travis?' Grace felt that her voice sounded strange, forced.

'Fine.'

'I knew him years ago.'

'I know.'

'He was in a commercial – for Javelin. The first we did actually.'

Emily sighed and sat back from the table, looking Grace in the eye and giving her all her attention in an exaggerated way. Grace dropped her eyes.

'Anyway. There you are. Small country.'

Emily made a sound, an expulsion of air that might have been a laugh.

'I know,' she said, 'he told me.'

Grace felt a pain in her stomach, like acid.

'What did he tell you?'

Emily got up and walked over to the sink with her mug. She laughed properly then.

'Look at Gramps. He's still trying to dig up that tree stump. Won't give up.'

Grace put down her mug with a clatter.

'What did he tell you?'

Emily turned round to face her and folded her arms.

'That he'd been in prison.'

The bones in Grace's arm seemed to melt with relief. She couldn't lift her tea.

'I see,' she said in a level voice.

'So you telling me about it is a waste of time.'

'I wasn't going to tell you about it.'

Emily made a contemptuous noise at the back of her throat.

'I wasn't.'

Emily came back and resumed her seat at the table.

'Yeah, right,' she said.

'It was his business. And it was a long time ago.'

Emily turned one of the many rings she wore on her fingers. She wound it round and round so that the silver glinted in the light.

'Were you really not going to say anything?'

'No.'

Emily thought about this.

'I like him,' she said finally. 'Did you like him?'

'I hardly remember him.'

'Well you had lunch with him. Did you think he'd changed?'

'He was different then. Very … very. Very intense – a bit scary really. Like a land mine. Everyone was very careful where they walked.' Grace laughed shakily.

'Were you surprised when you ran into him?'

'Yes. It was funny. A coincidence. Mike and I had just been working on the most recent Javelin commercial so it was strange running into him like that.'

There was a rap at the window. Grace's father was standing there, mouthing something through the glass. He was very red in the face, either from his efforts with the tree stump or from irritation at not being able to make himself clear to them. He mimed the action of lifting something and drinking. Emily giggled and went to the kettle. Outside the window, Grace's father threw his eyes up to heaven but he was smiling.

When Emily had delivered his tea, she returned to the table.

'So how did you think he'd turn out?' she asked.

Grace paused. If she'd thought about Travis at all during the years between the shoot and their meeting in the pub, it was probably to think that he'd end up back in prison. She'd known at the time that he hadn't much future as an actor; that he was a one trick pony, capable of conveying an air of menace, of threat coupled with a certain boyish charm, but not much more than that.

She tried to explain this to Emily, not very successfully.

'So you think he's a loser?'

'I didn't say that. Some people have qualities when they are young that don't travel. Age diminishes them.'

'What?' An explosion from Emily.

'I didn't mean "diminishes" them as a person — what I meant was that those bits of them that have no place in a person who's older, disappear.'

'Like what?'

'Well he doesn't need to appear to be that dangerous, that unpredictable anymore. And he's a bit old for boyish charm.'

'You think he's too old for me?'

'No I don't.'

'You think being a bouncer is some nothing job?'

'Jesus Emily, stop interrogating me. I couldn't care what he does. I've never cared about things like that. You know that.'

Emily let her shoulders slump and gave the slightest shake of her head.

'I don't know what you care about.'

Grace rubbed at the ring her mug had made on the table.

'I care about you.'

'Yeah …' Emily started to say.

'Don't say "Yeah, right",' Grace imitated Emily's breezy cynicism.

The back door opened with a clatter and Grace's father appeared, holding his mug as though it were something he'd come upon by chance.

'What we need is a good downpour,' he said, staring out the window, 'a flood. Something to shift that tree stump.'

'Why don't you just leave it?' Emily said. 'It's not doing any harm. It looks nice. You could train a few climbers over it. Would you like me to get you some?'

'I would not. I've more to do than fiddle around with clematis and rubbish thank you very much.'

'Please yourself,' said Emily, not put out.

'It's it or me,' her grandfather said. 'I'll shift it or die trying.'

'Die is right,' Emily told him. Grace's father laughed.

'You can't kill a bad thing,' he said swiftly followed by, 'Where's Mother?'

'She's gone for a lie down.'

'Ah well,' said Grace's father, hopping around on one leg as he tried to extricate himself from his wellingtons. Emily got up and went over to him. She grinned at him and then bent over slightly, close to him. Gratefully, he rested his hand on her shoulder and slipped out of, first his good boot and then the one he'd cut down to accommodate his bandage.

'Thanks pet,' he said, patting Emily on the shoulder. Grace felt a stab of jealousy.

'You used to like clematis,' she said sharply, as though defending a person rather than a plant. 'There was a clematis on the front of the house. You loved it.'

Her father frowned.

'I don't think so,' he said.

'Yes there was. It was white. It came out in May. It covered the whole house.'

Her father placed his boots tidily together and put them beside the cooker.

'That was next door,' he said, 'next door had clematis.'

Grace took a mouthful of her cold tea. Of course. Yes. It *was* next door. Why had she been so sure it was this house? Maybe it was because when she was a child she had seen the whole street as her home, as hers. She had always thought of her childhood as solitary but in fact it was filled with people – all the people in this street whose houses she would wander into, always assuming that she'd be welcomed with open arms.

The clematis-covered house had been owned by the Cohens, an elderly couple who kept themselves to themselves. He had been a jeweller and now worked at home. Grace visited him almost daily, sometimes ringing the doorbell but more often climbing over the wall into their garden. She'd tap on the French windows until she got Mr Cohen's attention. He'd look up appearing almost frightened and then let her in. He always said the same thing, 'What a nice surprise.'

Grace perched on a chair opposite him as he laboured over his task with his tools laid out with a surgeon's precision. She told him about girls at school and minutely detailed the plot of things she'd seen on television. She asked his advice on matters important to her: his assistance in choosing a name for her dog if, that is, she ever got a dog. Mr Cohen would nod and purse his lips, making only an occasional contribution to the conversation. He'd say things like, 'I bet I know how this one turns out,' when she was acting out a scene from a TV play. But he never did know. He was always as surprised as anything to discover the identity of the murderer or to find out which of the two dashing young men stood beside the heroine in a church decked with flowers in the final reel.

As for the naming of her dog, he thought Rover was a poor choice because you might get it mixed up with the car of the same name. Grace listened to everything he said with great attention.

At some point during Grace's visit, Mrs Cohen would appear with small cups of very sweet coffee and almond biscuits which Grace didn't like but ate out of politeness. She longed to be asked to stay for dinner because she wanted to see what Jewish people ate, but whenever she stretched her visit up to dinner time, the Cohens found a pressing need to go to the shops or to visit someone and all three would leave together.

Once or twice Grace had watched the Cohens from her bedroom window. On those occasions they must have forgotten something because they only went a little way up the road and then they returned to their house with its tea-cosy of flowers.

Sitting at the kitchen table with Emily sitting opposite her, Grace laughed.

'I bet the poor things just invented an errand to get rid of me,' she said.

'What?'

'It was next door that had the clematis. The Cohens.'

'Decent enough fellow for a Jew,' said her father.

'Jesus Gramps!'

'For God's sake Dad!'

For a moment the two women were united in the face of Grace's father's casual racism.

'What did I say?' he demanded, mystified, and he padded out of the kitchen in his stocking feet. They could hear him whistling as he went up the stairs.

'He doesn't mean it,' Grace said. The two women regarded each other gravely for a moment and then burst out laughing.

'Yeah, right!' they carolled in unison.

Their laughter died almost as soon as it had begun and Grace felt a familiar unease descend. She stole a glance at Emily and saw that Emily was watching her narrowly. It was like finding yourself in front of a camera. Grace's face fell into a stiff expression, one of mingled worry and expectation, underpinned with a tight smile – the face that looked back at her from photographs. Her shoulders felt hard and angular, as though they didn't belong to her. She wanted to ask Emily if she'd slept with Travis yet. This was stupid – of course she had.

The curious thing was that Grace herself no longer felt fearful or guilty. This was because the incident had taken on the quality of a dream. It didn't seem real at all. If the worst happened, Grace knew she would be able to lie about it with absolute conviction. It startled her when Emily seemed to have read her thoughts.

'I like him because he's real – because he never lies. You know where you are with him.'

'Telling the truth is an over-rated virtue,' Grace said, conscious that she might have said those words before.

'That's because you're a born liar. It's your job to lie.'

'Not any more.' Grace looked up towards the ceiling from where the sound of her father's heavy tread could be heard – one solid step followed by the lighter, dragging sound of his injured leg.

'Did you mind losing your job?'

'I don't know. Yes. Yes. Of course I did. I was stupid – I should have fought it. Still, the Olga thing mightn't have happened if I had. Everything's for the best I suppose.'

'You always fall on your feet, don't you?'

Grace felt around in her pocket for cigarettes and found a crumpled packet.

'Oh yes. Everything's been easy-peasy for me.'

Emily snorted and looked away.

From the stairs came the sound of Grace's father.

'Just going for a walk,' he shouted. Emily smiled.

'He can't be still poor old thing.' Then she laid her hands on the table so that all her rings were visible against her callused fingers and dirt-encrusted nails.

'Do you mind if I ask you something?'

Grace did mind. She felt little skitters of fear race around her body.

'No. Not at all.'

'Have you started drinking again?'

Grace's reply was cold.

'No.'

'I just thought I smelt drink when you were here a week or so ago.'

'You imagined it.'

'I know how hard it is.'

Grace smiled.

'And how would you know?' she said.

Emily smiled back, her expression as pleasant as Grace's.

'Forget it.'

Grace was going to say something but then she became aware of an acrid smell. She looked round and saw a coil of smoke around the oven door.

'Oh shit.' She ran to the cooker and threw open the door, drawing back as a billow of blackness gusted out.

'Christ, how could we have forgotten them? Oh poor Mum.'

Emily reached for her tea, unmoved.

'She won't remember making them so it's no big deal.'

Grace lifted out the scorched scones and put them on the sink.

'I suppose not,' she said. She opened the window to let the smoke escape.

At the end of the garden she could see a wrought-iron chair, almost obscured with foliage. For a moment she fancied her mother sitting there as she used to do during summers long ago, a paperback upturned on her knee, face turned to the sun, eyes closed, smiling at the day.

TWENTY-FIVE

GRACE WOKE out of a deep sleep unsure where she was. Olga was sitting on the side of her bed in the half-light that glowed through the heavy, drawn curtains.

'What is it?' Grace had got up for work that morning and then, inexplicably, felt so tired – so exhausted – that she had phoned Mike and said she wouldn't be in till after lunch. She'd lain down on the bed just as she was and immediately had fallen asleep. She tried to remember what she had been dreaming, something vivid and real – more real than real life. In the dream everything had fallen into place. She'd seen the solution to everything with such clarity, and it had been so simple that she'd laughed. Laughed out loud – maybe that's what woke her. Or maybe it was Olga's hand on her neck. Because Olga was stroking her neck very gently – just as Grace's mother had done long, long ago. Grace closed her eyes tight and then opened them. Everything seemed an effort.

'Grace? Are you awake?'

'Yes,' said Grace, not sure if she was or not.

'It's your mother. She's ill.'

Grace felt suddenly very thirsty. Her tongue seemed swollen, stuck to the roof of her mouth. She reached for the glass on the table and drank half the tepid water it contained. Olga got up.

'She's had a stroke Grace.'

'What? What?' Grace tried to get up but for some reason she couldn't. While sleeping, her arms had become entangled in the sleeves of her jacket. She wrenched it off and lifted herself on one elbow, then managed to get her feet on the floor.

'Travis is coming,' Olga said, 'he'll be here in a minute.'

'What?' Grace's voice was gathering strength – her head clearing.

'He's coming to bring you over to the house. Can I get you anything?'

Grace shook her head and got up and went to the bathroom. She threw cold water on her face – avoiding her eyes. She'd gone to bed with her make-up on. She went to get another jacket and, while she was doing this, the doorbell rang. She could hear the sound of quiet voices – too quiet for her to hear what was being said. Travis was waiting in the hall. Grace didn't greet him, just went outside and got into the car. Travis followed her. As they drove away, Grace looked back. Olga was still standing in the doorway. Neither of them said anything for a while and then Grace said, 'Why are you here?'

'Emily rang me.'

Grace could barely speak – her throat filled with rage like mucus.

'Emily rang you? To tell you that my mother had had a stroke?'

Travis answered evenly.

'She didn't want you getting a taxi. She rang me so that I could pick you up.'

'Oh.'

Travis drove rapidly, threading his way deftly from lane to lane. The traffic was lighter than usual. As they passed a pub, Grace noticed crowds milling outside in the sunlight, some holding pints – laughing, excited.

'What's happening?' Grace asked.

'Ireland versus Germany.'

'What?'

'World Cup.'

Emily opened the door before they'd got out of the car. Grace brushed past her and went straight to the kitchen. She could hear her father whistling tunelessly and the clatter of a fork against a Pyrex bowl. Her father was beating eggs. He held the bowl against his hip and flopped the raw yolks through the white. He smiled brightly at Grace for a moment before returning to his task. He added salt and pepper and then scissored some chives into the beaten egg. In a pan on the cooker, butter sizzled and spat.

'Dad?' Grace put her hand on her father's shoulder. He shook it off and poured the contents of the bowl into the frying pan. The butter hissed. Her father drew a wooden fork through the eggs as they congealed, letting the raw mixture run underneath.

'Shouldn't we get to the hospital?' Grace said.

'I am of no use to your mother if I haven't eaten,' he said, not turning round.

'Keep your strength up,' Travis offered.

'Exactly!' Grace's father looked at Travis gratefully.

Grace sat down at the kitchen table; Emily stayed where she was, leaning against the kitchen door, her face unreadable. Then she said, 'The ambulance came twenty minutes ago. They took her to Vincent's.'

Grace's father brought the pan to the table and slid the omelette onto the plate that was waiting. It was thick and yellow and barely cooked. Her father buttered some bread and cut it into neat fingers. He put a sliver of omelette on one of the fingers and handed it to Grace. After a moment she took it and put it in her mouth. It tasted very good.

'I make a first-rate omelette,' said her father, 'first-rate!' and then he began to eat, slowly and methodically in time to a mental metronome. Halfway through the omelette, tears started to slide down his cheeks. Some fell on the plate; some flowed down under his chin and were lost in the frayed neck of his pullover. He made no sound. The only sound was the scrape of his fork, and the tremble of his dentures at each tentative chew. When he'd finished, he took his plate and placed it in the sink. Then his shoulders sank and he walked towards Travis. He stopped and looked around at them eagerly, pleased to have found a question so normal – so everyday.

'Will I need a coat?' he asked.

'No,' Travis said, 'you'll be all right.'

The streets were deserted because of the match even though this was a working day. Grace opened the car window. Paused at traffic lights, they heard a huge wave of cheers burst from a nearby pub – a cheer that rose and rose.

'I hope this is the end for her,' her father said and, as he said it, the cheer dropped into a deep-throated sigh – a long, falling 'Aaaah' from thousands of football crowd voices.

'Must have missed a goal,' Travis said, in explanation.

A man in a green and white scarf ran out of the pub, yelling something into a mobile phone. Impatient, he finished the call and went back in. For a moment, through the open door, a whole sea of people was revealed before the door swung shut again. It was as though the world had taken a fork in the road so that Travis, Emily, Grace and her father were travelling alone, the only people in the whole country who were not part of the football frenzy. The lights changed and they turned into the hospital – past the mortuary chapel, past the car parks and up to the crescent in front of the A & E. Once in Accident and Emergency, her father seemed unsure. He hovered around the waiting area.

'You again!' a nurse called over her shoulder as she ran past, her thick-soled shoes making a sucking noise against the linoleum. Moments later, she returned.

'Well?' she said in a jolly voice. 'How's the patient?'

'I don't know,' Grace's father said, lost and uncertain.

'I'll take a look at it in a while. We're very busy.'

While she was talking, she was looking past Grace's father to the TV, high on the wall where the match was being played out, the sound turned down so that the cheers were muted. A man with a blood-soaked handkerchief held over his eye tried to follow the action on the screen.

'What? Look at what?' Grace's father said querulous, uncomprehending.

'Your leg!' the nurse said. Grace had forgotten all about their last visit here just days before. So, apparently, had her father. He looked down at his leg, puzzled.

'My father's all right,' Grace said to the nurse, 'it's my mother. She was taken in about an hour ago? Stroke?'

The nurse consulted a clipboard she held in her hand.

'Oh, yes.' She dropped her voice to a different level that was low and sympathetic.

Was that something you learned? Grace wondered. Was there

a whole song sheet of voices to suit different circumstances: the jolly 'get well soon' for a gardening accident and the lullabies of words for a stroke or a heart attack. Was there a special voice for cancer?

'She's been taken up to intensive care,' the nurse said. 'Just go across to the main entrance. The lifts are straight ahead – and then follow the signs.'

It was the dying moments of the match. Grace saw Travis's eyes drift back to the TV. Something was happening. The man with the handkerchief over his eye rose to his feet dropping the hand-kerchief to reveal a bloody mash of face; a nurse whooped. Outside they could hear a gathering thunder of cheers from the pub across the car park. People were spilling out into the street. Horns were blaring.

'Did we win?' Grace asked.

'A draw,' said Emily who up to now had sat in a corner of the waiting room as though she wasn't with them.

'A draw? Aren't we the cheery little lot all the same.'

Grace's mother lay on the pillows, a tube coming out of her mouth and another attached to her hand. She looked tiny in the iron bed – reduced to the size of a seven-year-old. The hand with the drip was almost skeletal, the veins standing out like ropes. Her hair was the colour of paper, thin and wispy. Between each breath, there was a long pause and then another rasping breath as though she were making a decision – will I bother with this one?

Emily and Travis waited in the corridor. Grace stood beside her father. A nurse whispered, 'The doctor will be here in a moment.' Her father started and looked around wildly imagining, perhaps, that she was talking about him. A young man in a white coat came in. Grace couldn't hear what he was saying – couldn't concentrate. She wanted to hear but every few seconds, she felt a sort of rushing in her ears. She could just discern occasional phrases: 'massive stroke', 'little hope', 'stats', 'comfortable'.

And then she was on the floor, her cheek resting against the linoleum – cool and slightly sticky. A nurse was taking her pulse. High overhead she could see her father looking down at her. His head was silhouetted against a fluorescent light, his hair standing out like a halo. He looked heroic, monumental.

They sat her on a chair and someone gave her a glass of water. It tasted of chlorine and plastic. Occasionally, her father stole glances at her over his shoulder, as though surprised to see her there – puzzled by her presence, as he would be by that of a stranger. The next few hours passed both slowly and quickly. A minute seemed to take forever and yet an hour passed in a flash. Grace's father sat by the bed. He sat very straight in the chair staring straight ahead.

Her mother died at six o'clock. She died just as the echo of the last stroke of the church bell died. At some point during the afternoon, Emily had cried. Grace didn't cry and neither did her father. When it was over, he got to his feet and strode out the door as though he had a pressing appointment. Emily, Travis and Grace had to hurry to catch up with him. Nobody spoke in the car until they were almost at her parents' house.

'Well that's that then,' said her father.

It was a small funeral: Grace and Lionel, Travis, Emily, Mike, Josh and Olga. There were a few old people, former patients of her father's, colleagues; rheumy-eyed old men who shook hands with each other gravely, recognizing in each other the one thing that they still shared – they were alive.

Her father didn't talk to anyone. When people shook his hand it was like a new gesture to him, a novel piece of social intercourse he found both fascinating and repellent. When they went back to the house, her father clambered from the car almost before it had fully stopped and raced into the house. Grace found him in the garden. He was digging around the rose bushes, turning the earth that was rich and dark after the rain.

Her father thrust the spade deep into the ground and left it there. Then he sat down heavily on the garden seat so that the slats bent underneath his weight. He ran his hand gently over the peeling paintwork.

'It seems only five minutes ago since she was sitting here,' he said.

Grace sat down beside him. The roses were overblown and lollopy from the rain. Their scent shifted around in the breeze so that one moment her nostrils were filled with it and the next it was as if it she had imagined it. Something she had dreamt.

'What will you do?' she asked after a while.

'Oh, I'll probably just have an early night,' said her father.

And the answer comforted her.

TWENTY-SIX

IF THERE COULD BE SAID to be an upside to Grace's mother's death it was that Grace's going-away party was cancelled. Unfortunately, when Andrew had said cancelled he had actually meant postponed. So it was that two weeks later, Grace found herself in the upstairs bar of a pub near the agency surrounded by her colleagues and holding on to a going-away card, the cover of which was adorned with a peculiarly cruel cartoon. The annoying thing was that it was pretty accurate. Inside the card were various messages signed with names, many of which she didn't recognize. 'To a colleague and a friend,' Andrew had written. He had chosen another word before 'friend' but had crossed the word out. Grace squinted at the page trying to decipher it. Maybe it was 'stranger'. Stranger would have been more accurate. A number of people had written 'Amazing Grace' – with an exclamation mark. Mike had written 'Agent Provocateur', which made her smile.

There is something unutterably sad about an agency going-away party. This may have to do with the choice of venue. They tend to take place in a room over a pub and, while down below in the pub proper there is a heaving, jolly throng of merrymakers, upstairs in this gloomy, little-used room, voices echo and, even in high summer, the air is dank and cold. There is a particular carpet which covers the floor in every upstairs 'function room'. It is of a serviceable, dark hue scattered with roses or possibly something less pleasant. The pile has been beaten into a matted, greasy skin and smells of packet soup and, as Mike pointed out, 'Ooops!' When her father looked puzzled, Mike explained that it was the accumulation of all those tiny spillages from overfilled pints.

'Ooops!' Mike repeated and her father nodded out of politeness.

Grace had brought him along because she couldn't think what else to do with him. Emily was going out and she didn't like to leave him. He stood with a glass of whiskey in his hand looking lost, surrounded by uneasy groups of her colleagues, none of whom was drunk enough yet to relax. Grace shifted her feet. The carpet sucked at her shoes like a peat bog after rain.

'This is ghastly. Sorry Pops,' she said to her father.

'Oh, it's the best you can expect from this crowd,' her father said.

Since her mother's death, he'd moved around in a dream and one place was much the same as another to him. She'd brought him out for dinner one night and, absent-mindedly, he'd gotten to his feet when he'd finished and started tidying up the table. He'd stood beside the table with a stack of plates in his hands looking around the crowded restaurant for the kitchen sink – for the window overlooking the garden. Then he'd sat down again, quiet as a child, and waited for her to pay the bill.

Myles made a long, largely inaudible speech that must have amused him because, occasionally, he paused to chuckle at some particularly well-chosen bon mot. But in spite of his spurts of laughter, there was a haunted look about him and Grace thought she could detect a nerve in his forehead that throbbed like a tiny heart. This was the result of a series of incidents with his car. Over the last few weeks, he had received several parking tickets and had been clamped four times. One of the clampings had taken place when he was personally serving a meter attendant with tea and the chocolate biscuits reserved for clients.

The whole thing was a mystery really. Myles would park his car and feed the meter for the maximum time allowed, but when he returned to move the car, it wasn't there. On a couple of occasions he'd reported it stolen but the police were sceptical, given that the car was found two spaces away on an unpaid meter. Several people in the agency suggested that Myles might be getting forgetful. Angela started popping a couple of ginkgo biloba into his vitamin C. His speech finished, Grace saw him order a double at the bar. He no longer needed to worry about Breathalysers. He had sold his car for a knock-down price.

Myles was lucky to get a price for it at all. Grace's final small revenge – it was Red's idea – had been to empty a carton of milk over the back seat. It was a smell that lasted forever, the car dealer explained to Myles, handing him a cheque for a fraction of the cost of the one-year-old Jaguar.

Then it was time for Grace's speech. She shouted a few words over the noise about how much she'd enjoyed working there and thanking them for her present, a weekend at a health farm. She mentioned Olga and her new career as an agent. Then, as an aside, she'd said that Olga was Russian but, and she looked straight at Myles, she was also a British citizen. Myles smiled tightly. She said she might take up new things now that she had time on her hands – learn to drive for instance. She beamed at

Myles. During the incidents with his car, he had become increasingly paranoid and had begun to suspect everyone in the agency. Everyone except Grace of course – the non-driver.

Then, before she could stop him, her father was on his feet and amidst clapping and much laughter, made a short speech full of puns about the Civil Service, allusions to famous people who had started life in the Civil Service and sweeping comments about bureaucracy in general. No one found his theme in the least odd.

In the taxi on the way home, Grace said,

'Pops, I actually worked in advertising – you know?'

'Really!' said her father, astonished. 'Isn't that the strangest thing.' He looked out the window into the dark made darker still by the pools of light shed by windows and streetlights and after a while asked carefully, 'And when did you leave the Civil Service?'

Grace smiled. 'Oh, ages ago,' she said.

When the taxi dropped her at her house, Lionel was out in the front weeding the overgrown flower-bed by the light of the hall lamp.

'There's whatshisname,' said her father.

'Lionel,' Grace reminded him.

'I know,' he said crossly.

'Are you sure you'll be all right?'

'Emily will be home by now,' he said, his breath smelling of whiskey.

Grace kissed him on the cheek.

'Yes, yes,' he said impatiently, as though she was delaying him.

'What are you up to?' she asked Lionel as the taxi drew away.

'I was bored,' Lionel said, 'and now,' he slung a weed up to the step, 'I'm even more bored. Where's Olga?'

'She's staying over at Josh's.'

'So how did the party go?'

Grace told him about her father's speech. Lionel chuckled. Then she showed him her going-away card.

'Who is it meant to be?' he said disarmingly.

'Oh, fuck off!' she said.

'Well, "Olga's Agent", I don't think it's a bit like you.'

'Olga's agent. It's nice to acquire a new job description overnight.'

'You'll have to change your passport.' Lionel sat down, exhausted by his attempts at weeding. Grace sat down too.

'How do you feel about her and Josh?' Grace asked.

'You know me,' Lionel said.

Grace lit a cigarette and took a long slow drag. 'Too bloody well,' she said.

'It's best to just leave things alone, I find,' Lionel said.

Grace took another pull at her cigarette and then she smiled.

'Good luck to them,' she said.

And that is how Grace found herself sitting in a field, in the rain, swaddled in a variety of heavy-weather clothing while, in the distance, Olga, clad in a purple ballgown, walked towards the camera, her hair aflame, her skin pale as china. Even at this distance, Grace could see that Olga was not pleased. She watched the silent ballet of filming, the electricians fighting with diffusers against the wind, the camera operator arguing with the director. Olga's hands were on her hips and her hair was whipping around her as her head moved angrily. The agency people were leaning towards her, their hands outstretched, pleading. A young man with a golf umbrella was vainly trying to keep Olga dry, scuttling after her as she stamped around in a circle. Then Olga looked across at Grace, hoisted up the yards and yards of purple silk, and started to march towards her. She was wearing green wellingtons. As she strode through the field, the material worked itself free of her hands and got caught on the thistles in this remote farmland.

Olga arrived, eyes flashing. Grace's first instinct was to say something conciliatory – to point out how much money Olga was making and that film was a delicate and slow-moving medium and that everyone must be patient. But then she remembered that things had changed.

'I don't work for them, I work for you,' she said, in wonder.

'Yes!' said Olga, furious. 'You're my focking agent. Do something.'

Grace got to her feet and set off through the thistles, crushing them underfoot with her moon-boots. She followed the same route Olga had taken. Every few steps, she came upon a fragment of purple silk. She could hear Olga muttering behind her, her wellingtons sinking into the marshy ground.

'What the fuck is going on here?' Grace said. Andrew turned around, startled.

'We are trying to shoot a commercial,' the director said.

'My client is frozen. You have her standing out here in the rain and you're not even lit yet.'

'Well we need her standing in while we're lighting,' Andrew reminded Grace who a few weeks ago would have seen the necessity for this.

'I'm not having her freezing to death. It's like Siberia here.'

'Well she should feel right at home then,' the director was unable to stop a little smile at his own witticism.

'Excuse me?' Grace said dangerously.

The director turned his back and, as an afterthought, folded his arms.

'Get a stand-in or we walk.'

'I think you'll find that your contract …' but Olga and Grace were already in one of the jeeps with the heating turned on full.

Grace lit two cigarettes and handed one to Olga. Through the window they could see the crew milling around the director and occasionally stealing glances at the car. Olga's dress spilled out over the seats and into the back so that the two women seemed to be reclining in a huge purple silk bed.

'I don't think we're going to get too long out of this,' Grace said.

'Focking waste of time. Finish contract, get out. I don't like model. Is stupid thing and not very comfortable.' Olga stretched and rolled her bare shoulders. Outside they saw that a solution had been found. Andrew was standing in for Olga. He stood with his shoulders slumped in the rain, occasionally turning this way or that at the behest of the director. Grace sighed. It was all extremely satisfying.

'So what are you going to do when it's all finished?'

Olga snorted in exasperation.

'I tell you what I want, Grace. You never listen.'

TWENTY-SEVEN

'HI POPS.'

Her father didn't answer. 'Just thought I'd look in.' Grace sat down on an upturned terracotta pot. Her father was dividing seedlings. They trembled green and thick on egg-boxes.

'I'm fine, thank you,' he said finally. 'I'm not morose or suicidal. I'm eating well, I'm sleeping.'

Grace realigned a pile of ancient newspapers that lay on one of the shelves. 'You're always in the garden when I come, like a dad from an old English black and white film who potters in the potting shed – oh and takes nips of whiskey from a bottle he's got stashed in the compost.'

Her father's eyes lit up. He reached behind a pile of baling twine and plucked out an almost empty naggin of rum.

'There you are, rum – you don't know everything smarty-pants. Actually I'm quite rarely out here. It's just that you always seem to come at the same time, Grace. If you were to visit at other times, you would not find me out here. You might find me cooking. If you came on Thursday evenings, I'd be playing bridge. If you troubled

293

yourself to come on Monday evenings, you would not find me here at all because I'd be visiting my ex-receptionist who is kind enough to have me to dinner on Mondays. She makes a very fine stew.' Her father pondered on this, 'Although stew can pall after a while.'

He turned the remains of the rum in his hands with some distaste. There was a piece of bark caught in his hair. Grace reached over and plucked it out.

'Do you miss Mum? It'll be a year next week.'

'I've missed her for a great many years.'

He went back to thinning his seedlings. 'So how's life? How's the Ruskie?'

'Olga? Oh, she's fine. She bought a pub in West Cork – well they bought a pub.'

'Josh and her?'

Her father smiled.

'Good for them.'

'And Emily's pregnant apparently.'

'I know.'

'They seem happy enough. Travis is …'

Grace lost the thread of what she was saying. Her father passed his hand gently over the seedlings remaining in the box so that they sprang back under his hand like close-cropped hair.

'There!' he said, proud of them.

'And what about you?' he asked.

'I'm good.'

Her father pushed his picked-over egg-boxes into a line. It seemed very important to him suddenly that they were arranged just so. Grace looked at the ordered row of boxes and then, with a child's angry impulse, pushed one askew.

'I'm nearly fifty and I don't remember my life. I can't seem to concentrate.'

Grace got up so suddenly that the terracotta pot scraped on the slate and a red tear of clay rolled across the floor. Her father made an irritated sound between his teeth.

'I'm sorry.'

'It's only a flowerpot, Grace.'

Her father lifted it up to examine the damage.

'I'm sorry!'

'Oh, do stop saying that.'

'Sorry.' The word caught in her throat and became a laugh. Her father looked at her, his face serious, and then he started to laugh too. He laughed the way she remembered him laughing when she was young. Helplessly, tears starting to his eyes.

She remembered the bandit of his humour, how it crept up on him, how the silliest things would tickle him. She remembered being in church and some small thing would hijack her father into chuckles. It might be the words of a hymn or the petal of toilet paper on the priest's face where he had cut himself shaving.

'I'm sorry,' he would mouth to her mother, 'Sorry.' Trapped in the agony of his laughter, a prisoner behind the big, white billow of his handkerchief.

'Oh, dear, oh dear, oh dear,' said her father, supporting himself against a rake. 'I haven't laughed like that since …'

And of course that's when he'd forgotten how to laugh: years ago, when Grace's mother stopped laughing – or if she did laugh, no one knew what she was laughing at, least of all herself.

'I don't know what to do. Everything's opaque. Out there in the distance.'

Her father looked out the grimy window of the shed to where the last of the sun span off the roof of the greenhouse next door.

'Do you want my advice? Go away. Far away where everything

is so – so unexpected that you *have* to concentrate to know what to do next.'

'Like where?'

'I'm not a bloody travel agent.' He started to oil the garden shears with unusual thoroughness.

Grace started to tidy the topmost shelf, moving the boxes of nails, the slug pellets, a yellowed packet of seeds.

Her father unscrewed the cap of the rum and sniffed at it experimentally. He passed it to Grace.

'Does that smell like rum to you?'

Grace put the bottle to her nose.

'I don't know. I don't drink rum.'

Her father sighed.

'Well does it smell of weedkiller then?'

'I don't know. I don't drink that either.'

He put the cap on the bottle.

'Better safe than sorry.'

'You shouldn't put poisons in bottles that people might mistake for something you can drink. And you a doctor!'

He seemed not to have heard. He started to roll a piece of twine round and round his fingers, taking care to align the strands so that as it grew it resembled something solid like a piece of pottery.

'I'm glad the drink didn't get you again.'

Grace looked away.

'No need to talk about it,' he said.

'It was just a …' Grace couldn't think of a word.

'A glitch,' he suggested.

'Yes.'

Her father finished rolling the ball of twine. It was now bigger than his fist. He admired it for a second before moving on to another. Grace fingered the packet of seeds. Age had obscured

the illustration and the print. All that remained was a capital 'P'.
Pansies? Peonies?

'Why did you never say anything at the time?' she asked finally.

'I don't know. I'm not one for big things.'

'How do you mean?'

'Oh you know,' he threaded the string round and round, 'conversations where people end up shouting or tearful.'

'You and Mum shouted enough.'

'Oh that's different,' he caught himself, 'that *was* different. We understood each other.'

'And we don't?'

Her father smiled.

'Of course we do. We understand that it's best that people work things out for themselves. And I was right. You did.'

'Olga's always saying I should talk to Emily. About it I mean. Because we both, we both ...' Grace couldn't bring herself to put it into words.

Her father laughed. 'Talk about "it".'

'You know what I mean.'

'You'll talk to her when you're ready.'

'When she's ready, you mean.'

'Don't be so hard on her.'

'Do you think we're alike? Olga thinks we're alike.'

Her father gave this some thought.

'You're as alike as you need to be,' he said, which Grace didn't understand at all.

They walked back to the house. The grass was damp underfoot. Grace looked over at the roses – an early variety, pale pink, teetering on delicate stems, while one with sturdy, dark stalks and scimitar-shaped thorns had been dead-headed ready to flower again.

'They look as though they'll be good this year.'

'Oh I don't hold out much hope for them. Your mother was the one for the roses.' He squinted at a worn piece of plastic affixed to the base of one of the flowerless stems.

'Floribunda,' he said. 'She was fond of those.'

TWENTY-EIGHT

THE WOODEN BENCH that lolled against the wall of the West Cork pub could do with painting but Grace was too exhausted to care. She lay back against the curved slats and allowed her eyes to close so that the clatter of pots from the kitchen and sound of tap water gushing against the enamel sink faded into muffled and rather comforting background noise. The afternoon sun was strong and kaleidoscoped against her lids with pinpricks of light.

'Nice ping,' she murmured.

'What?' Lionel asked, sitting heavily down beside her so that the seat bounced in protest.

'It's what the camera operator would say when the lighting got this sort of glint off … oh, someone's eye, a ring, a piece of metal … "nice ping".'

'Mmmh,' Lionel said, interest waning. 'God I'm whacked.'

'She's a hard taskmaster.'

From the kitchen at the back of the pub, they could hear Olga's voice.

'Take all the shell off prawn, Josh. You leave half them on.'

'Poor Josh,' Grace laughed softly, letting her arms hang down behind the slats of the seat, totally relaxed.

'Ah, the holy family!'

Grace opened her eyes. Up the laneway across the road from the pub, she saw Travis and Emily approach. Travis's arm was draped over her brown shoulder.

'How did lunch go?' Travis called across the street.

'Busy,' Grace said and then, lowering her voice, lest Olga hear, 'Börscht didn't go too well.'

'Looked like someone had vomited,' Lionel explained.

'Someone with an ulcer,' Grace added.

Emily stood with her hand supporting her back. Grace noticed that she was beginning to show and that the tan of her stomach was rounded out against the open top button of her jeans.

'Go in and give Josh a break,' she told them, 'his fingers are beginning to bleed. He thinks Olga has been lying about her past and was definitely a prison guard in Stalag 19.'

'We're visitors,' Emily pointed out. 'Oh, all right,' she said grabbing a piece of Travis's shirt and dragging him behind her. Grace could hear them arguing as they made their way towards the back door of the pub – about names probably.

'It's quite feudal really, isn't it?' Lionel said when they were alone again.

'Olga?'

'No, the way we arranged our children's marriages – well, relationships. I found Olga for Josh and you found Travis for Emily. Quite neat.'

'Mmmh.'

They were silent for a while and then Lionel said, 'It's nice here.'

Grace stiffened, suddenly alert as Lionel continued, 'You wouldn't like … you know … you and me.'

'What do you mean?' Grace said.

'Getting together again.'

'We are together. Here. On this seat.' Grace peeled a ribbon of white paint from one of the slats.

'You know what I mean Grace.'

Grace looked out across the roofs of the houses across the street to where the sea began, sun shining off the waves, the white slash of seagulls swooping over a shoal of fish or sewage.

'Go home to your wife Lionel – your wife and your other two children.'

'No. That's over. Well over. She's with someone else now. Some social worker.'

'Oh – I'm sorry.'

'Right.' Lionel laughed, as though he'd been joking earlier. 'I might try writing a book.'

Grace allowed her eyes to close again. Lionel became animated: 'I mean, I've seen, I've lived through extraordinary times. I've met the people who've written history – talked to them, known them.'

'I take it this will be a work of fiction then,' Grace said.

Lionel looked offended for a moment and then relaxed back in the seat enjoying the afternoon sun.

'What happened to that bloke in your office – Mike?'

'He left.'

'And you never blew the whistle?'

'No harm was done at the end of the day.'

Once Grace had assured him she had no intention of turning him in, Mike had taken his courage – and two bin bags – in his hands and left Annalise. He'd also left advertising and was now a very successful actors' agent with offices in Dublin and London. The London office was run by two of his old school-chums – one of whom was twenty-sixth in line to the throne. When you've got

Warren Beatty's private telephone number, it no longer matters that your father kept greyhounds.

'What about that fellow who taught you to drive?'

'Red? Oh, he's married with hordes of children. Well, three children but it seems like more. I dread him coming down with them. It's like kicking over an anthill. Olga likes them, though. Puts them to work. You're never too young to earn your keep, she says.'

A shadow fell over the garden seat. Lionel and Grace looked up. Olga stood there, her hair a tumble of fire, escaping from the many pins and clips supposed to keep it in place.

'Lionel, if you come here you have to do some work, you know? You could paint that seat for a beginning.'

'I could start weekend after next.'

Shouts from the kitchen made her hurry back. Grace and Lionel relaxed again on the unpainted bench.

'Will you stay here with Olga?'

Grace sat bolt upright.

'Christ, no. I'd murder her. Or vice versa.'

'I thought you liked it here.'

'I do. But this is Olga's dream – not mine.'

'And what's your dream?'

Grace closed her eyes again. Behind her lids the memory of the dappled sea glittered and flashed. She smiled.

'I don't know. I'm waiting to find out.'

A while later, Lionel left, shouting his goodbyes through the open door of the pub. Grace sat where she was as the sun sank and the air cooled.

'I'm exhausted.'

Grace opened her eyes and squinted into the light to where Emily was a dark silhouette.

'Shove over.'

Grace moved along the bench to let her sit down. They sat in silence for a while, Emily's hands resting on the round of her stomach.

'Bet you could murder a pint,' Emily said after a bit.

'Very funny.'

Because of course by then, Emily and Grace had had the conversation that Grace was so dreading. At the time, Emily had said, 'Is it hard for you?'

And Grace had said, 'About the same as it is for you.'

Afterwards, they'd never mentioned it again except at moments like these, when they were alone, and then mostly as a joke they shared rather than something terrible.

'Do you want a water or something?'

Grace shook her head.

'No. You're all right.'

The sun sank lower still and long fingers of black crept out across the horizon.

Grace looked down at her apron that was speckled with prawn shells and slashed with a long stain of tomato sauce. Lazily she started to pick off the pink fragments, placing them in a tidy pile on the bench. After a while, Emily joined in.

SARAH WEBB

Some Kind of Wonderful

PAN BOOKS

Rosie's life has become one long string of exhausting worries and stresses: getting her four-year-old daughter Cass to school, getting to work on time, conjuring up 'clever' and 'original' ideas for marketing campaigns. She's only twenty-eight, for heaven's sake, so why does she feel 101? And her husband, Darren, is no help, always working late and at weekends.

When Darren announces out of the blue that actually he's been having an affair, Rosie goes into shock. But then she takes a deep breath and decides that he's not the only one who can make life-changing decisions. Opting out of Dublin's rat race, Rosie sets up a small gallery in Redwood, a stately home in Wicklow that boasts its own wildlife park. Run by enigmatic entrepreneur Conor Dunlop and his good-looking son, Rory, every day at Redwood is full of surprises – and some new friends.